When Strawberries Bloom

A novel based on true experiences from an Amish writer!

LINDA BYLER

When Strawberries Bloom

LIZZIE SEARCHES *for* LOVE
· *Book 2* ·

Good Books
Intercourse, PA 17534
800/762-7171
www.GoodBooks.com

When Strawberries Bloom includes material originally published by
the author as these books: *Lizzie, Lizzie's Carefree Years, Lizzie's Teen
Years, Lizzie and Stephen.*

Cover design by Koechel Peterson & Associates, Inc.,
Minneapolis, Minnesota

Design by Cliff Snyder

WHEN STRAWBERRIES BLOOM
Copyright © 2010 by Good Books, Intercourse, PA 17534
International Standard Book Number: 978-1-56148-699-1
Library of Congress Catalog Card Number: 2010030943

Library of Congress Cataloging-in-Publication Data

Byler, Linda.

When strawberries bloom/Linda Byler.

p. cm. -- (Lizzie searches for love ; bk. 2)

Summary: Will Lizzie Glick, a high-spirited Amish teenager, give up her dream of teaching
so that her wish for a family and marriage can come true? Based on the true experiences of
the author's extended family.

ISBN 978-1-56148-699-1 (pbk. : alk. paper)

1. Amish--Juvenile fiction. [1. Amish--Fiction. 2. Teachers--Fiction. 3. Love--Fiction.
4. Courtship--Fiction.] I. Title.

PZ7.B9882Wh 2010

[Fic]--dc22   2010030943

Table of Contents

Chapter 1

"AND SO..." LIZZIE FINISHED HER STORY, "that's how it was!"

"Oh, I wonder how this will all turn out?" Mandy sighed.

Lizzie loved Monday evenings when she could tell stories about her weekend, interesting bit by interesting bit, to her younger sister Mandy who always listened with wide-eyed admiration. With dinner over and the dishes done, the sisters worked outside with Mam, planting flowers in the new rock garden that Dat had built beside the house. Lizzie mixed peat moss into the topsoil while Mandy set up the rubber garden hose from the water hydrant by the barn.

Spring had arrived, filling the days with warm, mellow sunshine. Buds burst forth from the maple tree in the front yard, and even the old walnut tree beside the sidewalk shone with a light green mist which, if Lizzie looked closely, was actually thousands of tiny green buds erupting from the dark branches. The swollen creek churned on its relentless way to the river, already muddy brown from all of the April showers. Little green shoots emerged from moist brown earth, stretching through the blanket of wet, decaying leaves.

During the warm days, Dat worked the horse hard, preparing the soil for another crop. Clyde, the big workhorse, was back in the harness, still bouncing around as if he had springs in his legs, but now he was settled down enough to pull his share of the plow.

In the evenings, barn swallows dipped and whirled through the air like little acrobats, chirping their evening song as they caught mosquitoes for their baby birds in the mud nests inside the horse barn.

"Ach, Lizzie, you're still so young. I wouldn't get too serious about either Amos or Stephen or too worried about Ruthie. You have plenty of time to run around yet. Besides, more importantly, you need to pray about this," her older sister Emma said, as she gently pushed the porch swing back and forth with her foot.

Lizzie flicked some dust off her black bib apron, adjusted the navy blue sleeve of her dress, and shivered. The cool evening breeze reminded her of the evening before when she had paddled across the pond with Amos, handsome Amos, who had always paid more attention to her friend Ruthie than to her until last night. Everything had been perfect until

Stephen appeared as they were pulling the boat to shore.

One moment she had felt warm and a little confused as she watched Amos tie up the canoe. The next moment, Stephen had stepped beside her and told her she was the prettiest thing he had ever seen.

Lizzie shook her head and snorted impatiently. Something about Stephen bothered her. They had become friends, real friends, in the year since his family moved to Lamont County. But even though Lizzie saw him every weekend, she never quite felt like she knew what he thought about her. He was too quiet, not as outgoing and funny as Amos or her Uncle Marvin, and sometimes she caught him watching her as if he knew something more than even she knew about herself. He bugged her!

Besides, how could she know that Stephen liked her in that way? Maybe he didn't really. He was just teasing her, or he thought she was pretty but nothing more. Or what if he wished he hadn't said anything to her now? She certainly wished he hadn't because she felt all mixed up inside.

"Emma, I do pray. You know I'm not as scared of God as I used to be. And you have nothing to say. How old were you when you started dating Joshua? Huh? How old?" Lizzie turned her head and squinted teasingly at Emma.

Emma reached down and playfully pulled at Lizzie's *dichly*, the little kerchief on her head. Lizzie grabbed the top of her head to stop her, but Emma was too fast, and she snatched it and flung it over the porch railing.

"Emma!"

"You should have a real worthwhile project in your life like drawing, crocheting, embroidering..."

Lizzie pretended to gag, and Mandy threw her head back, whooping and laughing. Emma may enjoy crocheting and embroidering, Lizzie knew, but not she or Mandy.

"I know what I would like to do more than anything in the whole world!" Lizzie said.

Mandy and Emma looked at each other, rolled their eyes, and said simultaneously, "Teach school!"

"Yup. That's right. Teach school," Lizzie said.

They had often listened to Lizzie's vivid accounts of what her classroom would look like, her methods of discipline, her way of teaching, the songs the children would sing, and on and on until both of her sisters became quite weary of listening and started to tease her. It wasn't that they scoffed at the idea of Lizzie teaching. It just seemed a bit improbable to them that the very proper school board would even think of asking 17-year-old Lizzie to teach school.

"But Lizzie," Mandy protested, "you're too young."

"And too fancy," Emma finished soberly.

"What do you mean?" Lizzie wailed. "I'm not fancy!"

"You're way too fancy with your hair, your clothes, your covering. The school board will not ask a girl like you to teach," Emma said quite matter-of-factly.

"I'm not fancier than any other girl in our entire church," Lizzie argued.

"Well, you could wet your hair down and roll the sides more sleekly. You often look so... well, I hate to say 'sloppy,' Lizzie. Maybe you'd like it better if I used the word 'fancy,'" Emma said.

"The school board shouldn't judge me by my hair," Lizzie said, her hands on her hips.

"They don't really, Lizzie. But... well, I don't know quite how to describe it."

Lizzie plopped down beside Emma on the swing. The chain of the porch swing creaked against the hooks in the ceiling as they swung silently together. Across the lawn, the girls' twin sisters, KatieAnn and Susan, were playing in the freshly mowed grass by the clothesline, while Dat whistled as he swept the horse barn floor with his wide broom. The sun was sinking behind the hills in a grand show of yellow, orange, and red. Streaks of dark blue and lavender made the colors seem almost like heaven, Lizzie thought.

Mam clapped her hands, brushing off the dirt as she straightened her back. Lizzie eyed her newly planted petunias. The old farm had been vastly improved in many different ways since they had moved in. It was their home now, and a cozy, homey one which Lizzie had learned to love with all her heart. Her heart always sang when she returned home to Mam's comfy kitchen, whether she had been at work or coming home from running around during a weekend in neighboring Allen County.

Lizzie truly yearned for only one thing now, and that was to become a real teacher. So if the school board thought she needed to change some things about her dress, she would. She knew there was nothing else in all the world she wanted to do more than be a teacher, so she would show them she could be a plain, old-maidy kind of person, quiet, sober, and very, very mature for a 17-year-old. She made a mental note of who was on the school board, wondering how she could persuade them that she was capable of doing the job.

Lizzie could still remember her first day of school. Emma was six years old then, and Lizzie was only five. Actually, Lizzie was almost too young to go to school, but Mam wanted the two girls to start together. They were only a little over a year apart in age, so she thought it was good for them to start first grade the same year.

On that first day, when the little white one-room schoolhouse came into view, Lizzie's heart had done a complete flip-flop. There was a porch and a fence with a gate that was pulled open. A horse shed and two outdoor bathrooms stood in a corner of the schoolyard. There were already lots of children at school, and Lizzie felt very afraid.

Emma said, "Good morning," to the teacher, but

not very loud. Lizzie didn't say anything. She had just stared at the teacher. She was very thin with a long black dress. Her forehead was wide, and she wore glasses, and her white covering was bigger than Mam's. She looked friendly enough, but she also looked scary. Lizzie wondered if she spanked little first-graders. She looked like she could really spank.

"Come, girls, we'll find your seats," the teacher said. "You'll find your name written on a piece of tape. Let's see if you can find your seats. Can you write your own name?"

Emma nodded her head. Lizzie was too shy to do anything except walk along under that hand on her shoulder. It had seemed so far across the classroom, and she felt like many pairs of eyes were staring at her. She hoped her dress was buttoned properly and that her bob was not falling down.

Lizzie squirmed a little to make herself more comfortable on the slippery varnished seat. She tucked her legs underneath, and her new shoes crinkled at the toes. Teacher Sylvia handed out blue songbooks to some of the children.

"Now we're going to take turns picking songs," she said. The singing started and welled in the room, growing louder and louder. Lizzie bit her lip, trying hard not to feel lonely.

"My Lord, what a morning,
My Lord, what a morning,
My Lord, what a morning,
When the stars begin to fall."

On and on the children sang, and lonelier and lonelier Lizzie became. She tried to think of happy things, of good things to eat, and of silly things, but the huge lump in her throat only grew bigger. She looked down and bit her lip, shuffling her feet, but the lump in her throat would not go away. She glanced at Emma, and Emma smiled a weak smile, trying to cheer her up.

In that moment, huge, wet tears coursed down Lizzie's cheeks, and a harsh sob escaped her bitten lips. She was soon crying uncontrollably, wishing she could go home to Mam before the stars fell and the end of the world came. Wouldn't it be awful if the stars fell from the sky and she was in school and Dat and Mam were at home?

Emma took Lizzie's hand and tugged gently. Lizzie followed Emma across that big expanse of schoolroom to the door while the singing went on. Emma led her across the porch and down to the little outdoor bathroom. They huddled together while Emma tried to console Lizzie in earnest tones.

"Lizzie, it's okay. What's wrong?"

Lizzie cried horribly. She couldn't tell Emma about the deep black loneliness she felt when they sang that song. So she just shrugged her shoulders, and Emma wiped her eyes and told her to be quiet. She said Lizzie would have to be a good girl and grow up now and not cry in school. Lizzie gulped and choked and nodded her head. She would be all right, she assured Emma. And much to Lizzie's surprise, she really was.

And soon she learned to love school, in spite of sad songs.

❧

The next morning when Lizzie combed her hair, she made sure it was all put up neatly in an orderly fashion. Dat looked at Lizzie once, then followed up with closer scrutiny before he gave Mam a bewildered look.

Mam checked Lizzie's neat attire, her covering pulled forward to cover her carefully combed hair. Lizzie's eyebrows were raised in a quite pious expression, her eyes downcast in her Herculean effort at humility.

Mam's eyes met Dat's and she shrugged her shoulders. Dat cleared his throat.

"Well, Lizzie, to what do we owe this change of heart you're displaying?"

Lizzie looked up at Dat, her eyes as meek and docile as a sheep's.

"Oh, the girls told me if I want to be a schoolteacher, I need to mend my ways. I mean, comb my hair more severely and act more responsible. How do I look?" she asked, batting her eyelashes demurely.

Mam sputtered. She made a brave attempt to keep from laughing, but in the end her shoulders shook until she gave up helplessly. Dat looked a bit stern, then seeing Mam wiping her eyes, he laughed with her.

When Emma came down the stairs, she was startled to hear everyone laughing so early in the morning until she saw Lizzie's hair and covering.

"Oh, my goodness!" she gasped.

Lizzie was a bit insulted to see everyone laughing at her real effort to appear grown up and responsible.

"Well, go ahead and laugh then," she said.

"We weren't laughing at you, Lizzie. But you are laying it on a bit thick," Dat said. "After all, Lizzie, you have to be yourself. You can't purposefully turn yourself into a whole other sort of person. I do admire you for dressing more respectfully, but I have a good feeling about the school board. If they know you truly want to teach school, they'll be kind enough to give you a try. I'm pretty sure they will."

"Of course, they will," Mam agreed.

Lizzie sighed. It was almost unbelievable that Dat actually thought the school board would ask her to teach! In this community there was only one school for Amish and Mennonite students, and as far as Lizzie knew, its teacher was getting married in the fall. That meant they would need a new teacher, and she knew of no one else who wanted the job. So maybe ... just maybe ...

Chapter 2

THE NEXT SUNDAY, LIZZIE DRESSED QUITE soberly. During church, she sang along with the congregation, singing quite purposefully, listening to the preacher with no fidgeting or whispering. She wanted the men on the school board to think she was a mature young woman, capable of teaching in the fall. She knew that the responsibility and seriousness of teaching could be completely overwhelming, which, really, sometimes if she thought about it, was about as frightening as … well, as lots of things about the unknown.

Emma was very supportive, always being positive when they talked about it. She even told Lizzie that she thought she would be a teacher herself someday, but the way things were turning out, she just didn't know if that would happen. Lizzie knew exactly why Emma didn't seriously pursue teaching. It was because she still held the dream of being married soon. She probably thought that if she didn't commit herself to teaching, Joshua would ask her to marry him.

After services were over, Lizzie helped the other single girls carry trays of bread and pies, ham, soft cheese spread, pickles, and red beets to the long tables where the traditional Sunday dinner was served. She caught sight of Stephen standing on the other side of the room, laughing at something Uncle Marvin had said. Stephen smiled at her and Lizzie's heart sped up. But when Uncle Marvin turned to see who had caught Stephen's attention, Lizzie ducked her head and walked away.

Dat was talking with an unfamiliar man who looked to be about his age. Lizzie wondered if he was part of the Beiler family who had recently moved to the area. She remembered that Dat mentioned one evening at the supper table that this Jonas Beiler was pushing for the development of an Amish school board to help the Mennonites run the local school.

"Who's that?" she asked Emma.

Emma smiled and shrugged.

"I don't know," she said.

Lizzie sighed and went on with her duties, hoping with all her heart that she was making a good impression.

By the next week, Lizzie had almost forgotten about impressing the school board with her good behavior. She was so busy working as a *maud* for a local family, and her days and evenings were full of spring cleaning and planting. She didn't have time to worry about teaching school. Mandy said they probably wouldn't ask her anyway, because she was only 17 years old. Lizzie quickly reminded her that she would be almost 18 in the fall, and that was plenty old enough to teach school.

She was upstairs cleaning her closet one warm evening, just as the birds were twittering their good-night songs, when the door of her room burst open.

"Lizzie, get down to the kitchen! The school board is here!" Mandy hissed.

Lizzie dropped the dress she was holding, her mouth open in disbelief. "The real school board?"

"Of course!"

Lizzie felt her heartbeat accelerate, and the color drained from her face. Quickly she dashed to the mirror, checking her hair and covering before she nervously wiped a few fuzzies from her apron. She could think of nothing, absolutely nothing to say. For some reason it felt as if they were there to spank her, like she was still a little girl who had done something mischievous in school, and the stern-faced school board had come to tell her what her punishment was going to be.

Her knees hardly supported her as she went slowly down the stairs, clutching the sides of her covering, checking that it covered part of her ears. Who knew? They might change their minds if she didn't look too fancy.

In the kitchen, Dat and Mam sat at the kitchen table with three men. Lizzie recognized Jonas Beiler from his conversation with Dat at church. The other two men, Elam Glick and Elmer Esh, had lived in the community much longer, and Lizzie knew them well. In one glance, Lizzie could see that Mam was nervous because her hands were closed with her thumbs tucked under her fingers. That's what Mam always did when she was worried about something.

"H...Hello!" Lizzie said in what she hoped was a sweet and humble way.

"Good evening, Lizzie," they all said, looking at her closely.

"How are you?" Jonas Beiler asked.

"Good," was all Lizzie could think of before she swallowed fitfully.

He looked at Dat before he asked how old she was. For all the world I feel like I'm a young cow or horse being taken to an auction, Lizzie thought.

They all talked about the weather, the price of milk, the price of the farm that had been sold recently, until Lizzie felt like screaming. Why didn't they say what they wanted? She began chewing on the inside of her thumbnail until Mam looked at her with lowered eyebrows. Lizzie quickly put her hands under the table and pressed them together as tightly as she could.

Finally, Jonas Beiler looked at Lizzie and cleared his throat.

"So your father says you'd like to try teaching school?"

Lizzie's heart jumped to her throat. But she looked steadily at him, meeting his clear gaze.

"I'd like to," she said.

"Well, that's good. We are going to need a teacher this fall because the Mennonite girl, I forget her name, is getting married. So..."

He left that sentence hanging in the air, and Lizzie felt as if she had been holding a balloon which the wind had suddenly whipped away, completely out of her grasp. He had only mentioned the fact that they needed a teacher; he hadn't really asked her to teach the school.

Just as suddenly, the departing balloon drifted back firmly into Lizzie's hands when Jonas said, "Would you consider being the new teacher in the fall then?"

"Yes!" Lizzie breathed, her eyes shining.

"That's good," Elam Glick said, smiling.

"Yes, we're glad you want to," Elmer Esh added.

"You'll need these," Jonas said, handing her a small orange booklet and a few other papers.

Lizzie flipped through the pages as the men talked about the date school would be opening, the book order, the rules of conduct for a teacher, and many other things that Lizzie hadn't considered before. But nothing deterred her. Not one thing they talked about gave her the blues. She was so thrilled about sitting right there in the kitchen, reveling in the delightful knowledge that the school board had really honest-to-goodness asked her to be a teacher.

Before the men left they each wished *der saya* for her, or God's blessing, which brought tears to Lizzie's eyes. Wasn't that the nicest thing in the whole world for a school board to say? She didn't feel worthy, but their words made her feel as if she could conquer anything. She would do her very, very, absolute best to become the teacher they expected her to be.

After saying good-night to them, Lizzie turned to Mam and clasped her hands to her chest. "Ma-am!"

"Looks like you're a teacher, Lizzie!"

Emma and Mandy clattered down the stairs, congratulating her as she twirled joyously around the kitchen. Jason thought she was making an awful fuss about it, and the twins danced funny little steps of their own.

"Jason, you may as well not look so sour! I'm going to be your teacher, too, you know!"

"I know!" he said, but Lizzie could tell he was pleased. She loved Jason, grown boy that he was now. He was turning out to be a good-looking young man and his curly hair was his most adorable feature, she thought.

Lizzie could still remember the day Jason was born.

"Emma, look at your brother. His name is Jason, and he looks a lot like Lizzie," Dat had said.

Emma whispered, "Jason? Aww, he's cute! Can I hold him, Dat?"

Dat had smiled and lowered the blue bundle into Emma's lap while Emma stroked the little cheeks and touched his downy hair.

Lizzie peered under the flap of the soft, woolly blanket. She was suddenly overcome with horror. He was so ugly and so bright red she couldn't imagine ever letting Mam take him to church. His eyes were closed, but he had lots of deep wrinkles around them. Lizzie could not imagine how he could ever see around all that skin. His nose was big and puffy, and his mouth was much too big for his face.

She felt Mam come up behind her and put her arm around her shoulders. Lizzie leaned against Mam and tried hard to smile—at least to smile enough to be nice. But she wished so much her new baby brother wasn't so ugly.

"Isn't he sweet, Lizzie? You may hold him, too. Emma, may Lizzie hold Baby Jason now?" Mam asked.

"I—I don't want to hold him. Emma may." And much to her shame, Lizzie started to cry.

"What's wrong? Come, Lizzie." Mam sat down on a soft chair and just held Lizzie till she finished crying. "Now tell me what's wrong."

But Lizzie never did tell Mam the real reason she cried. She just told her that her head hurt, because it wasn't nice to say Jason was ugly. But he really was.

❧

Now Jason had grown into a strong young man with even features and wild curls that caught the eye of more than one girl Lizzie knew. He was a good brother, and Lizzie hoped he was well-behaved at school because he was about to become her student.

Dat smiled, pleased that Lizzie would be a teacher. That afforded him some status in the community, one of his girls being the first Amish teacher in this school. That fact made him smile, Lizzie knew. Mam was beaming as well, although when everyone quieted down she said she hoped Lizzie was aware of the responsibility that was involved.

"I know, Mam!" Lizzie assured her. "I can handle 20 children. I know I can. I just wish it was the end of August and I could get started. I can already begin on some artwork, can't I?"

"Probably when you come home from work in the evening," Mam agreed.

That evening Lizzie did not sleep for a very long, long time. Thoughts and projects she would try the next year whirled through her head like a child's pinwheel on a stick, turning in the wind until she couldn't make sense of anything.

She did remember to thank God from the bottom of her heart for the chance to be a real schoolteacher before she drifted off to a happy slumber.

Chapter 3

THE SUMMER FLEW BY, LIKE A TRAIN GOING SO fast you had to turn your head to be sure and see the engine at all. Lizzie continued working part-time as a *maud*, but only part-time because she also needed to prepare for the upcoming school year.

Weekends in Allen County with her friends were still the highlight of her life, marred only by her growing obsession with Amos. He had become the center of her weekends—his attention, or lack of it, was now her main reason for going to Allen County. Of course, she didn't want to miss being with her Uncle Marvin, who was Dat's brother but almost the same age as Lizzie, and the mysterious Stephen, who was her friend, but who had also told her once that she was pretty but never mentioned it again.

Sometimes Lizzie thought it was easier to think about Amos and Ruthie than it was to figure out what Stephen really thought about her. In fact, Lizzie had begun to think that if it wasn't for Amos, she would have genuine fun with lots of other guys every weekend. But because she was never quite certain whether Amos liked her or Ruthie, she could think of nothing else.

On the surface, Lizzie remained good friends with Ruthie. No one but Mandy knew about the cold, hard jealousy that so often consumed Lizzie. She wondered how long God would have patience with her awful feelings of jealousy. Every Sunday night when she came home, she asked Jesus to forgive her and wipe away her sins and make her as clean and brand new as tablet paper with no marks on it.

Sometimes the whole sinning and forgiving thing was hard to figure out. How could Jesus keep forgiving her if he knew she'd just get jealous again the next weekend? Maybe he recognized that she was still young. She was pretty sure about one thing, though. After she became a member of the Amish church and gave her life to God really seriously, she either had to be dating Amos or quit going to Allen County on the weekend if she wanted to have any peace at all.

On Sunday night she was so positive that Amos would ask her for a date that her heart beat so rapidly and loudly she was sure he could hear it. After the singing and while she waited on her driver, he sat in the yard beside her, just sat there, talking about lots of different subjects. His teeth shone white in the dark, his head outlined against the starlight, and Lizzie was so nervous, just waiting to hear him ask her for a real date the following weekend. But he didn't. Lizzie was mad all week just thinking about it.

Finally, Mam had had quite enough of Lizzie's crabbiness, her pouting and short answers, her eyebrows raised in anxiety, her obviously being in the center of a great personal crisis of some sort.

"Lizzie, I do wish you wouldn't be so grouchy all the time. The twins are almost afraid of you," she said after Lizzie had shouted at the two girls to leave her alone. The twins stood against the sofa, tears in their eyes.

Lizzie didn't say anything. She just gazed miserably out the kitchen window. Mam sighed and went to the kitchen to make some lunch.

"Oh, dear," she said.

"What?" Lizzie asked.

"I'm out of butter."

"Do you want Mandy and me to drive Billy to Bittle's?"

"It's late!"

"Not that late. We can."

So Lizzie found Mandy, and together they led Billy from his stall and hitched him to the cart. It felt good to brush his coat and his oatmeal-colored mane and tail and to throw the harness across his round, sturdy little back.

As they rounded the corner and headed out the lane in the buggy, Lizzie held tight to the reins so the buggy wheels wouldn't slide. Billy always wanted to run, and to run fast, every time they hitched him to the cart, although he was much easier to control now than when he was a very young pony.

Mandy sat beside Lizzie, happy and talkative, content to let Lizzie drive as she talked about one subject after another, without too much comment from Lizzie. But as they turned onto the main road, Mandy glanced over at Lizzie.

"What a crab you are this week!" she suddenly said.

"Oh, be quiet. Can't I be a crab all by myself without you noticing every little thing about me?"

"It's Amos, isn't it?"

"No!"

"Mm-hmm. Oh, yes, it is, Lizzie. You know it is. What happened now?"

"Nothing!"

Mandy just shook her head. Billy trotted rapidly down the road, and the sisters waved at a lady mowing her lawn. It was one of those perfect summer evenings, not too hot or humid, not too windy, just perfect to be driving down the road with Billy. Lizzie wished she could tell Mandy the whole miserable story, but so far, she was too proud to admit even to herself that Amos was her problem. So they silently drove on through the little village situated on the side of a long, winding hill, with Billy lunging into his collar steadily until they reached the top.

Lizzie had to hold him back as they started down the opposite side. Billy loved running downhill at what was clearly an unsafe speed. Even as Lizzie firmly held Billy back, the buggy slid to the left as they pulled into the gravel parking lot of Bittle's Store.

Bittle's was a tiny store situated on the edge of a dairy farm. They sold milk, butter, cheese, and ice cream, among other things. It was a fairly new building, clean and shining on the inside, and the girls always loved driving Billy there because they could each buy a huge ice cream cone after they had made their purchases.

Lizzie tied Billy to the adjacent hitching rack. She quickly grabbed a pound of butter before she met Mandy at the ice cream counter where she was already deliberating over the ice cream flavors. Finally, Mandy chose mint chocolate chip while Lizzie decided on butter pecan.

"Let's sit here at the picnic table," Lizzie said as they left the store. "I always have a problem driving and eating my ice cream at the same time."

"I'll hold your ice cream for you," Mandy offered.

"No, let's stay here and eat it," Lizzie said. She threw down the bag containing the butter on the picnic table before sitting down on one of the benches. A young man drove up to the store, got out of his car, and nodded at them before disappearing through the doors.

"He looks like Amos," Lizzie said.

"Everybody looks like Amos to you," Mandy said, taking her napkin and wiping her mouth.

Lizzie didn't answer. She just gazed across the rolling farmland, watching the black and white

Holsteins grazing as she steadily ate her ice cream.

After awhile, Lizzie said dully, "I wish I was still 15 like you!"

"I'm 15, almost 16."

"So? You're still not 17 like I am."

Mandy bit off a huge chunk of mint chocolate chip ice cream. Lizzie watched her with narrowed eyes.

"Doesn't that hurt your teeth?"

"Nah. So what's wrong with being 16?"

"Oh, I don't know. Nothing, I guess. I mean, I have fun most times but… Mandy, why do you think a guy acts like he likes you and you're really, really, really good friends, but he never asks you for a real date? You know, a date where I can go tell all my friends that I have a date?"

"I don't know, Lizzie. How can you expect me to know if I'm only 15. Almost 16."

Lizzie nodded. She wished that she could ask Mandy about Stephen, too. But what could she say? Amos' interest in Ruthie really upset her, but Stephen bothered her almost as much. He told her he was pretty, but then went back to acting like they were just friends.

Lizzie wasn't sure what she'd do if Stephen asked her on a date. Amos was one thing. He was handsome and fun and interesting, but was he really her friend, she couldn't help but wonder. Stephen was, even if he was too quiet and a little mysterious. What if he decided he didn't like her as much as she was starting to like him? Or what if he wanted to

get married? That had happened to Emma. Lizzie
wanted to get married sometime. Probably. But not
yet.

Lizzie sighed. Customers drove up to the porch
or drove away, some of them with ice cream cones
and others with dishes piled high with the cold,
creamy confection. Some carried gallons of milk
or chocolate milk or bags containing ice cream or
cheese and butter.

Lizzie thought that milking cows wouldn't be
nearly so bad if you could operate a farm on this
level. She could have fun milking a hundred cows a
day in a fancy milking parlor and running a beautiful new store like this one with electricity and huge
coolers with shiny new tile on the floor. Then Dat
could hire men to do the milking, and all Lizzie
would have to do would be to comb her hair nicely
and look neat and pretty, smiling at customers all
day while she rang up sales on the up-to-date elec-
tronic cash register.

When they had finished their ice cream, Lizzie
and Mandy climbed back into the buggy and headed
towards home. Lizzie was glad she had eaten her ice
cream on the porch of the store. Billy was in one of
his running frenzies, as they called it, and it took all
of Lizzie's strength to hold him to a trot.

He bent his head so he could hold the bit better,
his ears turned forward, his mane thick and heavy,
bouncing solidly along the nape of his neck. His
muscular little haunches flapped rhythmically with
every clacking step. He had never been shod, which

meant he ran on the hard, unrelenting macadam with no iron shoes tacked to his hard little hooves. He never slipped or fell, being as surefooted a pony as Dat had ever seen.

Once, when Lizzie's family was attending a church service 13 miles away from their home, Dat had allowed Lizzie and Mandy to drive Billy. Little Billy moved in line with a row of other horses and buggies, running steadily up hill and down, his legs taking two steps to the larger horses' one. Dat would tell this story to anyone who would listen, how his little feet went "Blip-blip-blip," and how he kept up perfectly, arriving at church services without being winded.

"He wasn't even blowing. He could have run 10 more miles," Dat would say, waving his hands for emphasis.

Lizzie always felt like crying when Dat told that story, her love of this plucky little pony stirring up an emotion that choked her and melted into tears. He was the best, the strongest, the sweetest pony they had ever owned, and Lizzie hoped with all her heart he would live forever.

They moved down the hill through the village at an alarming pace, Lizzie hanging on to the reins with all her strength. They hit the concrete bridge, bouncing off the seat as they flew across the creek.

Mandy burst out laughing, and Lizzie joined in.

"Don't make me laugh, Mandy!" she gasped. "I can't hold him!" But the harder they tried to hold back their laughter, the more helpless they became, until Lizzie actually was struck by a panicky feeling that Billy was running away.

"Stop it, Mandy!" she shouted.

"Wheeee!" was Mandy's response, which caused Lizzie to fall into helpless giggles again.

As Billy broke into a gallop going up the opposite hill, the sisters became serious as Lizzie wrapped the reins around her hands and pulled with all her strength. He slowed, but none too obediently, Lizzie thought, sensing through the reins that he would break into another gallop the second she let up on them.

Mandy reached over and slapped her hand down on Lizzie's arm. "Good driver!" she said, grinning.

Lizzie grinned back. She was overcome with a feeling of love for Mandy. Dear skinny, green-eyed Mandy. The love of her life, besides Mam, Dat, Emma, and Jason. She loved Susan and KatieAnn too, of course, but not like Mandy. There was just something about having a sister close to your own age that was unlike any other blessing in life.

When Lizzie said something funny, she knew instinctively that Mandy would find it hilarious. She always did. And when Mandy was joking or in a silly mood, no one caught on faster than Lizzie.

The evening sun shed its warm golden light all around them and around the surrounding woods, fields, and houses. Even the telephone poles etched against the evening sky looked pretty as they wound their way home.

Lizzie momentarily forgot her troubled feelings about weekends, Amos and Ruthie, and running

around in general as she laughed happily with
Mandy, skidding the pony cart wheels as they turned
in on the country road that took them home.

✍

The following Sunday evening, not very long
after Lizzie arrived at the supper crowd, Rebecca,
Stephen's sister, came running toward her.

"Come here, Lizzie!"

"You'll never guess what?"

"What? What? Don't keep me guessing!"

Lizzie's eyes shone in anticipation, her heart beating, her thoughts going instantly to Amos. Maybe...
just maybe...

"Amos asked Ruthie for a date this weekend!"
Rebecca said. "It's her first one!"

Lizzie felt as if Rebecca had hit her in the stomach with a boxing glove. All the air surrounding her
lungs pushed up against her throat, constricting it in
an awful choking sensation. She leaned back, reaching for the support of the chair behind her, feeling
as if the whole floor was somehow going completely
crooked. She hadn't expected this kind of news to
hurt this much.

"Lizzie, aren't you happy for them? You look as
if you'd seen a ghost!" Rebecca burst out.

"Oh! Oh, no... No, of course I'm happy for
Ruthie! It's just such a total shock! I mean... I
mean... I didn't know Amos liked her," she ended
lamely.

"They liked each other since they went to vocational class together," Rebecca said, absolutely beaming. "It's so-o cute!"

"Oh, yes! Of course, I think so, too," Lizzie said. She felt as dishonest and untruthful as she had ever been in her whole life. Only her pride kept her standing there, knuckles white against the dark wood of the chair, a false smile pasted on her face.

The rest of the evening at the supper passed as if in a haze for Lizzie as she kept trying desperately to control her emotions. When Amos appeared in the kitchen door looking more handsome than ever in a sky-blue shirt, his black vest and pants setting off his very dark hair and skin, Lizzie almost burst into tears of frustration.

She slowly put down her plate and calmly walked to the bathroom where she sat down on the side of the bathtub, held her head in her hands, and cried great tears of annoyance and bitter disappointment. Why? How could he act as if he liked her one weekend and the very next Sunday have a date with Ruthie? She sat up and sniffed, grabbing a tissue from the box on the sink and honking into it loudly. She dabbed viciously at her eyes, going to the mirror to see the damage her tears had done.

Taking a deep breath, she braced her shoulders, pulled up her cape, and adjusted her covering. I don't want him anyway. I hope he marries Ruthie and she gains 50 pounds the first year. I hope he dates her awhile, and then they break up because he wants me. I'm not going to congratulate her. I'm not even going to talk to her.

No one will ever like me, she thought. First Joe and John, the handsome twins who were in her class at vocational school, who had paid much more attention to their pretty Mennonite classmates. Now Amos had picked Ruthie instead of her. I'm just fat and ugly. I have pimples.

But really, what does Ruthie have that I don't? She can't drive a fast horse or swim. Lizzie's thoughts collided against each other like bumper cars at an amusement park as she struggled with jealousy, self-pity, a low sense of self-worth, and, most of all, her first real disappointment in love.

"Who's in here?"

A resounding knock on the bathroom door propelled Lizzie into action. Dabbing desperately at her eyes with a cold wash rag and answering in a muffled voice, she sprang to the door to unlock it.

"You heard," Emma said.

She stepped into the bathroom and closed the door behind her.

That was Lizzie's undoing. All the pent-up frustration and bitter defeat emerged in one low sob which caught in her throat, bringing a real, little-girl hiccup with it.

Emma put her arms around her, stroking her back, talking in soothing tones, for all the world as she had done so many years before in the privy at school when Lizzie had the blues because of a mournful song the pupils were singing. The thought hit Lizzie, and in the middle of her tears, her shoulders started shaking uncontrollably as she began to laugh hysterically.

Emma stepped back, her eyes wide with concern. "You're laughing and crying at the same time!"

Lizzie blew her nose, sniffing, and smiling ruefully as she said, "Emma, this reminds me of us in first grade! Remember?"

Emma laughed with Lizzie, saying, "I guess we're still in first grade, as far as lessons in life go."

They sat side by side on the bathtub before Lizzie lifted her head and said, "Oh, well, I guess he wasn't meant for me."

"I guess not."

"Why do you suppose I don't have any luck with finding a husband? I don't really, really think I'm so awful looking. I mean, there are girls homelier than me who have boyfriends, aren't there?"

"Of course, Lizzie. You know you're even better looking than me."

"No, I'm not, Emma."

"Lizzie, please don't think you're ugly and worth nothing at all now. I knew you were going to do this. Listen. You know how Mam always says God knows best, and he already knows that somewhere there is a special young man for you. You just haven't found him yet. Sometimes he takes a long winding road around to teach us valuable lessons on the way."

"Evidently *you* didn't need any."

"Well…"

"Emma, it's always been like this. You don't seem to need lessons in your life, hard ones like this, and I get one right after the other."

"Not everyone's life is the same, Lizzie," Emma said, smiling at her reassuringly.

Lizzie sighed as she intently pleated her black apron across her knee. "Yeah, I guess, but I'll tell you one thing. I'm glad getting to heaven doesn't depend on luck, or I'd never make it. I hardly ever won in Chutes and Ladders even, because most times I landed on the square where you go down the longest chute."

Emma laughed. "You'll land on the square that takes you right back up the longest ladder soon, Lizzie, just you watch!" Emma said, squeezing Lizzie's hand affectionately. "Come on, you can go with Joshua and me to the singing."

Lizzie brightened noticeably. "All right, I will. Then no one will know where I am when I'm not around. Amos will think I walked home, and he'll feel so guilty it isn't e-e-even funny!"

They muffled their giggles in their handkerchiefs as they heard another knock on the bathroom door.

Chapter 4

AFTER AMOS BEGAN DATING RUTHIE, LIZZIE threw herself into her much anticipated year of teaching school. She helped the parents clean the old red-brick schoolhouse, washing down the freshly painted plaster walls and rubbing the old windowpanes with a solution of soap and vinegar until they shone. The men dabbed fresh putty outside the windowpanes and put a new stovepipe in the well-worn wood furnace. They varnished the old school desks for the 20 pupils who would attend school that year. After the cleaning was done, the men poured fresh oil on the wooden floor, which the boards partly absorbed, making it an easier task to sweep the dust and dirt from it.

There was just something about a freshly oiled floor, Lizzie thought, as she breathed in deeply after everyone else had gone home. It reminded her of her own Teacher Katie and her yellow apple, of a piece of fresh chalk in the blackboard tray, of clapping erasers in the sunshine while holding her head to the side as she squinted through the white dust at her friends who were doing the same thing. School was just a wonderful place to be, especially now since she was the teacher with so many new plans and ideas floating about in her head. She had a list of all her pupils. Some were Mennonite and some were Amish children, but to Lizzie there was no difference. She looked forward to having each one as her pupil.

Sitting at her desk, she clasped her hands in front of her and took a deep breath of absolute delight. Imagine! This was her very own teacher's desk with a wooden chair that had arms at the side and swiveled just like Teacher Katie's chair. Lizzie reached down and lifted up a plastic bag from the floor which contained new bookends, a pretty apple mug for her pens, and a basket to hold papers that had been corrected. She arranged each item, stacking her teacher's answer keys in sequence, starting with eighth grade on the left through third grade on the far right. First and second grades had workbooks with different answer books, so they went into her deep drawer on the left.

She hung name charts on the wall, each one a covered wagon designed with each pupil's name stenciled on it in black marker. Then she adjusted the A-B-C and 1-2-3 charts that the first-graders used and began taping name tags on each pupil's desk. Eighth-graders in the big seats along the back wall, followed by seats for the seventh-graders, and on down to the little first-graders at the front of the room whose desks seemed to be only knee-high.

Lizzie smiled to herself as she pictured the incoming first-grade class. Those little Mennonite girls were so sweet in their flowered dresses, with pigtails and barrettes in their hair. She could hardly wait to be their teacher. She frowned a bit, thinking about the upper-grade boys. Only a few years ago she had been a pupil here, playing baseball with some of the boys who would now be her pupils this year. She hoped with all her heart that they would respect her enough to behave most of the time. They weren't openly disobedient boys, just mischievous like all boys.

After everything was in order she stepped back and looked at the classroom, smiling with satisfaction. It was old, no doubt about it, with mismatched desks and chairs, cracked plaster ceilings, and an old wood furnace, but it was sparkling clean with a freshly washed blackboard and long pieces of white chalk lying in the wooden tray waiting to be used. Carefully she took a piece of chalk and wrote, "Monday, August 25," across the top of the board.

Oh, my, she thought. That is the grandest thing, writing on a blackboard like a real honest-to-goodness teacher. She stepped back and admired the teacherly slant to her handwriting, which bolstered her courage to begin teaching. She may not be very good at finding a husband, but she sure could write like a teacher.

Lizzie woke up early on the first day of school. She put on a forest-green dress, pinning the cape carefully into place, wetting her hair so she could roll it back neatly on either side of her head. When she finished combing her hair, she adjusted her black belt apron before turning around at least half a dozen times in front of the mirror to make sure everything was tucked, pinned, and pleated perfectly. Twenty pairs of eyes would be checking her out very closely, and she wanted to appear as neat and teacherly as possible.

Lizzie choked on her pancake before giving up on eating breakfast. She just wasn't hungry with all those butterflies in her stomach. Every time she thought of standing behind her desk to read the Bible story book, her stomach did a perfect flip-flop.

Emma glanced at Lizzie's uneaten food and raised her eyebrows.

"Butterflies?" she asked.

"Sort of," Lizzie admitted, laughing.

Mam put down her coffee cup.

"You'll do fine, Lizzie. You have more gumption when it comes to something like this than any of the other girls," she said.

That was all it took to calm Lizzie's nerves. If Mam placed so much faith in Lizzie's ability to face a classroom filled with eight grades, then Lizzie knew she could do her job well. She sighed, beaming at Mam, and then pulled up on the shoulders of her cape and went to the front window to watch for her driver.

The driver was an older gentleman who made a good living as a driver for Amish people in the community. Lizzie knew him well so she didn't mind sitting up front and chatting with him on the way to school. Jason sat in the back seat with a group of his friends as the van stopped at different Amish homes, picking up more of Lizzie's students en route to the brick schoolhouse.

There was a small group of Mennonite children on the playground when Lizzie arrived. As she unlocked the door she smiled at a few small children who stood in the background. Lizzie's worries faded as the students entered the classroom. The children just took over, crowding around her desk, introducing themselves, oohing and aahing about the name charts on the walls, admiring the cup where her pens and pencils were kept, and finding the desks with their names written on the tags.

Lizzie discovered to her delight that she could move quite unself-consciously about her classroom, the children's unabashed happiness making her forget all about her shyness. It's just like being at home, she thought happily. Oh, this will be so much fun. I'm going to teach school and never, ever get married.

When she rang the hand bell, everyone went quickly to their seats—so quickly, in fact, that Lizzie almost burst out laughing. They were so eager to please her. Surely this wouldn't last for long. Lizzie cleared her throat.

"Good morning, boys and girls!"

The whole classroom, except a few scared first-graders, answered, "Good morning, Teacher!"

Lizzie bent her head and read the very first story in the Bible story book about creation and the Garden of Eden. After she finished, the children stood beside their desks, and they all said the Lord's Prayer. Lizzie was desperately afraid she would forget a line, but she closed her eyes and concentrated, finding it harder to get through the prayer than she had thought.

Next, the children all filed up to the blackboard behind her desk and stood hesitantly while Lizzie sorted them by height for singing class. Jason and the other upper-graders stood in a row along the blackboard, followed by a second row of fifth- and sixth-graders who were a bit smaller, and so on until the first-graders stood beside the second grade in the front row.

"There, that looks pretty good," Lizzie said. "Maybe... Jason, would you trade places with Robert?"

She switched a few more children until the biggest children stood in the middle and the shortest stood on each side. Lizzie handed out the songbooks and picked the first song, an easy hymn that most children knew well, "Life's Railway to Heaven." After she started the song, they joined her, singing along as well as you could expect a group who wasn't accustomed to singing together.

Lizzie smiled at them reassuringly, noticing the one little first-grade girl looking a bit sad. If that little girl cries, I'm not going to sing one more song. I mean it, Lizzie thought, remembering the time she had been in first grade, so absolutely terrified about the stars falling that she could not wait to go home to Mam. But the little girl soldiered bravely on, trying her best to remain upbeat and positive, although the display of emotions on her small upturned face was heartbreaking. Lizzie couldn't stand another minute of seeing that poor, brave, little girl putting forth so much effort to keep from crying, so she said, "All right, we'll just sing two songs this morning because we only have a half-day today. It's our very first day, of course."

As the pupils filed to their seats, she smiled at the frightened little girl who dipped her head shyly and scuttled to her seat.

Lizzie asked the children to introduce themselves, saying their full names so she could begin to memorize who sat in which desk. The first-graders were Rosa, David, and Arlene, who whispered their names so quietly Lizzie could barely hear them.

The remainder of the day flew by on wings. She barely had time to look at the clock. She helped the pupils with their books and workbooks, passing out clean new tablets, pencils, and erasers. She showed the first and second grade where the scissors was kept on a hook low on the wall. She told them they'd have lots of cutting and pasting to do, which brought a shy smile to Rosa's face.

What an adorable child, Lizzie thought. But I'm not allowed to have teacher's pets. That doesn't work at all.

There were so many things to do, assigning the next day's work, finding the proper pages for the lower grades, answering raised hands in between her other duties, that the clock showed eleven-thirty before she was finished.

They had only half-days that first week, an old custom that allowed the children to go home and help their parents with the end of the summer's harvest. So at noon Lizzie quickly told everyone to put their books away just as the school van driver pulled into the schoolyard. Oh, dear, we haven't even swept or cleaned up a thing, she thought. Oh, well, it's my first day. I'll keep getting better, I hope.

She told everyone they would learn their good-bye song the following day and tapped the bell to dismiss them. She was shocked to hear everyone shout, "Good-bye, Teacher! Good-bye. Good-bye!" as they scrambled for the front door. Lizzie tried to answer, but there was no use. They would never have heard her over the din, even if she had yelled at the top of her lungs. She would have to try and quiet down this enthusiastic parting. But then, maybe the children would be insulted and think she was some doddering old maid who lived a joyless existence. Quickly, she packed a few things in her book bag, locked the door, and climbed into the front seat of the school van.

She sighed as the van pulled away from the school, and the driver smiled at her.

"Big day?" he asked.

Lizzie nodded.

They talked most of the way home, and, as usual, Lizzie could hardly wait to get there because she was bursting with lots of things to tell Mam. Emma and Mandy were away working, she knew, but it was lunch-time, so Dat would be in the house.

"How did it go, Lizzie?" he asked, as she hurried in the door.

"Oh, good! Really good. Except a little, first-grade girl almost cried, and Dat, I mean it, they're so loud after I dismiss them, it isn't even normal. They yell good-bye with all their might."

Dat chuckled as he took a bite of homemade vegetable soup.

"I guess they're glad to be out of there," he said.

As he crumbled a handful of saltines into the soup, he started to blink his eyes rapidly. He bent his head to take off his glasses and rub his hands across both eyes as he continued to blink.

"Can't figure out what's wrong with my eyes this morning. Everything seems a bit fuzzy, especially my one eye," he said, as he put his glasses back on while blinking over and over.

"Didn't you sleep well?" Mam asked.

"Just as good as usual," Dat answered.

"Which must be pretty good by the sounds of your snoring. I can hear you from my upstairs bedroom sometimes," Lizzie said, laughing.

"That's Mam you hear!" Dat said.

"Oh, I wouldn't say that, Melvin. Who knows? We both snore."

Jason slid onto the bench beside Lizzie.

"I'm starved!" he said.

"Here. Take some vegetable soup," Mam said, hovering over him, seeing that he had bread, cheese, and sweet bologna. Jason slapped bologna on a slice of bread, threw a piece of cheese on top, smashed the second piece of bread down on the cheese, and stuffed half of the dry sandwich into his mouth.

Jason's eating never failed to amaze Lizzie. He took bites twice the size of an ordinary person and swallowed promptly. You could hardly ever see him chewing; well, not very much, anyway. He ate so fast, Lizzie could never understand how he didn't upset his stomach when he swallowed his food without chewing properly.

"Pickles!" Jason said loudly.

"Your sandwich is too dry, isn't it?" Lizzie grinned at him.

"No, 'course not. I'm just hungry for a pickle."

"How did it feel to have Lizzie for a teacher?" Mam asked.

Jason's mouth was stuffed with pickles, so he nodded his head before bending it to eat the other half of his sandwich in one bite.

Dat shook his head, watching Jason eat.

"As soon as you have time, you can answer Mam," he said, his eyes twinkling.

Jason swallowed and nodded his head again. "Good. I think she's going to be all right. She's a good teacher!"

He started slurping soup, so Lizzie knew that was as much as he would say. She looked at Mam, beaming, and Mam smiled back.

"Good for you, Lizzie. I knew you could do it. Do you think you'll like it? This is only the first day, you know."

"I love it, Mam. I really do. I can't imagine getting the blues from teaching school. It's so much more challenging than standing at that egg-grading machine or working as a *maud*."

"There'll be times when you wish life was as simple as grading eggs, though. You can't teach school without occasional troubles along the way," Dat said wisely.

"How do you know?" Lizzie asked.

"Because I taught school one year," Dat said.

"Did you really? I never knew that."

So Dat launched into an account of his one year of teaching school when he and Mam were first married and living in Ohio. It was fascinating to listen to him tell the story of serious discipline problems, among other troubles he had encountered. But Dat's stories didn't worry Lizzie. She was quite sure that teaching school was the single most wonderful thing in the entire world, and there wasn't too much that could happen to change her mind. It was a whole lot easier than finding a husband.

Chapter 5

LIZZIE NARROWED HER EYES AS SHE LOOKED over her shoulder, pinning her white cape neatly into place.

"That's crooked," Mandy said, around a pin in her mouth. Lizzie sighed with exasperation before saying loudly, "Take that pin out of your mouth this second. I hate when you put a straight pin in there. Mam used to do that when we were little girls."

"I won't swallow it."

"Take it out!"

"Grouch."

Lizzie looked over her opposite shoulder, trying to get the pleats in her white organdy cape straight. Of all the clothes they wore, white organdy for church was the hardest to handle.

"Mandy, fix this!" Lizzie said, unable to get the whole thing straight. Mandy helped, adjusting a few pins, before saying, "Lizzie, aren't you thrilled about our new friends we'll get to meet today?"

More new families were moving to Cameron County that fall, including the Marks family with four girls near in age to Lizzie and her sisters. A young man had also recently moved there to help his brother, a bachelor, with the farming.

"Of course! Maybe if we have a few more teenagers we'll start to run around here in Cameron County and not bother going to Allen County at all anymore. Marvin was talking about it last weekend."

"Really?"

"Mmm-hmm."

"Goody, Lizzie! I'll soon be 16, and I don't really want to go to Allen County. It's too far away."

"Hurry up, girls. Time to leave," Mam called up the stairway.

Hurriedly, they pinned their black coverings to their heads, grabbed their black woolen shawls and bonnets and skipped down the steps. Emma ran lightly down the stairs behind them, a bottle of lotion clasped in one hand. In the kitchen, KatieAnn and Susan put on their coats and shawls, followed by their navy blue bonnets, while Mam hurried to get everyone out the door to the waiting carriage.

Lizzie scooped up Susan and planted a kiss on her little cheek. "You look so cute in your shawl and bonnet," she said.

"Let me down!" Susan said, wiping her cheek as she glared at Lizzie. Everyone laughed as they hurried out the door, while Dat stood wiping the mirror on the buggy with his clean, white, Sunday handkerchief.

❧

At church, Lizzie sat next to Mandy on the long, backless bench on the women's side of the room. As the boys filed into the room, they bent slightly to shake hands with the ministers before going to the men's side of the room to sit. A tall boy whom Lizzie didn't recognize joined the group. That must be the new boy who's moving in with his bachelor brother, Lizzie thought. She dug her elbow into Mandy's side.

"Is that him?" she whispered.

"Probably," Mandy whispered back.

He was taller than Uncle Marvin, with long, jet-black hair which hung in loose waves. His eyes were almost as dark as his hair, and he had an almost perfect nose and mouth. His face was expressionless and polite, but Lizzie was fascinated by his dark, good looks. Mandy must be, too, she thought, watching her. Oh, well, no use planning about this one as a husband. He'd probably go the way of Amos and of Joe and John, the twins who had caught Lizzie's eye in vocational school. Or he'd act like Stephen. He'd tell her that he thought she was pretty once and then never mention it again.

Stephen, Joe, and John filed into the room. The twins, once small for their age when they were in Lizzie's vocational class, had grown to almost normal size. They were still as blond and blue-eyed as ever. Stephen stood tall and dark beside them, his blue eyes flashing around the room until they landed on her. He smiled. Irritated, Lizzie turned away.

During services, Lizzie considered the possibility of staying here in Cameron County on weekends. Allen County had lost much of its charm since Amos and Ruthie were dating, she had to admit. Now there were enough young people in church to have their own supper crowd somewhere nearby and have a singing in the evening each weekend. That would be exciting, something new, and she bet they would have lots of fun once everyone became acquainted.

Doddy Glick stood up to give the main sermon, and, as usual, he preached with fervor. He always became quite loud, waving his arms for emphasis as he exhorted the congregation, adding Old Testament stories as examples for their everyday lives. Lizzie never tired of listening to Doddy preach, enjoying his stories of Gideon, David, and other Old Testament heroes.

After services, Lizzie asked Uncle Marvin if he was planning to stay here for the rest of the weekend. He raised his eyebrows and nodded toward the Marks sisters and said he guessed he'd have to since they had more young people now. Lizzie laughed and hit his arm playfully.

"Oh, you! I know exactly why you aren't going to Allen County!"

"Should we try and have a singing here? Do you want me to ask if Aaron Fishers want to hold one? Or what? What could we do this afternoon?" he asked.

Stephen and the new young man, John, walked up to Marvin.

"Hello," they said, nodding to Lizzie.

"Hi!"

"So... do we want to go boating?" Marvin asked.

"The water's too low," Stephen said. "We need more rain."

"Volleyball?" Marvin asked.

"We can go down to my brother's place," John offered.

Lizzie watched him speak, quite impressed with this tall guy. Of course, she wanted to go to his brother's place, and now she had several girlfriends and Mandy to go with her, all of whom had recently turned 16.

"I have to do evening chores because Leroy is in Allen County," John said.

"Good! We'll help you!" Marvin volunteered. "Do we want the girls to go along? There are only three of them."

"They can make supper," John said, smiling shyly.

Lizzie was ecstatic! She walked as calmly as she possibly could to the washhouse and almost shrieked as she grabbed Rebecca's hand.

"Rebecca, I'm so glad you're 16. And Mandy and Mary Ann just turned 16! We're going to have so much fun together. First of all, the boys are doing chores at Leroy Zook's place. You know, that old guy that's dating Emma's friend. They want us to go along and make supper!"

"Does that mean we're going to start having suppers and singings here now?" Rebecca asked.

"I guess that's up to the parents, but I think everyone would be glad to have singings, even if the group is small. Should we ask Aaron's wife if they want a hymn-singing this evening after the boys have finished the chores at Leroy's farm?"

❧

And so plans were made, with the small group of youth being "officially" started in Cameron County. The girls had great fun cooking supper through trial and error at Leroy Zook's house as the boys did the evening chores. Mary Ann was easy to talk to and, after a few hours together, Lizzie felt as if they had known each other for a long time. Rebecca was also talkative and good-natured with an easy laugh, and her antics never failed to send Lizzie into rounds of helpless laughter.

The boys came in for supper, filling their plates before sitting in the living room to eat. The girls ate around the kitchen table, laughing about the lumpy gravy on the mashed potatoes.

"This is a nice farm," Mary Ann said.

Lizzie agreed. The house wasn't new, but it had four good-sized rooms with a porch running along the front of the house. The view was nice, overlooking rolling pastures and neighboring farms. Leroy had recently built a new cow stable, and a new silo jutted up against the looming mountain, giving the whole farm a prosperous look.

What would it be like to marry John and live here in this farmhouse, milking cows every morning? Lizzie thought she could marry a farmer if he looked like John. It wouldn't be so bad to stumble out to a cow stable at five o'clock in the morning if a husband that good-looking was beside you, helping you milk cows.

Was John a farmer, or was he only helping out his brother for a little bit before returning to Lamton with its big community of Amish folks? Did he have a girlfriend? She wondered how he was going to the singing that evening, and if she might be riding in the same buggy.

❧

But when it was time to go to the singing, Marvin, of course, offered to take all three girls in his buggy. So Lizzie knew there would be no riding to the singing with John because it wasn't fair to make the other girls go alone with the boys. Mary Ann was still new, and she couldn't do that to her. So she told Marvin, all right, they would all go with him.

How unexciting, she thought, as she sat in the back seat of Marvin's buggy, slouched down and pouting just a tiny bit. Maybe if Marvin wouldn't have been quite so eager to ask us, John would have gone with me and Mary Ann. Oh well, she decided, that made no sense either, so there was no use being upset.

When they arrived at the singing, the kitchen table was already spread out long enough so everyone could sit around it, boys on one side and girls on the other. Some parents had come to help sing as well. Aaron Fisher's wife set pitchers of water and some paper cups on the table so no one would get thirsty. Since Lizzie was a schoolteacher, the girls said she could start the first song, an old German hymn she knew well from school and from singing it in Allen County with the youth there.

Glancing nervously at John, she cleared her throat and started the song. Marvin was a good singer, and he joined in heartily. The parents helped along immediately, realizing that there were only a few youth to keep the singing going smoothly. They sang one hymn after another, old German songs that had been sung by Amish youth for years and years. Lizzie especially enjoyed these old hymns, and she loved to sing. The evening sped by.

Mrs. Fisher served a snack of pretzels and cheese, leftover snitz pie, and grape juice after the singing was over. Lizzie and her friends laughed and talked with the parents easily. In this small budding community, the two generations had a close relationship. Some of the parents asked Lizzie how teaching was going and if the children were causing any trouble.

Marvin said he could take Lizzie home after the singing, which puzzled her. Stephen and Rebecca lived closer to her than Marvin, and she was sure they wouldn't mind dropping her off. She told Marvin so, but he insisted, telling her he really wanted to. It was time they had a good old chat to catch up again, he said.

That warmed Lizzie's heart, and she was glad he wanted to take her home, even if it meant many extra miles for Marvin. They hadn't gone very far before Marvin blurted out, "Lizzie, it's no wonder you don't have a boyfriend."

Lizzie's heart thudded and sank to her shoes. A heart couldn't sink to your shoes, she always thought, but sometimes when something shocked her, she had that kind of sensation, a sinking, downward feeling.

"Whatever makes you say that?" she breathed.

"Well, you know you are my dear 'niecely,' but you need to sit up and take notice. I don't want to hurt your feelings, Lizzie, but I can hardly stand to see something that you are so blind about."

"What on earth are you talking about, Marvin?"

"Well, hey, fix that rearview mirror. When a car comes up behind me, the headlights are blinding."

Typical proper Marvin, Lizzie thought as she opened the door of the buggy and adjusted the mirror.

"Right. Turn it a little to the right. There."

Lizzie closed the door, and Marvin continued.

"Just like now. This John guy coming out from Lamton, I can just see how he thrills you, and you bat your eyelashes, and you're all nervous and giggly when he's around."

"Every one of us girls was!" Lizzie burst out.

"I know. I know. I can see why. I mean, it's only normal, but that really bugs me, and since John is here, I have to say something. Lizzie, don't you even notice Stephen?"

Lizzie was dumbfounded.

"What do you mean, notice him?"

"Well, it's as plain as day, Lizzie. He adores the ground you walk on, he would do anything for you, and you notice him as much as... as an insect!" Marvin said.

"Marvin! I don't!"

"You do!"

"I don't. I mean it. I like Stephen. We talk a lot. All the time, actually. He's one of my friends. I mean... I do not treat him like an insect."

"See, Lizzie. Maybe that's why Amos started dating Ruthie—because he wasn't meant for you. It seems as if you always want someone else, and it's so plain what's happening right under your nose, but you're too busy always chasing after someone else."

"I don't chase after boys!" Lizzie shouted.

"Not so loud. You know what I mean."

Lizzie said nothing, just leaned back against the seat and crossed her arms tightly. Of all the nerve! This was the worst! How was she supposed to know how Stephen felt? All he ever said was that she was pretty once. But what did that really mean?

"I'm sorry, niecely."

Lizzie didn't answer. She was too angry.

"But please, Lizzie. Stephen is a great guy, a really nice, genuine kind of person. He doesn't think highly of himself, and maybe that's why he acts kind of different sometimes. But, ach well, I guess I can hardly stand to see him like you as much as he does, and you're off on Cloud Nine somewhere."

"I like Stephen, Marvin."

"But not in that way, right?"

"Well… not really. I mean, I guess if I knew he liked me, but…" Lizzie was at a loss for words.

"All right. I won't push some big burden on you, Lizzie. But, seriously, try and pray about it and regard him in a different light. You know, maybe he has all the feelings for you because it's meant to be, and you're just not listening to God's voice."

There was silence in the buggy except for the wheels rattling over the gravel and the horses' hooves spitting it against the bottom of the buggy. When they rolled to a stop by the sidewalk, Lizzie couldn't believe they were at home.

"There you go, Lizzie. Sorry if I offended you." Marvin slid his arm around her shoulders and squeezed affectionately. "Just think about it. Okay?"

There was already a dangerous lump forming in Lizzie's throat, the kind that quickly dissolves into embarrassing tears. She hopped out of the buggy, choking on her "Thanks, Marvin!" as she ran up the sidewalk.

Dear, caring Marvin. Who can stay angry at him? He's so genuinely honest.

When she hurried through the kitchen without speaking to Joshua and Emma, who were having a snack at the kitchen table, they looked at each other and shrugged. It was hard to tell what had happened now.

Chapter 6

Ever since Mandy had turned 16 years old, Lizzie was very happy. She was enjoying running around even more now that Mandy was allowed to go away with her on weekends. To celebrate, they had a great time painting and redecorating a room for Mandy and moving Lizzie's old bedroom suite into her room.

One snowy afternoon, shortly after Mandy's birthday, Lizzie sat at the sewing machine, a frown creasing her brow as she used the seam ripper to open the seam of a sleeve she had accidentally sewed on with the inside out. Finally, she stuck a few stray hairs under her covering, pushed back her chair in exasperation, threw down the offending garment, and marched out to the kitchen.

"I hate that fabric!" she said, much louder than necessary.

Mam looked up from watering the geraniums in the window. "Now what?" she asked.

"Why don't they produce fabric that looks the same on both sides?" Lizzie said, reaching for a warm chocolate chip cookie.

"I don't know," Mam said absentmindedly, her attention on a vine that needed inspection. "Hmm. This thing has mealybugs, that's what," she muttered.

Lizzie watched her mother with narrowed eyes. "You're not listening to me," Lizzie whined.

"Hmm?"

The door opened and Dat came into the kitchen, closing the door firmly behind him as he shivered, pulling off his coat and hat.

"Brrr! That air goes right through to the bones. It's a good thing I fixed those cow stable windows this week. I'm going to warm up and take a bit of a break. I'm just plain cold the whole way through."

Lizzie munched her cookie, saying nothing while Dat rubbed his hands together.

"Oh, yes, the phone was ringing out in the shanty when I went to call the vet. It was Henry's Sharon. She's having a sledding party at their farm this evening."

Lizzie sat up, brightening noticeably. Saturday evening! Maybe they could stay at Sharon's house for the night!

"Oh, goody!" Lizzie shouted.

"You sound like a five-year-old," Mandy said, grinning.

"You're just as excited as I am!" Lizzie said. She stuck out her tongue at Mandy.

❧

The snow continued to fall all day, turning the outdoors into a winter wonderland as Lizzie and Mandy traveled to Sharon's house. When they arrived, they were surprised to see a few other buggies parked by the horse barn.

They knocked lightly on the kitchen door. It burst open, and Sara Ruth and Rebecca pulled them into the house.

"You're late!" they said in unison, enveloping both girls with mittened hands.

"Bess had a shoe missing, so we had to get a driver," Mandy explained.

"It's okay. Sharon's mom made pizza!"

The kitchen had a warm, spicy, tomatoey smell, which mixed well with the aroma of homemade yeast dough. Lizzie's stomach rumbled unexpectedly, reminding her of how hungry she really was. Always watching her weight, she hadn't eaten any lunch or supper, only breakfast and one chocolate chip cookie that afternoon. She always wanted to feel thin, especially on running around weekends, so often on Saturdays she ate very little.

Sharon's mother, Cathy, was bustling between the table and the oven, setting two huge, round pizzas on the table. She grinned at Lizzie and Mandy.

"Where were you?" she asked.

"Late, evidently," Lizzie said, smiling.

"No, you're just in time," Cathy said. She was a small, gray-haired woman, formerly from an Amish community in Indiana. She had a quiet smile and manner of speaking. Lizzie loved to go to Sharon's house, feeling very welcome to spend the night or just be with Sharon. Her father, Henry, was a farmer who was just as friendly and welcoming as his wife.

"Help yourselves. Pizza's done," Henry boomed to the group of young men who were seated in the living room. They wasted no time in heaping their plates with pizza, potato chips, cheese, bologna, and other snacks.

Lizzie said hello to everyone before helping herself to a slice of the thick homemade pizza. It was one of the most delicious things she had ever eaten. The crust was thick and springy, with hot tomato sauce and cheese melting off the sides. Sausage and pepperoni sat on top of the melting cheese.

Oh, well, we're going sledding, Lizzie thought as she took a big bite, so I'll work off all the calories in this wonderful pizza.

After they finished eating and had helped Cathy with the dishes, Lizzie and her friends zipped up their snow boots, buttoned their coats, and tied their white scarves securely. Talking and laughing, they wound their way across the road and up a long twisting path to the top of a hill. Since visibility was limited with the snow whirling past them, the boys set gas lanterns in the snow at different points to mark the trail they would sled down. The group pulled wooden sleds with runners, a toboggan, plastic sleds, round sleds — anything that would whisk them down the hill.

The girls mostly used the runner sleds and the boys piled on the long wooden toboggan, determined to see how many could fit on at one time and how fast they would go.

Lizzie wasn't normally afraid of sledding, but watching the toboggan streak past her at such an alarming speed terrified her. The boys whizzed by so fast in one long dark blur, often losing one or two riders before they slowed at the bottom of the hill.

Later in the evening, the boys started a roaring bonfire in a small patch of trees, protected from the steady east wind and blowing snowflakes. One by one, the girls tired of sledding and sat by the fire to warm themselves.

Lizzie hadn't realized that she and Mandy were the only remaining girls sledding until John Zook and Paul Esh asked them to try a toboggan ride.

Mandy quickly accepted, which really irked Lizzie. *She's probably as scared as I am, but if John asks her to go, she'll go,* Lizzie thought. *She'd try to fly off a house roof if he asked her to jump.*

"Come on, Lizzie!" Mandy shouted.

"I'm not going."

"Come on!"

"No!"

"We won't go as fast if you girls go," Paul assured them. He was new to Cameron County, but he was easy to get along with and really funny. He had quickly become one of Lizzie's good friends, and she often confided in him.

Lizzie looked at Paul skeptically. "I don't know

about you."

"We'll be careful. Come on, pile on. Ladies before gentlemen!" Paul laughed.

"How many are going?"

"Just you and Mandy, me and John."

"I'll push you," Stephen offered, as he walked up to join them.

Her heart hammering in her chest, Lizzie seated herself behind Mandy. The boys piled on the back, telling the sisters to keep their feet on the sled. When the boys yelled "right" or "left," the girls should lean in that direction in order to steer the toboggan. Stephen showed Lizzie how to hang on to the rope attached along each side of the sled. She bit her lip, sniffed, blinked the snowflakes from her eyes, and tried to stay calm.

Mandy was eagerly leaning forward. "What are we waiting on? Let's go!"

There were a few thudding sounds as Stephen pushed on Paul's shoulders before he leaped on the back. Then the only sensation was black, whirling, blinding speed. It was the most helplessly, horrifying feeling Lizzie had ever experienced. She could see nothing at all, except sometimes Mandy's white-clad head bobbing up in front of her. The wind whistled so fast it was almost like a huge, sucking void that took her breath away.

When she could no longer bear the feeling of falling into a dark, bottomless hole, she screamed. She continued to yell at the top of her lungs, afraid to keep going and afraid to roll off.

She sincerely hoped they would each remain in one piece when they came to the bottom of this gigantic, seemingly endless hill. When her mouth became too dry from screaming, she just clamped it shut and hated Mandy with all her might. It was all her fault. She was just showing off for John. Just when Lizzie thought she would faint from pure terror, the swishing sound slowed to a whisper and they swooshed to a stop.

Mandy was laughing helplessly. "Hooo-boy!" she said, scrambling to her feet and wiping furiously at her snow-encrusted hair and scarf. "Let's do it again!"

John walked over to her side, put a hand on her shoulder, and wiped snow off her scarf. Even in the faint lantern light, Lizzie could see the sincere admiration in his eyes as he bent his head and said, "You really liked that, didn't you?"

"Of course!" Mandy said gleefully, looking up at him, her green eyes shining. So John just kept his hand on her shoulder as they began walking back up the hill. Oh, great! Lizzie thought, seething. How cute. She just turns 16, and already they're this charming little couple who have eyes only for each other.

She was angry. Mostly angry at Mandy for making her go along, but also angry at herself for feeling so horribly jealous of her own sister. She loved Mandy, so why did she struggle with this anger toward her now? John Zook. No, she knew she had no chance with him, but... the truth confronted her nevertheless, raising its big taunting head, blotting out any happy thoughts of the future.

She tried hard to accept the fact that John had no interest in her, even praying earnestly that God would not let these ugly feelings take control of her. But when Lizzie was with John and Mandy and confronted with their evident admiration of each other, it was more than she could handle. Especially when Mandy acted so sporty. Lizzie guaranteed that Mandy had been just as scared as she, but, oh, no, she would never admit it.

Lizzie yanked off her head scarf, shaking the snow from it, wiping her face with her mittens as she watched the retreating figures. She dusted off the front of her coat, stomped her feet to shake off the snow, and started trudging up the long, winding trail.

Suddenly, there was someone beside her. She turned, alarmed, to find Stephen in step with her.

Lizzie laughed ruefully. "I declare, you have the most annoying habit of sneaking up on someone!"

"I didn't sneak up on you."

"Yes, you did."

He didn't answer and they walked side by side up the slippery slope. Lizzie's breath came in short, panting gasps until she gave up and stopped.

"Whew! This really tires a person, doesn't it?"

"Not like the mountain."

Lizzie peered through the darkness at Stephen's face. He was very nice-looking, she realized again.

He stepped closer to Lizzie and said, "Lizzie, you

should go hiking with me sometime. I love to go tramping around in the mountain. You can always see deer or grouse, squirrels, or just whatever."

Lizzie was quite taken aback. She looked up at Stephen and blinked rapidly. Was he serious? Did he mean that they, just the two of them, should go hiking together, like a real date sort of thing? Or did he mean just in the way he would ask Paul or John to go with him, as a good buddy type of thing? Stephen was just mysteriously different. That's all there was to it.

"You mean in the wintertime?" Lizzie asked, laughing.

"No, some time when it gets warmer."

He paused before continuing, "'Course, I guess we can't go this year anymore. I'm going to another county in northern Pennsylvania to work for my uncle who just moved there a few months ago."

"You mean to live there? You'll stay there on the weekends, too?" Lizzie asked, incredulous. She couldn't imagine weekends without Stephen.

"Yeah."

There was silence as Lizzie scuffed the toe of her boot into the snow, as the soft snowflakes fell around them in the velvety night. Suddenly she raised her head and asked, "Why?"

"Why do you care if I stay there or not?" Stephen asked shortly.

"I ... I don't. I mean ... I do ... I mean, I'm going to miss you. It won't be the same without you. But ... " Lizzie shrugged helplessly.

Suddenly, Stephen moved close to her, and she felt the weight of both of his hands on her shoulders. Her breathing stopped, fading away to nothing, her heart hammering even as she felt as if all the oxygen was knocked out of her. She could not look up so she stood quietly, her breath coming in small jagged whispers.

"Lizzie, I'm going away because of you."

She lifted her head in one quick fluid movement. His eyes shone with a light of love or of pain… She wasn't sure which, but she quickly bent her head against his gaze, wanting to defend herself against… against what? She didn't know. She just knew she couldn't go on looking into his blue eyes.

"You know how it is," Stephen continued. "I've always, well, admired you, or in plain words, wanted you for my serious girlfriend. Surely you can tell a little bit how I feel. And there's just never any sign of you returning that feeling. It's always someone else. You care more about every other young man than you do about me. So… I figure the best thing for me to do is leave for awhile and try to sort out my feelings."

Lizzie was speechless. How was she supposed to know how he felt? Okay, so Uncle Marvin had told her. But what did Uncle Marvin really know? Why hadn't Stephen told her, really told her, before now? Lizzie glanced around, wishing that Mandy was nearby. What was she supposed to do?

"I suppose I'm hoping you'll miss me, I guess, which is kind of dumb. But maybe you'll be able to... well, maybe someday you'll feel differently about me."

"But... but..." Lizzie was searching for the appropriate words. All in one rush she knew she didn't want him to go, but she also knew if he stayed she was not ready to commit herself to him before... Before what? She wasn't sure. Taking a deep breath to steady herself, she said, "Stephen, I do like you. You are a good friend, and I don't want you to go away if you don't want to."

"I do. I want to go," Stephen said.

That left her more confused than ever. He wanted to go. What if he found a nice girl in northern Pennsylvania and stayed there forever?

"Because you'll find another girl and marry her?" Lizzie asked.

Stephen made a derisive sound, stepped back, and started on up the hill. "As if you'd care," he flung back over his shoulder.

"Stephen!" Lizzie called. "Wait."

He stopped. She could talk better if she wasn't so close, especially if she could talk to the back of his head.

"Stephen, listen. Just give me some time. I need a few months to think and to sort out my feelings. Sometimes I feel confused, and I don't always understand myself. My... my mom says I run away from God's will, whatever that means."

Stephen turned, and taking both her mittened hands in his, he said, "Did she? Did your mom really say that?"

"Yes," Lizzie said, puzzled that it should mean so much to him.

"Well, I'll go now, Lizzie. I'm leaving in a few days. Be good, and don't forget about me."

And he was gone. Just as if the night and the swirling snow had swallowed him whole, he was suddenly no longer there. Lizzie searched the area where he had stood a moment before, but he had vanished into the blowing snow, leaving her standing by herself on the side of the hill, as alone and dejected as she could ever remember feeling. She lifted her face to the sky as her heart cried out to God for guidance. Just show me the way, she prayed. You have to make it very clear, because I don't understand very much about how you make your will known.

But she knew, more plainly than ever, that her heart yearned for God to direct her often shaking footsteps.

Chapter 7

A TOUCH OF SPRING SUNSHINE FLOODED THE Glick family's kitchen in a soft yellow glow. The stainless steel teakettle on the stove top sparkled and shone as the light bounced off the shining windowpane.

It was Saturday morning, when breakfast was always later and much more relaxed than on weekdays, because no one had to hurry off to their jobs or to school. Dat and Mam were contentedly sipping their steaming mugs of morning coffee as they laughed at the twins. KatieAnn and Susan were dark-haired and very pretty. Dat said Jason was turning into a tall young man, his blue-gray eyes usually crinkling into an expression of humor. His curly hair was his most attractive feature as he grew older, something which never ceased to amaze Lizzie, having endured all that worrying about his looks as a little girl. She had been so certain that Jason would never know what to do with his head full of curls springing in every direction.

Lizzie sighed happily as she spread strawberry jam on a crisp piece of toast. Mandy and Emma were already doing the dishes, and when Lizzie finished eating, they started deciding whose job it was to do the Saturday cleaning, who would do laundry, and who would tackle the lawn-mowing.

"Mow grass!" Lizzie yelled.

"Do laundry!" Emma shouted, imitating Lizzie.

"I'm not doing all the Saturday cleaning by myself," Mandy complained.

Lizzie looped one arm around Mandy's shoulders.

"I'll help you do the cleaning, and then maybe we can find some grass that's long enough to mow," she said.

Lizzie was returning from the back porch with the dust mop when the kitchen door opened and Dat came in, sitting down at the table, his eyes open wider than usual.

"Annie, I can't figure this out," he said, his voice rising. "It seems as if there is a fog over my eyes that just won't lift."

"What could it be?" Mam asked, turning to look at Dat with an expression of concern. "Do you have a headache? Are you sure you didn't get some sawdust or something in one of your eyes?"

Dat shook his head.

"Why don't you take off your shoes and go lie down for awhile? Maybe you overworked yesterday," Mam suggested.

Dat turned to go into the living room to rest on the sofa. Lizzie raised her eyebrows at Mam, who raised her shoulders in a gesture of "I don't know."

Turning, Lizzie went upstairs to join Mandy and Emma in cleaning the bedrooms. It was highly unusual for Dat to be in the house midmorning like this. Fear swirled around in her mind like an ugly gray vacuum, threatening to force her into its grip. What if there was something seriously wrong with Dat? What if he was going blind? Some people did. How would Mam manage the farm if Dat was no longer able to work? The vacuum of fear whirred noisily in her head until she found Emma plumping the pillows of her bed.

"What?" Emma turned, straightening her back, seeing the expression on Lizzie's face.

"Emma, Dat came in and said he has a fog in front of his eyes. He hasn't been able to see normally all morning. Suppose he's going blind?" Lizzie said, her voice squeaking with fear.

"Lizzie, now stop it. There you go again. Thinking the absolute worst. He probably just has a headache."

Emma returned to her bed-making, telling Lizzie to hurry up and get started. It was already late enough, and after all, this was Saturday, and Saturday evening came right after that, and Joshua was coming to pick her up at seven o'clock.

Lizzie turned on her heel, biting her tongue to keep the hot, angry words inside. No use letting it show, she thought. I do it often enough.

Her pride arranged properly, she hurried into her own room and started taking up rugs, yanking open the window to shake them outside. Her hand slipped and she tore a fingernail on the sharp, wooden window frame. The window crashed down on the rug as Lizzie hopped around her room, pinching the injured finger with the opposite hand.

"What in the world is going on?" Mandy asked as she stood in the doorway, her eyes wide.

"Oh, don't worry about it!" Lizzie yelled hysterically. "What do you care? I always make everything worse than it is. So who cares if Dat has a brain tumor or he's going blind? As long as the cleaning gets done and the yard looks nice!"

Great big tears of pain and frustration rolled down Lizzie's face as she continued hurling senseless accusations at her sister. Mandy stood in the doorway, her wide green eyes filled with alarm as she stared open-mouthed at Lizzie.

"Wha...what?" she finally managed. "Lizzie, what has gotten into you? You act like...like you're not even normal."

Lizzie sat down hard on the floor, still holding the injured finger. Sighing, she grabbed a few Kleenexes from the nightstand, honked loudly into them, and dried her tears. She pushed back a few strands of her brown hair, adjusted her covering, and straightened her black bib apron. Mandy sat down quietly, watching as Lizzie regained her composure. She knew it was better to remain quiet for awhile once Lizzie was in one of these moods.

"All right," Lizzie said finally. "Sorry."

Mandy still said nothing.

"I said, sorry," Lizzie repeated, glancing at Mandy quickly before her eyes fell at Mandy's pitying gaze.

"I know."

"Well, say something."

"What?"

"I don't know."

Lizzie took a deep breath before the words began tumbling out miserably. She was very, very worried about Dat. She had a feeling deep down inside that it was something more than just a fog in front of his eyes. And she couldn't stop thinking about what Marvin had said about Stephen and his feelings for her.

"Lizzie, I could just shake you," Mandy said sharply. "Don't cross the bridge before you get to it about Dat. Nobody knows, and it might not even be serious. What crawled over you?"

That was their favorite question to ask when they wanted to know what was wrong, or what had suddenly made the other person act in a strange way.

Lizzie jumped up and started sweeping furiously. "Come on, Mandy. We'll never get done at the rate we're going."

So Mandy closed her mouth, turned and left, and resumed cleaning her own room. Lizzie swept and dusted her room, carefully arranging her pretty things a bit differently. She stood back to survey a basket of dried flowers she had placed in another area and smiled with satisfaction. That was better. Turning, she placed a candle on the opposite end of her dresser, only to frown at the emptiness beside it. She started whistling under her breath as she found a small wooden dish to place beside the candle, which really evened things out.

Catching sight of herself in the mirror, she leaned forward to check her complexion. The dreaded blemishes were no longer as evident as she became older, so that was comforting. Same brown hair, plain, mousy, homely old brown, same as 75 percent of the population, she thought. Blue-gray eyes that sometimes turned green when she wore a dark, forest-green dress, which still made no sense. Same old rabbit teeth, but very white and not too bad when she smiled, she thought. She tried smiling deeply to watch for dimples, but even if she had some, they weren't natural, quirky, cute dimples, instead more like an extra line in her cheeks.

She smoothed her bib apron over her hips, wishing she was as thin as Mandy. Oh, well, too bad, so sad, she thought wryly. I'm not thin, never will be, but I'm not fat either.

I wonder... I really wonder... She hardly let herself think. How did she feel? Why should she care? Why was she nervous? Why would she even think about all this? Stephen was just... well, he was just a good friend, that was all.

She finished cleaning the bathroom, her thoughts in a constant whirl. Maybe that was why she was so upset about Dat's eyesight. It was her yet unexplained, unaccepted nervousness about this evening.

She had almost nothing to say as they finished the kitchen downstairs. Mam had cleaned the refrigerator, stove, and cabinets, wiping down the countertops as she always did. Lizzie and Mandy got down on their hands and knees, a bucket of soapy, clean-smelling water between them, and scrubbed the kitchen floor.

"Good job, girls," Mam said. "That's a great feeling, having the cleaning done."

"Where's Dat?" Lizzie asked.

"He got up and went back to work. He said he'll just have to ignore it awhile, and maybe it'll go away. Oh, I certainly hope so," Mam said as she watched Dat through the kitchen window.

After lunch, the girls went down to the lawn shed for the mowers. Dat had eaten a hearty meal, saying his eyesight seemed a bit better and hopefully that would be the end of it. So Lizzie's heart felt lighter as she found her favorite red mower beside the one Mandy always used.

Before they pushed them out the door, Lizzie blurted out, "I'm not going away tonight."

"Why?" Mandy asked in disbelief.

"Oh, I just don't feel like it. I'm tired and ... and I ... well, I just don't think I will."

"Lizzie, that is so absolutely not *you*," Emma said. "You always love to go away and be with your group of friends."

"Mandy and Emma, do we have time to talk?"

"Of course."

Lizzie bent down and picked a piece of grass. She looked at her sisters, then looked down at the piece of grass in her hand. She opened her mouth, made a sound, then closed it again.

"What?" Mandy urged. "You are one strange person today."

"No, I'm not. Okay, promise me you will not laugh."

Mandy's serious green eyes looked directly into Lizzie's, and neither one wavered as Emma said, "I promise I will not laugh."

They all lifted their faces and howled with laughter. They laughed until tears squeezed from Lizzie's eyes. Then they looked seriously at each other once more.

"I trust you both. You're always so wise; you really are. Now let's not laugh. Okay?"

"All right."

"Marvin told me that Stephen really likes me. Then Stephen told me he likes me so much he needs to leave the County for a while to get away from me. He's going to help his uncle farm. How am I supposed to feel? I mean, you know how it always was with us. He... he..."

"Likes you," Mandy finished matter-of-factly.

"Yes."

"Go on."

"But the thing that really bothers me most is that I feel so nervous and worried. I don't really want to see him ever again. And yet I do. I'm afraid that when he comes back, he won't seem like plain old Stephen anymore. Not at all. How am I supposed to feel? How does it feel, Emma, when you're in love like you and Joshua? So how am I going to know if he's the right one for me? Suppose this nervousness is all wrong, and Marvin's wrong, and Stephen doesn't like me one tiny bit anymore when he returns, and I'll like him as much as I used to like Amos?"

All Emma said was, "You'll know." That was all.

Then she was gone, off with her lawn mower, whistling in the nearly spring-time air. Lizzie looked over at Mandy who shrugged. Lizzie got up and hurried after Emma.

"Stop, Emma! You can't just go walking off like that. How will I know?"

"Lizzie, you'll know. You already do. God probably knew for a long time. You were just too thick-headed to hear him."

"Now stop acting like a prophet of some sort, Miss Know-It-All!"

Lizzie grabbed Emma's apron strings and pulled the bow loose, then ran to her mower and started pushing it as fast as she could. Oh, my! Oh, my! I'm going to go out tonight after all, Lizzie thought. That Emma. She thinks she knows everything. But really, she does.

Lizzie's heart sang as the mower cut the light green grass in an even swath. She loved to mow lawn, and today's taste of spring was certainly no exception. She felt some heat rise in her face, but she was used to the exertion of lawn-mowing. She kept steadily at her task. Her concerns about Dat's eyes were pushed to the background of her mind as she watched him clean the cow stable. Surely there was nothing too seriously wrong with him or he wouldn't have the strength to lift those huge forkfuls of cow manure.

Jason whistled at her as she stopped to rest, and she waved at him, smiling to herself. What would Dat do without Jason's help? He certainly was a hard worker for his age, and Dat appreciated him every day.

She shook her head ruefully as if to clear it, then stood up straight, took a deep breath, and put her mower away. It was time to clean the flower beds, too, and trim around them, so that would be a good place to be for awhile. On her knees.

Chapter 8

As SPRING BEGAN TO WARM TOWARD SUMMER, Lizzie's concerns about Stephen were overshadowed by her interest in Emma's future. Mam had begun fussing to Emma, wondering when Joshua would ask her to marry him, or if he had any plans of marrying her this year.

"You're young, Emma, but you've been dating well over two years, and sometimes it's better not to be dating for too long," she said, hurrying between the stove and refrigerator, preparing a quick supper for Dat.

Some Amish youth weren't ready to settle down right away, but not Emma. She had always been conscientious, aware of right from wrong. She had become a member of the church the previous year, taking instruction classes during the summer until she had been baptized in the fall.

It was all very serious for Emma, and she did not have a hard time giving in to the instruction of the ministers. She seemed to understand about the new birth, and that the water poured on her head was the outward sign of an inward change of heart, of giving her life to God.

Lizzie and Mandy both knew very surely, like the button on the flap of a pocket being buttoned securely, that they wanted to do exactly the same thing as Emma did. It never occurred to them that they wouldn't be Amish their whole lives. They each had a deeply ingrained knowledge that when the time was right, they would become baptized members, the same as Emma. God was very real to Emma, and she calmly listened to Bible stories at a very young age without getting the blues like Lizzie did.

Sometimes church made Lizzie sad. The feeling had started when Lizzie was a little girl. Some daughters sat with their fathers on the men's side during church. Lizzie and Mandy often sat with Dat because they were both better behaved with Dat. When Dat walked into church, Lizzie would take Mandy's hand, and the three of them would find a seat on a bench along the wall.

Once an unfamiliar man sat down beside Lizzie, along with his two strange-looking boys. He looked a bit scary to Lizzie. His boys were wriggling around on the bench, trying to take their coats off. He didn't help them, and Lizzie guessed he was mean to them. Lizzie moved as close to Dat as she could and put one hand under Dat's arm. He looked down at her and smiled. Lizzie felt a bit better.

Someone picked a song, saying the number in German. Dat found the page, and soon the room was filled with the sound of the slow German singing. Usually Lizzie enjoyed that, but for some reason, she felt like crying today. She blinked and tried to think happy thoughts, or at least something funny.

Suddenly, the strange man reached over and pinched one of his little boys. Then he twisted the boy's arm as he talked to him quite sternly. The little boy opened his mouth and let out a crying howl of pain and surprise.

Dat looked over at the howling little boy, but then politely looked away. Lizzie sat and looked straight ahead, too. The boy's father did not try to comfort him or make him feel better. He just sang loudly as his little boy wailed beside him. Lizzie had the blues. She was so afraid of that strange man, and Dat was singing as if nothing was wrong at all. She felt more and more dejected, even though she knew she was much too old to cry in church.

Her nose started to run, so she got out her little flowered handkerchief and carefully wiped it. Even before tears formed, a sob tore at her throat. Dat looked down at Lizzie. He put his arm around her, bent low, and whispered, "What's wrong, Lizzie?"

With Dat's kindness, her blues dissolved into tears, and she sobbed quietly. She hid her face in Dat's *mutsa*, or suit coat, and cried. He patted her shoulder and asked her again why she was crying. Lizzie couldn't tell him, because maybe she was acting like a baby. But she really did not like that man and his little boy. So Dat just kept his arm around her and let her cry quietly.

Lizzie felt a bit better after she was finished crying. When Dat patted her shoulder, she relaxed. She thought of snitz pie and cheese bread and wished it was time for church to be over. She drifted off to sleep, dreaming that she was eating peanut butter bread and bologna, and that the black-haired man took it from her and dipped it in his coffee.

⌀

Emma had never had any hesitation about church, just as she seemed so certain about Joshua.

"Mam, don't you know that old tradition of being asked to marry when the strawberries bloom?" Emma asked, her eyes twinkling.

"Pshaw!" Mam snorted. "Never heard of such a thing."

Lizzie giggled. That was Mam, all right. Because she came from Ohio where the culture was a bit different, she didn't like "these eastern old wives' tales." If it was an old Ohio tradition, it was all right, which always made Dat smile and shake his head. Mam was born and raised in Ohio, and that's just how she was.

"Joshua's parents come from the real old traditional state of Maryland," Emma said.

"His mother doesn't," Mam argued.

"Wherever. She knows all those sayings and even abides by them. Her favorite saying is, 'We didn't use to do that in the old days.'"

"Well, if Joshua waits to ask you to marry him until June..."

"Not June, Mam," Emma broke in. "Strawberries bloom in May!"

And sure enough, the next Monday morning, the first in May, Emma fairly danced down the steps, her cheeks flushed as she whistled nervously under her breath.

Uh-oh, here it comes, Lizzie thought from her seat on the bench where she sagged wearily after a late evening at a singing.

Mam had her back turned, flipping pancakes on the griddle.

"Is that you, Emma? Come put the toast in the broiler," she said.

Emma obeyed, saying nothing as she pulled out the broiler drawer from the gas stove, arranging the sliced white bread in neat rows. Lizzie yawned, her eyes watering, and she dabbed at them with the back of her hand. It was nearing the end of school, and she was happily looking forward to sleeping in during the summer.

"Boy, I'm tired! Wish school was over this week," she mumbled.

"Why?" Emma asked, straightening her back.

"I could sleep later in the morning."

"You won't be sleeping late too many mornings if we have a wedding at our house," Emma said, blushing.

"Who's having a wedding?" Mam asked without turning around.

"We are, Mam. Joshua asked me to marry him this fall," Emma said.

"What?"

Mam's spatula clattered to the floor as she whirled around, her eyes wide. Emma was laughing with tears in her eyes.

"Really, Emma? For real?" Mam quavered.

"Yes, for real, Mam."

Mam returned to her pancake turning, but Lizzie knew she only went back to her duty to hide her emotions. After awhile, when the pancakes were arranged on a plate, she turned.

"So, Emma, this is what you always wanted, isn't it?" But there was a catch in her voice, and her eyes glistened.

"Yes. You know it is," Emma said, almost shyly.

The breakfast table that morning was absolute bedlam. Everyone congratulating Emma, everyone asking about the wedding plans, everyone talking at once while no one listened.

Dat was very excited. His eyes weren't bothering him as much these days, and Lizzie hoped that whatever had ailed a few weeks ago was gone. Dat could hardly wait to tear down the dilapidated old washhouse, add a new basement for the laundry, and build a large, new living room. He loved to remodel, fix things, and make them look nice. Mam always said Dat was never happier than the times he was building something.

They planned, laughed, and talked until Lizzie had only 20 minutes to put on her cape and apron.

She flew up the stairs, threw on her clothes, and hurried down just in time to grab her coat as the school van pulled up.

❧

That evening as Lizzie and Emma swung on the newly painted porch swing, Lizzie suddenly became a bit wistful. She could not imagine life without Emma, and that thought suddenly took away some of the excitement of preparing for her sister's wedding.

"Emma, doesn't it make you one teeny bit sad about moving away from here?" Lizzie asked.

Emma looked over at Lizzie.

"You sound sad, Lizzie. You're such a strange duck!" She pinched her arm affectionately.

"Emma, it isn't funny. Don't you kind of ... well, just sort of wish you weren't getting married and could live here with me and Mam and Mandy for always?"

"Li-i-zzie!" Emma shrieked.

"Well, don't you? Not a teeny weeny bit, even?"

"Of course not!"

There was a quiet calm as the porch swing creaked and Emma slid one foot along the concrete floor in a rasping noise.

Well, Lizzie thought, either I'm not ready to get married or else I'm just different. If I knew I had to move to Allen County, 50 miles away, into an old farmhouse with some strange person I hardly knew,

I would most certainly have the blues.

She looked out over the pasture that led to the creek near Charlie Zimmerman's house, then back at the new living room and the freshly painted wash-line poles. She loved her home so much, there was no one going to get her to move away.

Mandy came through the door with a cereal dish held in one hand and a spoon in the other. She backed up to the porch swing and looked down at Lizzie.

"Slide over."

"If you give me a bite of whatever's in your dish."

"Okay."

Lizzie sat tightly against Emma, and Mandy wiggled in on the other side. Lizzie peered into her dish. Chocolate cake and vanilla pudding. Mmmm!

"One bite!" Mandy said, knowing Lizzie's appetite.

"A big one."

Mandy cut off a huge piece of cake, loaded it with vanilla pudding, held it in front of Lizzie's face.

"Open wide!"

Lizzie did, and her mouth was promptly filled with a huge bite of cake, the whole spoon, and vanilla pudding squishing everywhere. Lizzie made funny noises, and Mandy threw back her head, howling with glee, as Lizzie struggled to keep everything in her mouth. After she had swallowed, Mandy jumped up, knowing from experience she would catch it from Lizzie.

Sure enough, Mandy tore down the steps and across the yard with Lizzie in hot pursuit. After racing circles in the yard, Lizzie plunked down on the porch swing beside Emma, panting.

Emma grinned.

"I don't know why you don't give up. You can never catch Mandy anyway."

"She's so skinny," Lizzie panted.

Mandy ran up to the porch swing, backed up, and said, "Slide over."

The peaceful swinging resumed as Mandy finished her cake and pudding.

"Emma, you're going to miss us when you move!" Mandy said.

"You'll come visit me, I hope."

"Yes."

"But you know very well how I always was, Mandy. This is what I wanted since I was a little girl, not much older than eight years old. To be alone in my old farmhouse, cooking and cleaning, baking good things and washing my very own dishes—it's just too good to be true."

"What if you get homesick? What if Joshua is mean to you?" Lizzie asked.

"He won't be. You don't understand, Lizzie. You were never in love."

"Oh, yes, I was!"

"With who?"

"You know. Remember?"

"Well, yes. But I mean, you've never dated anyone seriously for years like I have. I feel actually closer to Joshua than I do to you and Mandy. Or Mam, for that matter. I just look forward to spending the rest of my life with him. Growing old together and having a whole pile of children."

Suddenly, Mandy sat up very straight, blinking her large green eyes seriously. "I think I'm falling in love."

"Mandy!" Lizzie shrieked.

Lizzie looked closely at Mandy. She could tell Mandy was dead serious. She had that certain set to her upper lip when she was not joking at all. Lizzie called it her "professor" look, all smart and wise and knowing.

"John Zook comes to church every two weeks," she said, as matter-of-factly and rock-solid as a mountain.

Lizzie's heart sank. Don't tell me that Mandy will be exactly like Emma, she thought. Oh, please.

"I think he's very handsome, and I think he likes me," she said.

"How do you know? You never said a word to him, and he never talked to you either," Lizzie said.

"Oh, I just know," Mandy said. She started to hum in the most grating manner.

Emma got up, saying it was time for her to give KatieAnn and Susan their baths. Mandy and Lizzie continued to swing, watching the pasture as if their life depended on it. The tension between them was as thick as Mam's potato soup. Lizzie was still secretly hoping John would ask her for a date, and that's all she thought about Monday evenings. Well, she just had a feeling she knew why he didn't ask her out. It was because he was very likely Mandy's "meant to be."

"Lizzie," Mandy sighed, "I don't want to hurt your feelings, but you may as well not like John Zook. From the first moment I saw him, I had a little feeling that someday, if it was the Lord's will, John Zook would be my husband, just like Emma and Joshua."

"I don't like him anymore," Lizzie said, surprisingly quiet and reserved.

Mandy looked at her sharply. "You used to."

"Let's not talk about it, okay?"

"If you don't want to, all right."

The thing was, Lizzie had some thinking of her own to do. For the last few weeks she had been busy thinking of Emma's wedding and pushing all thoughts of boys and dating aside. Uncle Marvin's words about Stephen were stuck somewhere out of reach, failing to wake her conscience or reason. She wanted John to ask her, just as she had wanted Amos to. And now Mandy said she liked John, and it was almost scary with that Mandy, once she said something in that wise way of hers.

She sighed. Oh, well... if John liked skinny, big-eyed Mandy, then so be it. I'll just never get married. They are building the new Amish school, the school board has already asked me to be the teacher, and I can hardly wait to get started at the end of the summer. So if that's what God has for me, fine. At least if I'm an old maid, I can pack two whole sandwiches in my lunch with all the mayonnaise I want, and who is to care if I weigh 200 pounds?

She sniffed, and she shook her head.

"What's wrong with you?" Mandy asked.

"A fly flew up my nose."

They giggled and continued to swing.

Chapter 9

THE SUMMER BEFORE EMMA'S WEDDING WAS full of one busy day following another. Lizzie and Mandy often did the milking alone, since Dat was working on the new addition. Mam's garden was full of vegetables for Emma as well as for the wedding. Earlier that summer, Dat had plowed a large area behind the house, past the apple trees, and planted potatoes and sweet corn. Mam called it her "patch." Lizzie said it was more like an acre than a patch. It was huge, and often she and Mandy spent hours hoeing and weeding on hot summer days.

They also had a frolic on a Saturday in June, when they invited all of their relatives and friends to work on the addition to the house. Mam cooked and baked the week before, preparing huge amounts of food to feed the hungry workers. She made two roasters of fried chicken and filling. Emma was always proud of Mam's culinary skills and worked diligently to learn all of Mam's cooking and baking secrets. Lizzie didn't care. She just ate the food.

Of course, Mam made cream sticks for coffee break in the morning. They were homemade doughnuts, with the dough cut in rectangles, fried in deep fat, a slit cut along each top, and filled with creamy vanilla frosting. Golden caramel icing was spread on top, resulting in achingly sweet, oblong, filled doughnuts, which in Emma's words were so good it wasn't even right.

When the men finished eating, they paid Mam warm compliments. She dipped her head, her cheeks flushed, basking in the words of praise. Dat acted so conceited when someone praised Mam's cooking that the girls hid their smiles behind their hands. He wasn't very tall, but he grew a few inches whenever that happened, Emma would say.

After the frolic was over, the addition was well on its way. Just like a miracle, a new basement and the skeleton frame of the living room with a new roof and windows were put in place. All through the summer, Dat and Jason kept steadily on, building and finishing the new living room until the day came when Mam went to town for a few gallons of primer and semi-gloss paint for the walls. Mam was thrilled with the light shade of blue she chose, saying this old farm was looking pretty good of late.

It was a happy summer, an exciting one, with Mam being more energetic and enthused than she had ever been since moving to the farm, Lizzie thought. And when Dat put down the hardwood flooring, rented a sander to smooth it, and then put on three applications of polyurethane varnish, she was almost in tears of gratitude.

"What a lovely, lovely, big living room!" she exclaimed, as she finished the final coat of varnish. "I'm almost afraid to have a wedding in this beautiful new room!"

There were five new windows, all freshly stained and varnished, letting in the fresh air and sunshine. Mam hung blinds in the windows. In Ohio they hang white cloth curtains and tie them back, but here in the East that was considered too fancy, she said. Mam had lived in the East long enough to appreciate the blinds, so she only said it a bit wistfully.

After all the furniture was put in place and Dat set the woodstove on the brick platform by the new chimney, it was just like a brand-new house. The twins squealed and shouted as they raced each other across the glowing hardwood floor, sliding in their stocking feet until they crashed into furniture and Mam made them stop.

Mam and Emma painted the porch railing, the kitchen, the brick part of the house, and every doorway and windowsill to match the living room. Dat shook his head, saying it was dangerous to be in the house because you'd be painted to the wall if you held still long enough. He was only joking, his eyes twinkling, and the girls knew he enjoyed getting ready for Emma's wedding as much as Mam did.

They froze tiny little bags of corn, lima beans, and peas for Emma, in bags only big enough for two people. Emma beamed and giggled as she put one cup of vegetables in each bag, saying how cozy that would be, cooking supper for Joshua in their old farmhouse.

They filled little pint jars with pickles, red beets, grape jelly, and applesauce. They put peaches and pears in quart jars. Mam said two people could eat a whole quart of peaches before they spoiled. They canned beef, sausage, and little chunks of ham, all in pint jars that looked so cute, Lizzie found herself wanting to be married and making supper of her own.

Mam went shopping, buying sheet sets, towels, and washcloths. They made comforters from flannel patches—any color—orange, pink, blue, and hideous-looking patterns. Lizzie got all huffy about that, saying there was no way she would put anything like that on her bed.

"Oh, yes, Lizzie! This is exactly what I always dreamed of—patchwork comforters and quilts. Just wait until you see my old upstairs. It's so cold up there in the winter that these warm blankets will be exactly what I need."

"That's right!" Mam agreed, around the pins in her mouth. "Just wait, Lizzie. Your turn will come, and these comforters won't seem ugly then."

Lizzie snorted a bit, thinking how they wouldn't look any better at that point.

Mam had two quiltings that summer after the new living room was finished, inviting the women from church to quilt Emma's quilts. Mam had pieced one the summer before called a "Dahlia," blocks of small, star-shaped flowers made with lavender fabric on a background of white. Emma's favorite color was lavender, so after the quilt was finished and bound, she was absolutely delighted.

Late that summer, Lizzie helped the Amish parents of the community paint and varnish the walls of the brand-new schoolhouse. The small, square building sat on the side of a gently rolling hill on the edge of Elam Stoltzfus' farm. A little meandering creek wrapped through the pasture on the opposite side of the road, and pretty oak and maple trees lined its banks. The schoolhouse was about six miles from the Glick farm, so, of course, Lizzie had to go with the school van again.

Lizzie always thought it would be so much nicer to be able to stay at school later in the evening and arrive earlier than the pupils, but it would have been too expensive for the school board to pay for all that extra transportation. Sometimes, when there was a special event, she would drive Bess and the buggy to school, but Mam didn't like that too much, saying it was too far. Mam took good care of horses, always pitying them if they had to run too fast or too long.

When school started the last week of August, Lizzie was as excited as ever, only without quite as many sickening butterflies in her stomach as she had her first year. She had successfully taught her first year, loving every minute of it, so she had less qualms about the unknown this time around.

She couldn't believe her good fortune, being the first teacher in a brand-new classroom. The walls were so smooth, and the windows were all square with new trim. There was a brand-new blackboard, closets, and even new desks that were actually fastened to the floor. Her own desk was not new, but it was a good secondhand one, large and not as high as her old wooden one at the Mennonite school.

There were a few more pupils this year, all Amish children from homes and farms spread throughout a large portion of Cameron County. Some of them drove their ponies or horses and buggies to school, but most of them came with a driver.

The pupils were as excited as she was on the first day, exclaiming about and admiring the finished new school. There were Kings, Beilers, Zooks, Stoltzfuses, and lots of other common Amish names. The children were all loving, none of them causing her too much grief or worry those first few weeks. At home, with all of the wedding planning, there was no rest for anyone, so school was actually a welcome reprieve from the madcap pace in the Glick household.

By late September, the wedding was still six weeks away, but Mam was a nervous wreck, Emma said. Lizzie agreed.

Lizzie was secretly pleased to hear Mam and Emma argue and get upset with each other. All her life, it had been those two working together, and Lizzie was the different one. Even Mandy made Mam happier than Lizzie did most of the time.

Even when they were little and Dat taught the three girls to read the Scriptures in German, Lizzie had upset Mam. Each Sunday morning, Dat read from the Scripture, Emma read the verse after his, and so on.

Reading the German language was a bit more difficult for Emma, so it had taken her longer to read a verse. German had always been easy for Lizzie, so she zipped through her verse. Dat smiled at her each time she finished. But as Mandy faltered through hers, Lizzie noticed Mam's unhappy expression. Now what had she done wrong? Evidently something, because Mam's eyebrows were drawn and her mouth stern.

On they read, with the exact same results—Dat smiled at Lizzie, then sighed impatiently if Emma missed a word, until Mam opened her mouth.

"Melvin, I can hardly stand it. Emma and Mandy are trying to read just as well as Lizzie. You need to have more patience with them. If Lizzie can read so much better than the others, why does she have to read at all? She knows everything there is to know about German."

Dat had stared at Mam. Lizzie felt like running out of the room and never reading a word of German ever again. Her feelings were terribly hurt. She had always been proud of her German reading ability. Emma did lots and lots of other things so much better than she did, just not reading German.

That's how Mam is, Lizzie thought. She always likes Emma so much better than me. I'm not going to talk to Mam for so long she'll know she hurt my feelings.

They finished their session of German reading, and Dat told them they were free to do whatever they wanted. It was an in-between Sunday, meaning a day their district did not have church services. Old Order Amish have church every other Sunday. This is an old custom that allows ministers to visit other districts.

Emma and Mandy wandered into the kitchen for a snack, but Lizzie went straight up the stairs to her bedroom. She flung herself on the bed, stuck her face in her pillow, and pitied herself. She planned on crying, but the tears wouldn't come, probably because she was more angry than hurt.

After a while she felt a bit silly so she got up, smoothed her dress, and wondered what she could do to worry Mam. She didn't care what Emma said. Mam always took her side. Emma never did one thing wrong. Mam should be glad she has a daughter who can read German so well. If Lizzie was a boy, she'd probably be a preacher or a deacon, and then Mam would be so happy to hear her read German in church. Mam ought to be ashamed of herself.

❧

Now, years later, Mam told Lizzie she just couldn't understand what got into Emma, it was a fright how determined she was to have her own way. And Emma cried to Lizzie in sheer frustration because Mam put her foot down, saying there would be absolutely no more than 250 guests, the house was not big enough for more. Emma begged and pleaded, but Mam's nostrils flared, her mouth was set, and that was that. Lizzie felt very important, being in the middle of Mam and Emma.

A wedding was a mess. Everyone was on pins and needles all the time. Lizzie told Mam this wasn't right. When it was her turn to get married, she was going to run away and go to the lawyer or governor or whoever it is that marries you. Mam laughed at her, saying she'd have a hard time getting either of them to marry her.

Finally, the day of preparation—*risht dag* in Pennsylvania Dutch—arrived. Everyone was up at five o'clock, except for Mam who had been up since three o'clock to bake enough pumpkin pies to feed all of the relatives. Emma said that was too early. Now Mam would be too tired to enjoy the day. But Lizzie guessed that if she wanted to get up at three to bake pies, she could.

Relatives began to arrive very early that morning. The *risht leid*, or the four couples who made the chicken and filling, arrived first. There was lots of work involved in that process, and they had to start early to get the roasting chickens in the oven.

The *risht dag* was a jolly day, almost more fun than the day of the wedding, Lizzie thought. Everyone hustled and bustled, smiled and teased each other as they worked together. The farm was truly a beehive of activity.

There were so many old traditions to follow. Joshua and Emma and their bridal party cleaned the celery. An Amish wedding had celery in everything, Lizzie claimed, but Emma corrected her, saying only in the *roasht* and the stewed celery. Oh, yes, and in the afternoon whole stalks of celery to snack on were placed in tall vases and set on the tables.

"Why celery?" Lizzie asked, as she scrubbed yet another piece.

"Because over a hundred years ago, our ancestors served whatever was in the garden at the end of the season at their weddings. That's why we have chicken filling, mashed potatoes, celery, and cole slaw. The cabbage, potatoes, and celery all come from the late harvest," Joshua informed her proudly.

"They grew the chickens in the garden too, huh?" Lizzie cracked.

The aunts were in the kitchen, baking pies and cooking vanilla cornstarch pudding and tapioca pudding while they also chopped celery, baked rolls, and just fussed up a storm. What a day to remember, Lizzie thought, with everyone full of energy and enthusiasm because Emma was getting married.

After the celery was all washed and sorted, the whole group took a coffee break and snacked on all kinds of cookies and doughnuts. Lizzie was cold and wet from washing celery, so it felt good to be in the warm kitchen with all of Dat's sisters—the aunts—and Doddy Glicks.

The men measured rooms and set up tables and

benches. Since the wedding service would be held in the same room as the one in which the meal would later be served, they had to know the length of each bench, exactly which bench went where, and how many tables filled each room.

Everyone had a job. Usually, the older women of the church made the gravy, cooked the celery, and brewed the coffee, while the aunts bustled about setting out plates of doughnuts, cookies, and dishes of tapioca pudding.

Lizzie loved the whole whirl of this special day before the wedding. The kitchen sounded just like a henhouse when the chickens are afraid of an intruder and cackling madly. Mam's face was so red Lizzie was afraid she'd have heart failure if she didn't calm down. But then, this was her first daughter's wedding, and she did have plenty of reason to be nervous and flushed, Lizzie decided.

Amid the hubbub, Emma flitted about, looking radiantly happy and excited. She was to finally have her big day, the one she so looked forward to her whole life. Lizzie couldn't fully understand why Emma didn't mind moving so far away, but then, she didn't have to. She most certainly was not planning any future moves of her own.

❦

The sun shone beautifully on the day of Emma's wedding. Mam was so pleased to be blessed with a lovely day. Not too cold for November, she said, just a nice moderate day for a wedding. Dat smiled and smiled, hurrying about doing last-minute things in his white shirt and new black suit.

Lizzie wore the same new white cape and apron as Emma, because Lizzie was a *nehva-sitsa*, or Emma's attendant. Joshua's brother Ben sat with Lizzie on one side of the couple, while the other *nehva-sitsa* couple, Joshua's sister Mary sat with Marvin on the other side. Lizzie had worried that Mandy would feel left out since she wasn't one of Emma's attendants.

"Don't worry," Mandy said. "I'll be a *nehva-sitsa* for you."

"I'm not getting married," Lizzie said as she pinned her cape.

Emma, Lizzie, and Mary all wore identical blue dresses with white organdy capes and aprons and black coverings. Joshua, Ben, and Marvin wore new black suits and white shirts with black bow ties clipped to their shirt collars.

"Don't say things you don't mean," Mandy said. "I see how you look for Stephen every Sunday at church, even though he's still living up north with his uncle."

"Be quiet, Mandy," Lizzie said. She sat down on the bed so she could tie her shoes and hide her red cheeks. Mandy was right. She did check each Sunday to see if Stephen was attending church with his family that week. So far he hadn't, but Lizzie was certain he would return sometime soon.

They all took a long time to get ready before the

service. Lizzie's hair was plastered down so close to her head it would take a severe windstorm to remove one hair from its place. Marvin told her she should always be so neat, but Lizzie felt like her hair was greased with lard, even though it was actually hair spray.

The wedding party entered the kitchen and were seated side by side where they would remain for the whole service like six stick men, Lizzie thought. Dat smiled and told them they looked very nice.

Then he looked at Mam, she looked at Dat, and all at once their smiles melted into little watery pools in their eyes. Dat blew his nose, tears running over. Mam turned away quickly, dabbing fiercely at her eyes. Lizzie felt her own emotion welling up, prickling her nose. But the relatives started to arrive and everyone started to smile again.

"Do your shoes fit?" Mommy Glick asked as she entered the kitchen. She bent down to take a peek at Emma's shoes.

"Oh, yes!" Emma said, smiling at Mommy as they shook hands warmly.

"You have a lovely wedding day," Mommy said, clasping Emma's hand with both of her own.

Emma wore Mommy's high-top shoes that laced over her ankles like figure skates. Ministers' wives wore these shoes to church, and a bride tradition-ally wore them to be married as a sign of obedience and a humble spirit, virtues that are highly respected among the Amish. Joshua wore new shoes in the same style, which was really very touching, old-fashioned, and serious, Lizzie thought. Lizzie had to admit, she hoped someday she, too, could borrow Mommy Glick's shoes.

The guests began arriving in earnest. Aunt Vera's eyes swam with tears as she rushed in, wrapping her arms around Emma. Mam was so glad to see her sisters that she started openly crying, but that was all right because she didn't see her sisters very often.

Mam had asked a bishop from Ohio to perform the marriage ceremony. She always said it seemed so unfinished the way it was done in Pennsylvania, with the couple seated as soon as they were pronounced man and wife. In Ohio, the bishop asked the congregation to stand while he said a prayer for the couple, which Mam had asked for and Dat agreed to.

The bishop preached an inspiring sermon in his Ohio accent, which was all very interesting. Emma looked so dark-haired, petite, and pretty as she stood soberly beside Joshua, saying her vows in a soft voice. He answered in a deeper masculine voice.

When they stood to pray, Lizzie cried. She had planned to stay dry-eyed and serene. But this was Emma, her own bossy big sister who was taking this very serious step, and everything seemed so holy and good and right that Lizzie cried until she had to get out her handkerchief and silently wipe her nose. When they all sat down again, she was so embarrassed by her tears that she looked at Ben's shoes for a very long time.

After they sang the last swelling strain of the old wedding hymn, the festivities began. The new husband and wife with their *nehva-sitsa* went upstairs to change from their traditional, borrowed shoes into new ones they had bought for their wedding day. Emma, Lizzie, and Mary each took off their black church coverings and put on new white ones. Then came the best part of the whole day—sitting down at the corner table in the living room downstairs.

While the couples were changing their clothes, their helpers had set the bridal table with Emma's fancy tablecloths, her fine white china embellished with tiny garlands of flowers, the pitcher and glasses Joshua had given her, and the pretty silverware she had received from him, as well. Lizzie was even more excited by the food in front of them—bowls of fruit, cut-glass cake stands holding decorated wedding cakes, parfait glasses filled with a creamy gelatin dessert, and all kinds of other classy-looking dishes and food. It was a beautiful table with Joshua on one side and Emma on the other, both happier than Lizzie had ever seen them.

Tables were set up along every available wall, with aunts and uncles hurrying and scurrying, carrying steaming plates of *roasht*, bowls heaped high with creamy mashed potatoes, cooked celery swimming in a velvety white sauce, pitchers of thick gravy, and dishes of cole slaw. The food was delicious, but Lizzie tried to eat daintily, feeling almost bashful sitting at this lovely table with Ben.

Emma oohed about the cakes, carefully reading the small tags on their tops, which identified the name of each person who had baked a cake for Emma and Joshua.

"Oh, this beautiful white one is from Uncle James and Aunt Becca!" Emma said.

"They're both pretty, and this one is from your parents, Emma," Joshua said.

After the wedding dinner, it was time to open gifts. They unwrapped what seemed like hundreds of packages, carefully keeping a record of who had given each gift.

Then it was time to go back to the corner table again for the "afternoon table," the time of the day when the youth assembled at the tables to sing wedding hymns. Each young man asked a girl to accompany him and sit beside him during the singing. It was a thrilling, very jittery time for any young girl, because you never knew when you would be picked, or if any young man would pick you at all, Lizzie thought. You just had to stand there, trying to look calm and nonchalant, when all that time your face was devoid of color because your heart was beating so fast, it was all you could do not to drop away in a dead faint.

Lizzie had often heard of this practice from other girls, but she had never participated in it before. She could well imagine how absolutely unstrung she would become if Ben wasn't already her partner, her life so much like the Chutes and Ladders game with its constant ups and downs. With her luck, no one would find her attractive enough to choose her to accompany him.

The girls told Lizzie that the boys didn't really choose someone because she was pretty, but she never believed that. Of course, they did. All the pretty girls will be picked right off the bat, you watch, she thought. She wondered if Stephen would have chosen her if she hadn't already had Ben as a partner. She hoped so. She had looked everywhere for him, but she hadn't seen him yet. But with so many people in the house, she might just have overlooked him.

But she was pleasantly surprised to see when the couples filled in that the prettiest girls didn't automatically get picked first. Most of the boys chose their friends, and once everyone was seated, they seemed to be having a genuinely good time. In between songs, the youth snacked on the potato chips, candy, and fruit that was passed from table to table.

The relatives, parents, and other wedding guests were assembled in the center of the room in neat rows of folding chairs. The singing swelled to the ceiling, rolling around the room in great waves until Lizzie became quite bored. When would they ever stop? Just when she thought surely no one could think of one more song to pick, someone started another one, louder than the last one.

"Those Glicks can really sing," Ben said, leaning close to Lizzie so she could hear him.

"I guess so. I hope they soon run out of air. I'm getting tired of sitting here," Lizzie answered, smiling.

Ben laughed, telling her they'd sing for awhile yet. Finally it was supper-time. The young people at the afternoon table were free to go. Lizzie was glad to get up and leave, going upstairs with Emma and Mary where they talked with friends and some of the Ohio aunts until it was time to go to Dat's shop where the youth had already gathered. There Emma and Joshua assigned each young man a supper partner. Some of the men were pleased, and others were impolite enough to refuse. But it was all in good fun and, for the most part, Emma and Joshua did not have a hard time with anyone.

Then for the last time, the wedding party sat at the elegant corner table, watching the couples file into the room as their names were called. Lizzie felt a slight twinge of pain when Amos led Ruthie in and together they found their seats. Amos is just as handsome as ever, she thought wryly. I wonder what Stephen is doing, she thought. But she shook her head and pushed away those thoughts.

Then John Zook led Mandy to the corner table. He was so much taller than Mandy, and she looked as if she had seen a ghost and never got over it. Her face was colorless, her eyes huge and dark with nervousness, but she gave Lizzie a tight little grin as she found her seat beside John.

Supper was delicious, but no one was really hungry. Lizzie pushed the ham and potatoes around on her plate, wishing the wedding would be over now. It was interesting watching John trying not to watch Mandy. Lizzie talked and laughed with him since

she saw him almost every weekend, and he was a
good friend. Mandy was new to running around,
so she was unaccustomed to any of the young men
from the youth group, and she sat shy and quiet.

John was quite enamored with Mandy, Lizzie
could easily tell. He must have found her pleasant
company, too, since by the end of the evening as the
singing was winding down, they sat deep in a serious
conversation. As far as they were concerned, Lizzie
thought, there was no one else at the wedding.

Lizzie was not happy at first, but she had to admit
to herself, although grudgingly, that she hoped
Mandy could be blessed with a sure feeling about
finding a husband like Emma had been.

❧

After the house was quiet and the last guests had
gone home, Lizzie came down the stairs, shedding
her white cape and apron as she entered the kitchen.
Mam stood washing dishes at the sink.

"Mam, why don't you just go to bed? We'll do
these dishes in the morning," Lizzie said.

"Oh, I need to wind down. I've been wound up
as tightly as an alarm clock for so long that this
helps me relax before I go to bed. Wasn't it a lovely
wedding, Lizzie? What would we do at a time like
this without relatives? All the managing and the
work they did!"

"It was a nice wedding, Mam. It really was.
Emma looked so happy, and Joshua is so in love

with her."

"I know. I hope their love can continue to grow and flourish. We never know what lies before us in marriage. We just have to trust that God will provide strength for whatever we have to face together."

"Did you see Mandy with John Zook?" Lizzie asked.

"Someone said he asked for her. Imagine! I suppose that'll be another case like Joshua and Emma," Mam said.

Lizzie bit her lower lip, hard, then turned to Mam.

"Why doesn't anything work out for me, Mam? Am I just meant to be an old maid who teaches school, or what? I don't know how to understand God's voice or have the right feeling like Emma and Mandy do."

Mam took her hands out of the dishwater, dried them on a tea towel, laughed wryly, and said, "I don't think there's a dry dish towel in this entire house.

"No, Lizzie dear, now listen. I'll tell you a secret. I had lots and lots and lots of dates with boys in Ohio, and not one of them was my 'meant to be.' Then I met Dat, and I knew as sure as the sun rises, he was the one. And let me tell you something, Lizzie. I always feel the same about you. I think your 'meant to be' is right under your nose. You're just not seeing him." She patted Lizzie's shoulder affectionately. "You will someday. God just isn't finished with you or him yet."

"Who do you mean?"

"You know, Lizzie."

"I don't."

Mam looked deeply into Lizzie's eyes, and they fell before the certainty she saw in Mam's.

"Lizzie, I think you're trying to run away from God's will. We have to be very careful in blindly searching for our own will and not even trying to discern the difference. It's a very serious thing when God puts a true, undying love in a young man's heart for us, Lizzie, and we're too wrapped up in ourselves to see it."

Lizzie didn't say anything as Mam began taking off her cape and apron, laying the pins on the countertop.

"You mean Stephen, don't you?" she whispered.

"Yes, I do."

"I like him."

"But you don't love him."

"What is love?"

"You'll know when the time is right. Now go to bed, Lizzie. We're both tired. It's been a long day, and you have a whole lifetime to figure it out."

"Thanks, Mam."

"For what?"

"For being you."

Chapter 10

JOSHUA AND EMMA PLANNED THEIR MOVING day for the third of February. Although Lizzie was a bit worried about life without Emma, she told Mandy it would be a relief to have the upstairs back to normal with all of their wedding gifts finally out of there.

Even Mam had to admit that there was a time for everything. She didn't like this whole idea of newlyweds living at home with their parents. But it was an old Amish custom for a couple in Lamton County to visit the homes of most of the guests who attended their wedding before they moved into their own home. During each visit, Emma and Joshua received wedding gifts. Soon Emma's room and part of the second-floor hallway were filled with snow shovels, rakes, hoes, saws, hammers, flashlights, Tupperware, canister sets, brooms, and everything else you need to set up a new household.

Mam snorted and harrumphed quite a bit about these "Lamton rules," which really, if you thought about it, was no small wonder. She wasn't raised that way, and when all her brothers and sisters were married, they moved away from home within a few days, skipping, in her words, "all of this constant visiting and goings on."

That was just how Mam was, and no matter how often Dat sighed and shook his head, she didn't change. Oh, she visited homes along with Joshua and Emma, doing her level best to conform to Dat's ways, but she didn't genuinely endorse the whole traditional practice.

So in some ways, the day Emma moved away was a happy time. The family loaded all of Emma's and Joshua's belongings into a large truck early that Saturday morning. When the truck was full, Emma rode with Joshua and the driver in the truck, while the rest of the family followed in a van.

Lizzie hadn't been to Allen County in several months. She had many good memories of her weekends there, and she still wrote quite regularly to Mary and Barbara. The two girls had been dear friends of Lizzie's, and even if she didn't see them much at all, she wanted to stay in contact with them through letters.

On Joshua's farm were a large, red brick house with a huge bank barn and outbuildings. Joshua's parents had recently remodeled the kitchen. Emma had brand new kitchen cupboards and shiny new green linoleum on the floor. The living room had beautiful, glossy, hardwood flooring with freshly painted white trim and newly painted walls. The walls were old, uneven plaster, but with the cracks repaired and painted over, it really was a lovely room, especially with the long low windows along two sides.

A big bedroom ran along the back of the house, along with a spare room that could have been made into another bedroom. But Emma and Joshua stored their extra belongings in there instead and also used part of it as a pantry.

The upstairs had four large bedrooms, all empty and so cold you could see your breath in them. Lizzie didn't know which was worse, living here in Allen County with an old, cold upstairs or milking cows with your husband. The whole marriage deal just gave her the blues as she stood all alone on the second floor.

As the men moved beds and dressers, cedar chests and brand-new chairs up the stairs, they propped the front door wide open. The mild winter air warmed a few of the rooms on the second floor enough that Lizzie and Mandy could unpack Emma's things.

Emma was radiant and her cheeks flushed as she worked. Lizzie thought she seemed almost happier than she had been on her wedding day. She instructed Lizzie on which new sheet set went on which bed, and which comforter and quilt, showing her the proper way to make up a bed for guests.

Mandy smelled the fresh new quilts from Joshua's cedar chest. "His mom must be quite proper," she commented.

"Why?"

"Look at all this stuff!"

Lizzie peered into the opened cedar chest, smiling to see all the neatly folded items stacked carefully inside.

"You should feel this comforter," Mandy said.

It was the heaviest, warmest comforter Lizzie had ever seen. Emma told them it was stuffed with wool. The flannel cover on the outside was buttoned so she could take it off and wash it when she spring-cleaned the house. Emma was so pleased with everything Joshua's parents had given them, saying Joshua and she had more than enough to furnish this big upstairs.

"Emma, I can hardly wait to come here and stay for a weekend, sleeping under these wonderful heavy comforters," Lizzie said, patting a pillow to make it fit nicely under the quilt.

"I hope you come often, Lizzie. I'm going to miss you," Emma said.

Lizzie looked at her sharply. Emma still looked happy, but there was a bit of apprehension in her voice.

"Aren't you glad you got married, Emma?" Lizzie asked, her voice rising sharply.

"Ach now, Lizzie, there you go again, jumping to conclusions. It's no wonder you don't have a boy-friend. I honestly think you're afraid of getting mar-ried yourself," Emma said, sitting on the side of the bed and patting the area beside her for Lizzie.

Lizzie sat down close to Emma, and an

overwhelming feeling of nostalgia gripped her. Time moved on, bringing changes, and it didn't seem very long ago at all that they were little girls. They had been so close.

"To tell you the truth, Lizzie, being married is all I ever dreamed it would be. And today ... moving into our own house, and putting my quilts on my own beds ... it's just, well, it's just the happiest time of my life. Joshua is so good to me, and I can hardly wait for our life to begin here on the farm. But that new beginning still brings wistful feelings of the past, of you and Mandy and Mam. Especially you. I'm going to miss you. Promise me, Lizzie, that you'll write me a long, funny letter every week. Promise?"

"Promise," Lizzie whispered around the lump in her throat.

"Don't you cry, or I'll start!" Emma said, her voice shaking.

"I'm not crying," Lizzie said fiercely. "I'm just going to miss you. I wish I had appreciated you more already. Who is going to sweep the kitchen 10 times a day?"

Emma laughed. "I didn't sweep 10 times."

"Almost."

"I feel almost guilty with all I have, Lizzie, and you ... you ..." she broke off, looking earnestly into Lizzie's eyes.

"And I'm a pathetic old maid," Lizzie finished for her, laughing. "Don't worry about me, Emma. I know now, since I'm here today, that I'm not ready for this. You want to know something? This upstairs gives me the blues."

"Why? Whatever for? It's my very best place. The one I always imagined for my quilts. I love my upstairs," Emma said.

"Well, good for you, Emma. You know how very different we always were."

"We sure were and still are, I suppose. But yet, in our own way, we always had a special bond, as long as you weren't too lazy. Remember all the things you did to slip away from the jobs you had to do?"

"Or how bossy you were! Emma, you were so bossy, that's probably why I don't have a boyfriend. I have nightmares of him acting as bossy as you used to be."

Emma slapped Lizzie playfully. "Now, you know better."

They laughed together as they finished making the beds, and Emma went downstairs to help Mam with the kitchen cupboards, leaving Lizzie to hang up pictures and finish unpacking. She smiled as she came to a box filled with old copies of *Family Life*, *Young Companion*, and *Blackboard Bulletin*, monthly magazines published by Pathway Publishers in Ontario, Canada.

Emma loved the magazines, poring over each story and copying recipes as soon as they arrived in the mail. She saved each issue for future use, and she got upset if someone lost or tore one of her precious magazines. Lizzie enjoyed reading the magazines, too, but she also quickly became bored with them.

After stacking the magazines neatly in a dresser drawer, Lizzie opened another cardboard box, labeled "Spare Bedroom." Inside she found Emma's old diaries, letters, birthday cards, and even her get-well cards from when she had rheumatic fever as a child. Lizzie was fascinated. Sifting through all of Emma's old belongings, she felt a keen sadness, the same feeling she often felt growing up. It was sad that people had to grow up. Why did they have to? It brought so many more responsibilities, decisions, and serious weighty matters that just well... that just made you old. Old and fat and wrinkly.

But then, God made things that way. He invented the whole concept of time, and people had to go along with that because they were just people. And besides, that Peter Pan story about the children going to Never-Never-Land and remaining children couldn't be true. It was all a fairy tale, and would she even be happy staying a child? She doubted it.

She sat down on the floor, leaned back against the wall, then sat forward immediately as a chill crept up her spine. Cold air wafted in from cracks in the floor and baseboard, and she shivered. See, it's stuff like this that gives me the blues about marrying, she thought. They should fix up this old upstairs, but they could never afford it, so they'll just have to live with it. And who knows? Every year these cracks in the floor could get larger, letting in more cold air until their woodstove in the kitchen can't keep out the cold, and they'll just freeze. Oh, well, if she did get married, her husband would just have to make sure the house wasn't too old or damaged, because that would make her nervous.

Lizzie wondered fleetingly how Stephen felt about houses and wondered if he was happy way up north. It was brave of him to leave his parents and family like that. She had thought over and over about their conversation that night at the sledding party. Surely it wasn't as serious as he made it sound. The thing that really tormented her most, though, was why she kept fighting against his love for her. It had to be love, or he wouldn't be so serious. Why did she resist him? It should be so easy just to let the wall of defense down and become his girlfriend, and, of course, marry him in the end.

Maybe she read too many novels that made her expect some knight in shining armor to come along, some extraordinary person who would sweep her off her feet with such a great love that it wasn't even funny. Or, like Mam always said, maybe she was fighting against God's will.

Mam had always felt that Stephen was the one for her. But how could your mother know? That was so dumb it never failed to irk her. Just as if God could talk to Mam but not to Lizzie because she was too... well, too thick-headed. The whole thing just gave her a headache, so she didn't think about it too much.

But the thing was, how could Emma and Mandy be so 100 percent certain that this was the right one? They were taking an awful risk in Lizzie's opinion. Oh, that was another thing. Mam always said it was different for every person, no two situations were alike. Hmmph. That was not very reassuring.

∾⊱

"Lizzie! Where are you?" Mandy called.

"Up here."

"You're supposed to come down now. Mam said we're to rake the yard."

"I'm not finished with these things for the spare bedroom," Lizzie said.

"Come on, Lizzie. You have to help me," Mandy said.

So Lizzie put the lid back on the unpacked cardboard box and went downstairs where Mam and Emma were arranging things in the kitchen cupboards. They were talking and laughing with Joshua's parents and his sisters who were cleaning the pantry.

Lizzie was hungry, but it didn't look as if anyone was preparing any food. There wasn't even any coffee or tea on the stove or cookies for a midmorning snack. She couldn't remember anyone talking about lunch.

"Aren't we having coffee break?" Lizzie asked Mam.

"No, we got started a bit late, so we'll just have an early lunch," Mam answered.

"Are you finished upstairs?" Emma asked.

"Not quite."

"That's all right. I'll do that next week," Emma said brightly.

Lizzie looked closely at Emma. Yes, that happy answer was genuine, there was no doubt about it. But when Lizzie thought about being all alone in that upstairs the following week, it just made her heart drop so far she could almost feel it in her stomach.

Lizzie and Mandy headed outside. Patches of snow sat under the large maple trees, but the rest of the yard was bare. Sticks, leaves, and debris littered the brown grass. Mandy and Lizzie grabbed a rake and started cleaning up in earnest.

The brisk, cold air and exercise lifted Lizzie's spirits as she worked. Mandy's cheeks were flushed as she raked steadily, her scarf fluttering in the breeze.

"Mandy," Lizzie said. She stopped and leaned on her rake. "Do you think Emma will be all right?"

"What? Lizzie, of course. She was looking forward to this for a very long time."

"But... but I'm afraid she'll get homesick so much," Lizzie said, her brow creased in worry.

"Not Emma. You would probably, and maybe I would a little, but not her. You know how she is."

✌

That afternoon, as the Glick family packed their things for the return trip home, Mam was fighting tears. Lizzie couldn't look at her, certain that she would burst into big, choking baby-like sobs at the thought of leaving Emma.

Everyone piled into the van while Joshua and Emma stood close together, their faces wreathed in happy smiles. Mam put a few boxes under the seat, and Dat rolled down the window.

"Now come visit us soon. Take good care of Emma, Joshua," he said.

Joshua smiled and said of course he would, while Dat blinked back tears of his own.

"Good-bye, Lizzie! Don't forget to write! Good-bye, Mandy and Jason!" Emma reached through the window for the twins, hugging them good-bye, and still she did not cry. Lizzie wished the driver would just go now, because her tears might start to roll any minute.

Mam wiped her eyes as the van pulled slowly out the country road. Lizzie bit her lip and blinked steadily to keep the tears away. Her heart felt sad, almost as if a part of her stayed at the farm in Allen County. She would come visit them as often as she could, that was one sure thing.

"Well, there goes Emma," Mandy said quietly.

"Yep, there she went," Lizzie answered.

They grinned at each other, a special loving grin, so glad to have each other. Sisters were just the very best thing ever, Lizzie decided. Even better than boyfriends or husbands.

Chapter 11

DURING THE LATE WINTER, AFTER EMMA moved to Allen County, Lizzie struggled to remain enthused about teaching school. For one thing, she thought drearily, it's constantly raining, and the dismal playground is nothing but one huge muddy pigpen.

She stood on the porch, gazing out over the grayish brown landscape as more rain fell from a leaden sky. The children had already left for the day, collecting their muddy boots and coats before wending their way down the drive to their various forms of transportation—pony carts, buggies, on foot, or to the waiting driver.

It's high time for school to be over, Lizzie thought darkly. She had more than the usual discipline trouble that week, and her usual methods of control—keeping kids in at recess or asking them to apologize, or to write their misdemeanors over and over on tablet paper—were not solving the behavior problems. An undercurrent of bad attitudes was threading its way through the upper grades.

She sank wearily on a dry spot of the concrete porch, tucking her feet in away from the raindrops. There were patches of white strewn across the playground, evidence that the children were throwing their paper or little plastic bags of snacks on the grass again. She had been giving the children points on the blackboard for littering on the playground, but it looked as if that wasn't working very well either.

Huge tears welled in her eyes, spilling over her cheeks until they splashed on her black apron. She felt as if the ground beneath her feet was crumbling and she was going to fall headlong into a void of despair. She could not stop the tears, nor did she want to. There was no one to see her, no one to care. Her driver would not be arriving for another hour, so she let the tears flow until she was finished crying. Using the corner of her apron to dry her tears, she sighed deeply and shakily as she continued to watch the rain come steadily down. Rivulets of muddy water trickled over the gravel that surrounded the steps as she thought.

Suddenly her despair was swept aside by feelings of anger. I would love to see some of these housewives put up with all this dirt and mud around the entrances to their houses, she thought. They'd have a fit. I bet they would.

Getting to her feet, she swept into the classroom, yanking open the door with the force of her angry thoughts. I'm going to stop at Jonas Beiler's house on the way home and ask...no, not ask, *tell* him I need a load of gravel on this driveway and the entrances to the privies.

Then, she thought, as she clenched her fists on top of her desk, I am going to make a speech on Monday morning. I am going to talk to all the pupils and tell them exactly how I feel. This rebellion is going to stop.

Adrenalin flowed through her veins, giving her energy to finish her work while she thought about her speech to the pupils. Climbing up and down the rickety wooden stepladder to hang the student's new art on the classroom walls, she muttered to herself, thinking of the words she would use to convey her feelings of failure as a teacher.

Where has all the joy gone this winter? she wondered to herself. I always loved my teaching job, but lately something is missing. Maybe it's me. She didn't think the problems were entirely her fault, but she knew she had lost some of her enthusiasm, too.

When the van pulled up to the front door, Lizzie was ready to go, her jaw set in a firm line of determination. But as the driver turned in at Jonas Beiler's farm, Lizzie's stomach did a flip-flop of nervousness. She soon controlled it, knowing this was the only way to improve the school and hopefully her mood. She hurried up to the door and knocked timidly.

"Come in!" called a voice.

Stepping inside, she clasped her hands as she greeted the family who was seated around the table, ready to eat their evening meal.

"So, what brings you here? This is a pleasant surprise. Hopefully, you're not having any discipline problems or anything of that nature," Jonas said from his place at the head of the table.

"Uh ... oh no," Lizzie said. "I ... I ... Well, is it too expensive to have a load of gravel or stones of some kind put down at school? The ... the playground is simply a mess, and the entrance to the privies is just ... well, like a hollowed-out path of chocolate pudding," she finished.

Jonas Beiler burst out laughing, a sound of deep, rolling mirth that swirled around Lizzie's spirit, gently lifting and carrying her own thoughts upward. Her hesitant smile widened as she felt the black cloak of despair lifting like curtains on a summer breeze.

"Chocolate pudding! That must be some mud," Jonas chuckled, looking at his wife who smiled back pleasantly.

"Well, it is a mess. We all kind of peepy-step along the side of the enclosure to keep our feet dry," Lizzie said.

"Yes, I believe it. That new schoolhouse should have had more gravel put down at the beginning of the term. But you know it's not just me who makes the decisions, and we have to watch our pennies so the school tuition doesn't get too high. Let me bring this matter up at our meeting, all right?"

"The next meeting! You mean I have to wait for another month?" Lizzie said, trying vainly to hide her disappointment.

"It's tonight."

"Oh, I'm sorry. I don't mean to be imposing, but... well, the floor, the porch, everyone's shoes, it's just..." Lizzie said.

"It doesn't surprise me," Barbara Beiler said. "I told Jonas if we housewives had to put up with that kind of mud, we'd have a fit."

Lizzie smiled at her. So they did think about it, she thought.

"Well, thank you very much. I just hope the rest of the school board will agree to the cost of a load of gravel," Lizzie said.

"We'll see, but I would imagine we'll do something for you. It probably gets a bit despairing this time of the year."

"A bit."

"You sure everything else is all right?" Barbara asked.

"Well, not really, but I think it's nothing I can't handle by myself," Lizzie smiled.

Later at home, after supper was eaten, Mam lingered around the table with Mandy and Lizzie. She put another piece of peach pie on her plate, added a bit of ice cream and said, "Mmm!"

Lizzie grinned at Mam. "I know. That pie is still warm. Did you ever notice how it is with pie and ice cream? You don't always have quite enough ice cream to finish your pie, then you don't have quite enough pie to finish your ice cream, and it just goes on and on."

Mam laughed. "Oh, I know exactly what you mean. I could eat that whole pie!"

The door opened and Dat appeared, his hat pushed down on his head, his hair disheveled as if he'd been running. "Mandy, the phone was ringing. It's for you," he said, his voice breathless.

Mandy's eyes widened in surprise. She started getting up from her perch on the bench. "Who is it?"

"Don't know," Dat said, grinning.

"Is it a boy or a girl?" Mandy asked.

"She has an awfully gruff voice if it's a girl," Dat said.

Mandy shrieked, slapping Dat's arm as she rushed past him and out the door, running as fast as she could to the end of the drive where the Glick family's phone was housed in a small building. Amish families in their community kept their telephones outside because they didn't have electricity or many more modern conveniences in their homes.

Lizzie anxiously peered out the kitchen window after Mandy as she related her miseries to Mam, telling her about the thread of rebellion that was steadily growing among the upper grades and about the amount of gooey mud in the playground. Mam listened attentively, clucking her tongue in sympathy, nodding her head as she agreed with the Lizzie.

Finally, she said, "But Lizzie, you know we can't expect our children to be respectful if we aren't being the type of person who earns that respect."

"Whatever that means," Lizzie grumbled.

"What I'm saying is... Now, don't take this as an insult, all right? But you haven't been too happy yourself lately. I mean, around the house. Especially with the twins. They were playing dolls, and one of them kept slapping her poor baby, saying she was Lizzie."

Lizzie glanced at Mam sharply. "So?"

"Well, I'm just saying this as nicely as possible. I'm afraid your lack of enthusiasm and happiness in school goes a lot deeper than just the mud or the children's behavior."

Lizzie wrung the dishcloth over the sudsy water, turning to wipe viciously at the countertop. Then she straightened, putting her hands on her hips.

"So you think I have this deep depression or something?" she asked.

"No, Lizzie. No, I don't. It's just that..."

The door was flung open as if a whirlwind had hit it full force, and Mandy fairly danced into the kitchen. "I have a date!" she shouted, grabbing Lizzie's hands and whirling her around the room.

"Let me guess!" Lizzie said sarcastically.

"John Zook!" Mam finished for her.

"Yep!"

"Not much of a surprise!" Lizzie said, smiling at Mandy.

"Whew! I need to catch my breath. I'll faint," Mandy said, gasping as she folded herself on the bench along the wall. She lifted both hands to flap them in front of her face, as she breathed slowly in and out.

"So, where are you going?" Lizzie asked, trying to sound all excited and not even the least bit envious.

"Guess what? Just guess what? He's taking me to a really nice sit-down restaurant. Not just to McDonald's," she said, batting her eyelashes.

That did it. Lizzie gave in to all her envy and feelings of frustration about her own life, which at the moment was only one insurmountable mountain after another. "What's wrong with McDonald's?" she burst out. "If I had my choice, a big hamburger dripping with sauce, ketchup, pickles, onions, and all that good stuff or some fancy restaurant, I'd pick McDonald's!"

"Now," Mam said.

"You're just jealous," Mandy said angrily.

"I'm not jealous! I am not one teeny bit jealous. You can have John Zook. You're going to end up with a farmer and get up every morning at four-thirty and milk his sloppy cows for the rest of your life. You can just have him and gladly," she flung in Mandy's direction before opening the stair door and clomping up the stairs. She wasn't sure, but she thought she saw Mam and Mandy give each other that look, the one that meant Lizzie's pathetic.

Lizzie spent the remainder of the evening in her room writing letters, correcting papers from school, and mulling her sordid life around and around in her head. So a person had the right to be grouchy occasionally, didn't they? Schoolteachers were cooped up with dozens of noisy children all day in all kinds of weather, day in and day out, and nobody, not one single solitary person, appreciated it.

That's what was wrong. She wasn't sad or depressed. The parents should come visit school much more often than they did. Maybe if she'd get more praise and appreciation from the parents, she'd be a better teacher.

Then she thought of the Valentine's Day surprise that Rachel Beiler and Mary Lapp had brought her. She remembered the bouquet of carnations and roses Jonathan King gave her, and she couldn't help thinking about Samuel Glick's warm handshake and sincere thanks for teaching his children. All the kindness the parents had shown throughout the year slammed into her self-pity, sending it flying like sparks into a dark night sky until not one trace was left.

She sat back in her chair and blinked, the feeling of warm gratitude bringing tears to her eyes. Yes, Mam was right, she decided. Maybe there was something deeper.

"May I come in?" Mandy whispered, opening the door a tiny bit.

Lizzie grinned. "Of course."

Mandy tried to walk quietly and sedately, but there was an extra bounce to her step, one she couldn't quiet down. She plopped on Lizzie's bed, patted the pillows, and sighed. She rolled over, stared at the ceiling, and sighed again.

Lizzie glanced over at Mandy and smiled in spite of herself. "As soon as you're done passing out, you can talk to me about your date," Lizzie said.

"Oh, goody! Okay, I'm done passing out."

Mandy jumped up, bounced back down, and then arranged herself on the bed so she could see Lizzie better. "At least for now."

Lizzie smiled, twirling her pencil. "So, what did he say?"

"Oh, as soon as I lifted the receiver and heard his voice, I knew it was John." She rolled her large green eyes dreamily. "And, oh, Lizzie, I have to tell you, he was so polite, so manly, so... well, he knew exactly how to ask me out on a real date. It was the most... the most..."

Mandy clasped her hands to her heart, looked at the ceiling, and sighed deeply. "It was the most memorable moment of my entire life," she finished.

"What did he say?"

"Oh, he just said he knows he should wait longer to ask me out, but it seems like he's already waited forever. Imagine, Lizzie! He probably liked me from the very first time he saw me, exactly the way I felt. Oh, it's just all meant to be. I can just see God's hand in all of it. It's the most wonderful feeling," she said, sighing in rapture.

"That's nice," was all Lizzie could manage as she pushed the lemon tinge of jealousy away.

Mandy paused, watching Lizzie's face closely. Finally she said very quietly, "Lizzie, I'm sorry to go on and on. You're not really, seriously jealous of me, are you?"

Lizzie straightened her shoulders, briskly turning to sort through her stack of papers.

"Oh, no, of course not," she said airily, waving

her left hand as if to dismiss the very thought. "Of course not."

"I'm so glad, Lizzie. You are such an absolute good sport about me having my first date. You know what? You should help me pick out fabric for a new dress and make it for me. Would you?"

"That would be fun!" Lizzie said. "What color are you planning to wear?"

"Oh, my! I don't know. What should I wear?"

They opened Mandy's closet door and paged through the sleeves of Mandy's colorful array of dresses.

"This one would be perfect, Mandy. You really don't need a new one just to go out for supper," Lizzie said, taking down a soft dress of sage green. "This matches your eyes perfectly."

"You think so?" Mandy gathered the dress in her arms and held it up in front of her, turning left and right as she examined herself in the mirror. Lizzie watched as Mandy's slim figure floated back and forth in the glass, her bright smile emphasizing the green color of her eyes. "But... it's so green!" she said doubtfully.

"It's perfect, Mandy. You look lovely. I've hardly ever seen you wear it," Lizzie assured her.

"You really, really, honestly think so?"

"Yes, Mandy. I do. If I were you, that's exactly what I would wear."

"All right. I'm going to."

Lizzie smiled as Mandy went twirling across the room, the green dress flapping wildly. Who could be jealous of Mandy for any length of time? She was so young and happy. Her excitement kind of grabbed you and spun you along, like one of those little whirlwinds that went twirling across a dusty lane on a dry summer day just before a thunderstorm. Lizzie felt much like one of those pieces of dust. She was just swept along by Mandy's infectious joy.

"Mandy, let's ask Mam if we can go to Falling Springs on Saturday and go shoe-shopping!" Lizzie said, bouncing on her bed.

"Let's do! Do you have any money?"

"We'll ask Mam. She can give us some."

They sat side by side making plans, talking about boyfriends, school troubles, muddy playgrounds, self-pity, first dates, and anything else they thought of.

A comfortable silence fell over the room as each one became lost in her own thoughts. The kerosene lamp flickered as a lone ladybug buzzed into the lamp chimney, evidently banging its head as it fell to the dresser top.

"One more thing," Mandy said, clasping and unclasping her hands nervously.

"Hmm?" Lizzie asked, thinking more about the ladybug, her mind relaxing, slowly easing her hectic thoughts into a softer, dreamier state.

"Now don't laugh. Promise?"

"I promise."

"You know we don't eat at a restaurant very often?"

"Mmm-hmm."

"What if I don't know how to order? I mean ...
now don't laugh!"

"I'm not laughing."

Lizzie was still thinking about the ladybug, wondering how it had ever gotten into the house in the
first place.

"You know how awkward I feel when I do order
at a restaurant. Like I can't talk fancy enough or
don't know how to pronounce the words, or ... I
just feel so stupid," Mandy said miserably.

"Oh, you aren't that low class that you can't
order a dinner at a restaurant. You will do just fine.
I'm sure you'll be able to pronounce the words,
since Amish people don't go to places that are so
fancy you can't pronounce the name of the dishes
you're ordering."

"Are you sure? John comes from Lamton originally, and those people are classy."

"Not that classy."

"You don't know."

"Yes, I do know," Lizzie said quickly. "We are
only as pitiful as we allow ourselves to be. We are
someone, too. I mean, you can't always feel like a
nobody, being intimidated by the slightest thing.
You are a very attractive young girl who is being
escorted by a handsome young man, and you can
say fancy words just as well as anyone else."

Mandy looked at Lizzie with disbelief.

"You sound so English. Lizzie, stop it," she said,
frowning.

"I mean it. I don't want you to feel like a country

mouse, just because we're poor and live on this old farm. That evidently doesn't bother John Zook or he wouldn't have asked you out."

"True, true," Mandy said, her spirits visibly lifted. "That was dumb of me, wasn't it? Of course, I'll be all right. And you know what? I could always just tell the waitress I'm having whatever John orders."

"Of course. Good idea," Lizzie agreed.

"Thanks, Liz. I don't know what I'd do without you. You're my best friend, best sister, best advisor, best everything. G'night!" And with that Mandy was off in a twirl of green.

Lizzie sighed as she stared out the window to the tops of the old apple trees in the pasture. She decided she was truly, from the bottom of her heart, happy for Mandy. And then she admitted wryly to herself that what took away the worst of that awful sting of jealousy was John's plans to farm with his brother. John was handsome, and, of course, there had been a time when Lizzie would gladly have accepted his offer to go out, but those cows definitely put a damper on any romance.

Vaguely she wondered if Stephen's uncle in northern Pennsylvania was a serious farmer and if Stephen would want to farm after working with his uncle. She couldn't even remember what Stephen looked like anymore. She wondered idly if he had a girlfriend picked out by this time. Probably.

Suddenly, she picked up her pencil and started writing on a sheet of scrap paper. She scribbled her name, Elizabeth Glick, leaving an empty space beneath it. Slowly, she wrote Joshua and Emma, then John Zook and Amanda Glick. Smiling pensively, she drew a question mark in the empty space beneath her name. Slowly she erased it and lightly wrote "Stephen" in that space. Leaning back, she nibbled on the end of her pencil, wondering how she would feel if he called her and asked her to go with him to a restaurant. It would be nice, but... slowly she erased the name.

Dear God in Heaven, she prayed, You know the space is still empty. I am no longer running away from you. I'm just walking, and I think I am listening for real this time. Guide me and show me the way like you showed Emma, and now I think Mandy, too, so ... just show me the way. Amen.

Chapter 12

THE CLANGING OF LIZZIE'S ALARM CLOCK jolted her out of a deep, peaceful slumber. Turning over, she pressed the button to stop the annoying jangle before pulling the covers up over her shoulders and snuggling down for a last moment of comfort before facing her day. Just as she started to doze, the abrupt memory of what this day held jarred her consciousness, and her eyes flew open.

Today she had to make a speech to the pupils. She could no longer push things away or pretend that there was nothing wrong or hope that this rebellion would fade away. She had to face this problem head-on, not wavering in her ambition to correct it nor run away from it. Did God know how nervous she was? Was courage something he supplied at the last minute? Probably he would. Well, actually, he was going to have to help her, because just the thought of making a serious speech in front of those upper-grade boys turned her knees to jelly.

Dear God, please help me, she prayed, but then she couldn't think of any words to continue her prayer. She supposed that was enough anyway, rolled over, threw back the covers, and got out of bed.

Mandy was helping Dat and Jason in the barn, so the upstairs was quiet as Lizzie brushed her teeth, pinned her cape to her dress, and combed her hair. She took extra pains to make sure she looked nice, carefully rolling her hair sleekly along the side of her head before pinning her hair in a bob.

How would she start her speech? How about, I have to talk to everyone this morning? No, that sounded too... well, she didn't know. Before we start our work this morning, we need to have a discussion. No, that would never do. It wasn't really a discussion. The pupils were going to have to be told how it was.

Setting her mouth in a determined line, she leaned forward over her dresser to pin her covering, asking God again to help her, to go with her to school today.

Mam smiled at Lizzie, and they talked about the events of the day as she packed her lunch. The thought of food made Lizzie's stomach churn unexpectedly, so she didn't bother packing much.

"Are you on a diet, Lizzie?" Mam asked, as Lizzie clicked the lid of her lunchbox shut.

"No. Remember, Mam, this is the day I have to straighten out the problem in school," Lizzie said, nervously pleating her sleeve with her fingers.

"Oh, yes, that's right. Well, I'm certainly glad I'm not you. But you'll do fine, I'm sure. You always did have more pluck than Emma or Mandy when it came to something of this nature. God surely knows who the schoolteacher is in this family."

"Really, Mam? You really mean it? You think I'm an honest-to-goodness schoolteacher?" Lizzie asked, her mouth open in disbelief.

"Why, of course, Lizzie. You're doing a great job!"

And so Lizzie went off to school carrying Mam's encouragement like a banner of bravery, which really is what it was. It was amazing what a bit of praise from Mam could do, she thought. It bolstered her failing spirit and gave her a great big warm, woolly cloak of love that wrapped around her all day.

The children arrived in groups, chattering and laughing as usual. Their enthusiasm dampened Lizzie's, especially as they came in the door smiling their usual noisy, "Good morning, Teacher!" Oh, I'll just ignore it. They look so innocent and unassuming this morning, she thought for a moment.

But when the older pupils came in to put their lunches in the cloakrooms, some with averted eyes or mumbling an unintelligible version of "Good Morning," her resolve bounded back with more determination than before. Definitely something needs to be done, she thought.

Morning devotions went as usual, although some of the boys scuffled their feet on the way to singing class, punching each other, lifting smiling eyes to

Lizzie as if daring her to make them stop it, while the girls quietly giggled.

Lizzie's heart sank but she stared back steadily, saying nothing because she wanted to avoid a confrontation in singing class.

Singing was quite an accomplishment that morning, with her heart rapidly beating and her mouth feeling as dry as sandpaper. Tears threatened to spring to her eyes at the slightest thought of her speech, but she bravely withstood any sign of emotion, knowing there was no other way if she wanted to retain her dignity and authority.

After everyone was seated, the lower graders dipped their heads, reaching into their desks for their arithmetic books, knowing out of habit that their class came first.

Lizzie stood behind her desk, clutching the back of her chair until her knuckles turned as white as her face. She took a deep, shaking breath.

"This morning," she began, her voice quavering, "we're going to have to have an understanding."

The classroom became as quiet as the lull before a storm as the students sat up in their desks. They laid down their pencils and placed their books on their desktops. The students in the lower grades glanced uneasily over their shoulders at the older students.

Lizzie steadied herself before continuing. "I've noticed recently that there seems to be an atmosphere of rebellion among the upper grades, which is slowly filtering down to the little ones."

She paused to clear her throat, looking up to see some of the older pupils' faces turn pale. "I have no idea what started all of this or when it began. It's just suddenly very evident that some of you older boys seem to get a big kick out of irritating me, or rather, seeing how far you can push me until I lose my temper."

Lizzie found herself clinging desperately to her desktop for support, willing back the rising flood of tears. "Perhaps it's all my fault. Maybe I'm being grouchy every day without realizing that I am. At any rate, we need to understand each other, because I can't go on this way."

To her absolute horror, a huge, noisy, rasping sob caught in her throat, followed immediately by a torrent of genuine tears. There was nothing to do except stand in front of her class and let all the pent-up frustration and misery of the past month flow down her cheeks. Quickly, she reached for a tissue from the box beside her desk.

"What have I done to encourage you to, well … in plain words, just turn against me like this?"

Fresh tears rose unbidden as her eyes searched the older pupils' faces, hoping for, and yet dreading, their answers. There was dead silence. Lizzie waited, alarmed to see tears rise in the eyes of the most timid of her little girls. She tried to summon a reassuring smile for her, feeling sorry that she had to put her through this lecture.

Slowly, an upper-grade girl lifted her arm.

"Yes?" Lizzie said.

"It started with the boys."

Lizzie looked at the boys, her eyes never wavering, until one by one, they dropped their eyes from her gaze. "I know, Rachel. I know that's where the problem started, but you girls were willing accomplices these past few weeks. But, to be perfectly honest, I can't put the blame 100 percent on the boys. I know I don't have a happy, carefree attitude myself. I haven't come to school and remained enthused about ordinary, everyday lessons. Maybe I was a worse teacher than I thought I was."

The oldest of the boys, Melvin, raised his hand.

"Yes?" Lizzie said, raising her eyebrows.

"You give us too much work. You're always pushing us too hard, and we never hear one word of praise. That's what started it."

Lizzie's eyes opened wide in disbelief, and she struggled to maintain her composure. Of all the nerve! Spoiled child! He was so lazy, it wasn't even funny. How dare he?

"But... but..." Lizzie sputtered. "You're supposed to do all the assigned work the teacher tells you to do. I can't cut back on lessons just because the pupils think it's too much. Don't you have any spare time at all? Ever?"

Rapidly, heads began to shake back and forth, and a few of the boys snickered.

That's when a hot, white anger coursed through Lizzie's veins, and she pulled herself up to her full height, surveying her classroom much as an eagle watched its prey. "All right. That's enough. I made the mistake of being less than happy some days, grouchy really, and that is my fault. I'm sorry. But you boys are just not doing your job either. You are not trying to do your work nearly as well as you could. As for spare time, the library books are being used much more than necessary. How many of you have a book you're reading in your spare time?"

Every hand shot up.

"How many of you are finished with yesterday's vocabulary?"

Only a few of the girls raised their hands.

"And ... how many have finished the art I assigned you on Friday?"

Not one hand was raised.

Lizzie sighed before she began again, "So you see, what we have going all wrong is a vicious circle of me being grouchy and you pupils being lazy. None of us has the enthusiasm we should have. But as far as me assigning too much work, I find that extremely hard to believe. How can I offer any praise for lessons that are rarely completed on time or with so little effort put into them?"

Mary, an older pupil, shook her head slowly. That gave Lizzie the courage to continue.

"So there are going to be a few changes. There will be no recess for pupils with unfinished work. I know for a fact that every one of you is perfectly capable of completing every assignment on time, and if any of you has a problem with that, you may raise your hand."

No one raised their hands. Lizzie sighed as she searched the boys' faces anxiously.

"Now, does anyone have an idea about how we can all stay enthused and energetic with our work?"

Two of the girls raised their hands.

"Yes, Sally?"

"You could give us points for 100 percent, then have a prize after we have so many points," she said.

"Not 100 percent! Anything over 92 percent. It's too hard to get every single problem right," Allen, one of the boys, shot back.

Suddenly Lizzie saw the opportunity to win over Allen.

"Good idea, Allen! Of course, it is hard to get 100 percent in every subject. But 92 percent is a bit lenient, so why don't we say 95 percent, or anything over that, is a point?" she asked, smiling at him.

His face reddened, and he looked flustered but said, "Sounds good."

"All right. That's what we're going to do. Now how are we going to keep track of each individual's points? And, how many points are a fair amount before we have the prize? What will the prize be?"

Over half of the classroom's hands shot up, some of the children raising their hands as high as they would go while they opened their eyes wide with anticipation, bursting to tell Lizzie what they thought.

One by one, the pupils told her their ideas, until they had come up with a feasible plan. Stars were the answer, they said. Those little foil stars you licked on the back and stuck on a chart. After they each had over 500 stars, the whole school would go on a hike.

"That is just a great idea," Lizzie said. "Tell you what! The day of the hike, we'll ask permission to roast hot dogs and marshmallows!"

"Crackers and peanut butter!" shouted a fourth-grader, who instantly slunk down in his seat after receiving some lowered eyebrow looks from the upper-graders.

"I love a burned marshmallow between Ritz crackers with peanut butter on them," Lizzie said, smiling to reassure him.

❧

That evening, Lizzie found four notes attached to workbooks. Her heart swelled with love and gratitude to her pupils, especially the upper-grade girls who wrote endearing little notes of apology. The boys didn't write notes, but they may as well have, she thought.

One by one, they wandered up to her desk, starting friendly conversations with Lizzie until they were talking and laughing like old friends. Then they picked sides to start playing baseball on Monday morning, teasing Lizzie because she was no longer the first one to be picked.

❧

The change in Lizzie's enthusiasm was almost unbelievable. Every day she sensed the pupils brought equal eagerness to arriving at school, playing baseball at recess, raising averages during class, and bending their heads studiously as they all tried to receive good grades.

The weather was beautiful with soft breezes beckoning them all outside at recess. Often she allowed them 15 minutes extra playtime, mostly because the baseball games were extremely competitive, which Lizzie enjoyed more than anything. There were still minor discipline problems, but she no longer went home with a sinking feeling of failure, of not knowing which way to turn.

A few weeks later there was a knock on the schoolhouse door. Lizzie opened it to find the porch filled with the school board members and their wives. Her knees felt as if every bone and muscle had turned to gelatin. "Come in," she said, trying to smile calmly and naturally, although her mouth had instantly turned into the texture of a cotton ball.

She put out folding chairs and directed a few of the school board members to empty seats on a bench along the back wall while her heart hammered in her ears. Please, please let my pupils behave, she thought.

After everyone was seated comfortably, Lizzie resumed teaching her German classes. Good, she thought, I'm glad we're having German. Most of her upper-grade pupils were good readers in the German language, which Lizzie knew impressed their parents, and especially school board members.

As usual, Melvin read clearly and properly, followed by Rachel who did just as well. She stole a cautious glance at the men and was gratified to see them raising their eyebrows at each other.

That is a good sign, she thought. Hopefully, things will be all right. Next she reviewed flashcards with the fourth-graders, who loudly pronounced each German letter.

After the lessons were completed, the children all filed to the front of the room to sing for their visitors. The pupils minded their manners, walking quietly without whispering or punching each other. Oh, bless them, Lizzie thought. She chose songs that normally went well, and as the music rose in volume, swirling around the classroom with its warm melody and touching words, she was very grateful to her pupils for putting their hearts and souls into the singing.

She couldn't praise them with the school board there, but she rolled her eyes and hissed, "Thanks!" to the older girls, which brought a smile to their faces.

After the children were dismissed for recess, she talked with the visitors, answering questions and thanking them for the fresh gravel that had been put down in the driveway.

"Well, it looks as if you needed it," one of the women answered.

"Oh, we did. I even had the nerve to ask for it," Lizzie said, laughing.

Before the school board members left, they all mentioned that they hoped she would consider teaching at least another term.

"Oh, I don't know," Lizzie said, flustered. "Does this mean you're asking me seriously or ...?"

"Oh, no, we'll come around to ask you," Jonas Beiler said. "This is just to warn you."

Lizzie was left with a warm feeling of accomplishment after the school board members left. There was something satisfying about winning their approval that made her want to become an even better teacher, to exercise all of her ideas and plans because she was doing some good for the community.

Teaching school was like that. It continually held Lizzie's interest and fascination. It was like being at the helm of a little boat filled with children on an unpredictable body of water. You never knew what would happen from one day to the next, and you couldn't always depend on smooth sailing. But in spite of it all, every day was filled with love from the children. They were, indeed, such unique little individuals, each having their own separate needs. Each one teaches me something, Lizzie thought wryly.

She sat down on the front porch steps, her chin in her hands as she reflected on the past year. It certainly had not been without its ups and downs, its trials and challenges, but through it all, she wanted to continue teaching more than ever.

What else would I do, she thought. Grade eggs until I'm gray-haired and bent over from old age?

School gives me the blues sometimes, but not always. Not nearly always. Actually, only a small fraction of the time.

Now that she was 18 years old, she felt every inch a young woman, capable of handling her job, looking forward to another year of teaching, achieving goals, and finding fulfillment doing something she loved.

Lizzie watched the creek that ran beside the school, babbling over the rocks, winding its way to the river, meandering through the green, sleepy pasture. Yes, she decided, she was happy. Genuinely happy being a teacher. But deep down, she knew she did not want to be a teacher forever, or rather, until she died. She wanted to have a home of her own, a husband and children, just like every ordinary Amish girl. Just like Emma.

She shook her head, thinking about Mandy and John. Boy, if they weren't off to a running start. She accepted the idea of Mandy dating, no longer struggling with jealousy, thanks to John's farm and his cows, but still... sometimes she longed to have a special friend of her own. Not always. Boys can be so... immature sometimes, acting so childish. 'Course, I better watch it. Mandy says I act the same way at times.

She was just ready to get up and go inside when she heard the distinct rattle of wheels, along with the steady clip-clop of a horse-drawn buggy approaching. She watched as the black horse slowed and turned in, coming to a stop in front of the porch.

The door of the buggy was pushed open from inside, and Rebecca stuck her head out the door.

"Hi!" she said, her blue eyes sparkling from beneath her heavy, black lashes.

"Hi, yourself!" Lizzie grinned, genuinely glad to see her friend. "What are you doing?"

"Oh, I had to help Sarah for the day and finished early, so I came to talk to you for awhile."

"Good! Tie your horse to the fence and come see my classroom," Lizzie said happily.

"I can't. I have to get going. We're planting the garden tonight."

"Really? Already?"

"It's late this year."

"I guess."

"What are you doing this weekend?" Rebecca asked.

"I don't know. Why? Come over."

"Elmer Riehls have the supper for us on Sunday," Rebecca said, swatting at a fly that tried to enter the buggy.

"Good!"

"Did you know Stephen's coming home?" she asked.

Lizzie's attention was suddenly riveted on the horse's ears. For some strange reason, she could not meet Rebecca's gaze at that moment. She straightened her black apron belt, running her hand quickly across it to eliminate some imaginary dust. Wiping a hand across her forehead, she finally turned to face Rebecca.

"Is he? When?" she asked.

"Saturday. He's going to stay home, he thinks. I hope he does. I miss him too much when he lives so far away."

"I bet," Lizzie said absentmindedly.

"Well, see you, Lizzie. I really do have to go."

Before Lizzie could answer, Rebecca was off down the hill, rounding the turn at a dangerous speed before racing down the road on her way to plant the garden.

Stephen is coming home to stay. Oh, my word. Now what? How am I supposed to feel? She sat back down on the concrete steps of the schoolhouse and held perfectly still, lifting her face upwards to trace the pattern of two swallows who were dipping and weaving their way across the blue sky.

Quite unexpectedly, she felt the soft strains of music in her heart. The tune grew louder and louder, like an iridescent bubble beginning to form. It grew in volume until she thought of the mound of bubbles running over the side of the sink when she washed dishes as a little girl.

She wondered if God spoke to a person in bubbles. Or feelings like bubbles. She breathed deeply, sighing happily as all the imaginary bubbles floated toward the sky, joining the soaring swallows with music on their wings.

Chapter 13

LIZZIE STOOD IN FRONT OF HER OPEN CLOSET doors, flipping through the sleeves of her dresses, trying to decide what color she should choose. None of her dresses fit her mood. She should have made a new one for this evening.

She considered the light aqua blue dress. No. Too pale. Just wore it a week ago. Navy blue. Don't think so. Too dark for Saturday evening. Burgundy. Deep, dark red. Hate those sleeves. Too short. And on and on, until she was almost through her row of dresses.

"I have nothing to wear!" she wailed out loud, hoping Mandy would hear her and come to her rescue. She didn't like to admit it, but Mandy's choices were sometimes better than her own. That, or it boosted Lizzie's self-confidence to have Mandy say she looked nice in a certain color.

As nervous and edgy as she felt this evening, nothing, not one color, looked right to her.

Mandy's face appeared at the doorway, laughing. "Red. Deep, dark burgundy would look nice on you tonight with your tanned face."

She disappeared, swiping furiously at her wet hair with a fluffy blue towel.

Lizzie pulled at the sleeve of her burgundy dress, liking the feel of the soft satiny material, thinking that Mandy was probably right as usual.

She pulled on the dress, gazing at herself in the mirror, nervously biting down on her lower lip. She whistled under her breath as she combed her hair, wondering what the evening would bring. Her heart thudded, almost stopped, then went racing on every single time she thought of Stephen.

꩜

As soon as Lizzie and Mandy arrived at Jacob Beilers, Rebecca and Mary Ann raced out of the house, hopped into the buggy, and rode with them into the barn. Laughing and talking, the friends remained in the buggy, catching up on all the latest news, admiring each other's dresses, and laughing at Rebecca's antics as she imitated her failure at combing her hair into a bob earlier that evening.

Lizzie laughed along with the rest of them, although her laugh felt a bit forced and strained as she kept glancing furtively over her shoulder, wondering where Stephen was at that moment. Maybe he hadn't even come home this week, she thought. She didn't have the nerve to ask Rebecca, although her curiosity almost overwhelmed her common sense. Better to be quiet, she knew.

"And then," Mary Ann concluded, "she told me I have to chop my onions even *more*! Can you imagine? The tears were already running down my face!"

"Oh, I envy you! I wish my mom would let me work in the kitchen of a restaurant!" Lizzie burst out.

"It's okay. I enjoy it. But it's harder work than you think, Lizzie."

Lizzie smiled back at Mary Ann, thinking how fortunate she was to work in a restaurant. Mam was so strict. She always told them a restaurant was no place for her girls—too many men, too many temptations, which Lizzie thought was just ridiculous. What was the difference? She had dealt with temptation in the egg-grading room when that English truck driver, Don Albert, had flirted with her. She enjoyed teaching school, but a part of her longed to work as a waitress in a real-life restaurant. But Mam would never agree.

There was just something so glamorous about lifting a tray of glasses or dishes of steaming food in one hand while walking swiftly to serve a table of waiting patrons, she thought. When she was a little girl she had often practiced that maneuver, playing restaurant for countless hours, holding a small tablet, asking her "customers" what they would like.

"The volleyball net is set up," John called to the girls. "Let's play."

They clambered down from the buggy and headed across the neatly mowed lawn to the playing field where the volleyball net was stretched between two heavy poles. A few of the boys tightened the pegs holding the poles.

The girls called hello to the young men as the game quickly began in earnest. Lizzie didn't see Stephen anywhere. He wasn't here. Well, all right, he probably never came home. After all, Rebecca hadn't mentioned a thing.

As the evening wore on, the volleyball game became more intense. Competition was fierce, and Lizzie forgot about Stephen as she was swept up in the heat of the game.

"Time out!" one of the boys yelled.

"Game over!" John shouted.

Lizzie laughed and shook her head. Her breath was coming in short gasps from the exertion, the constant movement of the game, and all of the shouting. Her side had lost in spite of her efforts. The group drifted away from the volleyball net. The girls laid out the food while the boys carried out a cooler filled to capacity with ice and sodas. Lizzie bent over to choose a drink when she felt a tap on her shoulder. Straightening, she looked directly into Stephen's face.

Quickly she took a step back, her mouth open in disbelief. "Stephen!" was all she could say.

"Hello, Lizzie. How are you?" Stephen said, his face thinner and somehow, much older.

"I'm, I'm doing okay. How about you? It's been months since I've seen you."

"Yeah."

That was all he said. Lizzie glanced up nervously, not knowing exactly what to say to that. Did he mean it seemed like a long year and he was glad to see her again, or did he mean it was almost a year, but so what? Lizzie couldn't tell. She looked at him again but he said nothing, just stood there with his hands in his pockets watching her face.

Lizzie looked down at the top of her soda can and toyed with the top. Say something. Say anything. Just make him stay here. She snapped at the small silver ring to open her can of soda.

Stephen laughed softly. "Here. Give me that. You never could open a can of soda the right way."

Before she could protest, he reached down and took her soda. He opened it expertly and handed it back.

Her eyes met his as their fingers touched. His blue, blue eyes pierced her very mind, and this time there were no walls of resistance around Lizzie's heart. She looked at him steadily, knowing that her eyes told him how much she had missed him, had thought about him, and that she was very, very glad he had returned.

Her gaze dropped, shyness overcoming her need to let him know that she was not the same Lizzie he had left. Laughing a bit shakily, she said, "How do you know I can't open a can of soda?"

"Oh, I just remember. I remember how much you like fish sandwiches at Joe's restaurant, and I remember the habit you have of chewing on a plastic straw after your Pepsi is finished. I remember our ride to Dan Lantzes in the pouring rain, when I couldn't hold my horse and you were having a fit. I remember…"

They were startled by a resounding "Hey, Steve! Remember me?" A small dark-haired girl walked rapidly up to Stephen and shook his hand.

"Don't you remember me? Miriam! The girl from Lamont. Surely you remember. Was it a year? It wasn't that long, was it?" she asked.

She wedged herself firmly between them, and Lizzie backed away a few steps, watching closely as Stephen looked down and smiled, shaking his head and laughing when she said something much too quietly for Lizzie to hear.

Turning, Lizzie walked away blindly, furious to have been so rudely cut off from her conversation with Stephen. But he remembered all that! Sighing rapturously, she made her way over to Rebecca and Marvin who were sitting together at the wooden picnic table.

She sat down beside Marvin.

"Oh, my niecely! Here's my niecely!" Marvin crowed.

Lizzie ground out between clenched teeth, "Who is she?"

Marvin raised his head, looking over the crowd of young people.

"Who?" he asked loudly.

"That little dark-haired girl who is talking to Stephen."

Rebecca grinned and Marvin pointed at the new girl.

"You mean her? That one?" he said noisily, pointing with his forefinger.

"Shhh! Not so loud. She'll hear you!" Lizzie hissed. "And stop pointing."

"Oh, her. That's ... mmm ... What's her name? Miriam, I think. Stephen had a date with her one weekend when he was in Lamont with me."

Lizzie's eyes opened wide and she turned to face Marvin. "When was that?"

"Oh, I don't know. A year ago?"

"Why didn't I know about it?"

Marvin lowered his head, looking straight into Lizzie's eyes. "He can date whoever he wants to, Lizzie. You never wanted him."

"But ... but ... " Lizzie floundered.

"But, what?" Marvin said, clearly enjoying Lizzie's lack of composure.

Lizzie shook her head, cupping her chin in her hands as her gaze wandered over to Stephen who was bent down and talking to the dark-haired girl, clearly enjoying the way she animated her sentences with her hands. Her laughter reverberated through the lantern-lit darkness, and Lizzie snorted, getting up quite suddenly.

"Where are you going?" Rebecca asked.

"Nowhere."

"You want me to go along?"

"No."

Lizzie stalked off into the soft darkness, away

from the light of the gas lanterns and Stephen and the new girl.

Little flirt! She has the nerve. Biting down hard on her thumbnail, she kept walking across the newly mown hay field. So this was how it would end. Despair washed over her in long, drowning waves as she remembered Amos.

She was just unlucky in love, that was all there was to it. She was most likely cursed, like God cursed the different tribes of Israel in the Old Testament when they did wrong. She tried very hard to think of some major sin in her life, like stealing, hating someone, lying, but there was no huge thing she could think of that would cause the curse. Perhaps she shouldn't even try to think of such an unfortunate thing. Maybe all of this was to teach her patience, or maybe oh, horrible thought—maybe Stephen was not God's will for her life. How in the world were you supposed to know?

She had thought in the past months that maybe, just maybe, thinking about Stephen so much meant that she might be falling in love. She never told a single soul, not Mandy or Mam, not even Emma. No one. Then when she was so nervous about choosing the right dress, she was almost 100 percent certain that Stephen was the one. Then, finally, she had let her barrier of resistance down, trying to convey her feelings like some bold... Oh, my. She lifted cold hands to her flaming face, hating herself and her jittery nerves until she could barely breathe.

Stopping, she listened. Were there footsteps behind her? She froze, both hands covering her mouth, as solid footsteps followed her in the darkness. "Wait! Lizzie, wait up."

Stephen!

She remained frozen, her feet rooted to the ground as her strength left her body. Blood pounded in her ears, and she was seriously afraid her knees would no longer support her, that she might crumple to the ground.

Her breath left in one soft whoosh of sound as she felt Stephen's hands on her shoulders. She shrugged them off, wanting to run away faster than she had ever run, yet wanting to stay here close to him.

"Where are you going?"

She could not answer because of the huge lump in her throat. Tears pricked her eyelashes as she fought down the strong desire to tell him everything. She wanted to tell him how she felt, how different things were now, how grown up and mature and attractive he was. Suddenly he seemed so different now, but just as she finally came to this conclusion, here was Miriam, a small, pretty girl, appearing like a bad dream from the past.

Stephen turned her around to face him. His hands fell to his sides and his fists clenched as he stepped away from her. "Why did you run away?"

Lizzie lifted her chin. "I just needed to go for a walk. I have a headache," she said.

"Oh, well. I was afraid it had something to do with Miriam talking to me." He laughed a low laugh of derision. "I... I mean, I probably couldn't be so lucky that it would even matter to you whether Miriam talked to me or not."

Lizzie didn't know what he was talking about. She was too unstrung to understand him. Suddenly, she could no longer remain standing and she sank to the ground, her knees quite seriously refusing to hold her.

Instantly Stephen was beside her, reaching out to help her up.

"No," Lizzie said in a tiny voice laced with tears. "Let's just sit here awhile."

Watching her closely, Stephen sat down slowly on the grass beside her, staying a polite distance away from her.

Sighing, Lizzie watched the night sky as she struggled to dissolve her feelings of despair and regain control of her swirling thoughts and emotions.

Stephen didn't say anything. Lizzie remained quiet, too, listening to the night sounds. A dog barked hysterically somewhere in the distance as the youth group shouted and laughed as they returned to their volleyball game.

"Do stars blink?" Lizzie asked suddenly.

"I guess. I don't know. It looks as if they do," Stephen answered.

There was an awkward silence as Lizzie battled with her pride and her new feelings for Stephen. Quite suddenly she blurted out, "Who is Miriam?"

"Miriam? That short girl? Someone I know from Lamont."

"Do you like her? Marvin said you had a date with her."

Stephen went completely still. He did not move a muscle, until Lizzie felt quite sick in the pit of her stomach. Here it came. Now he'd tell her what he followed her to tell her. He loves Miriam. And sorry about that look you just gave me over that can of soda, but you waited too long, Lizzie, he would say. My heart belongs to Miriam. You'll find someone else.

Then he turned his head, his hair lifting on the soft night breeze. He ran a hand through his bangs, shook his head as if to clear his sight, and said, "Look at me, Lizzie."

"Just tell me," Lizzie whispered, a sob catching in her throat.

"All right. I will. I'll tell you everything. Maybe I'm just stupid enough to tell you because I'm feeling bolder right now since you seem to care whether I like Miriam or not. But you know how it has always been since the first time I saw you. There was never anyone else in my heart. Never."

"Until Miriam," Lizzie finished miserably.

"No."

"What?"

"No. She means nothing to me."

And then Stephen started talking. The flow of his words rippled and swirled around Lizzie's heart like a myriad butterflies flitting from one heaven-sent spring flower to the next. She listened quietly as he told her things he had kept in his heart for years, his memories of her which kept him at his uncle's farm in northern Pennsylvania because he knew she needed time and space to decide what she wanted. He loved the way she threw a baseball with her left hand, he loved the way she drove his horse and waded in the creek and ate stick pretzels two by two.

Lizzie threw back her head and let all the happiness escape in one long sigh that turned into smiles, and then into a mix of tears and laughter.

"Yes, Stephen, you were right. I needed time. I was blind for so long. I think I'm finally beginning to see how I am. I mean, that may sound like I'm a bit full of myself, but I truly think some young people are born with a nature that makes them want what they can't have, and *not* want what they can have. Or, in other words, I may as well admit it, maybe I've been resisting God's will. That's the way Mam puts it."

"Lizzie, does that mean that… Well, does this conversation really mean anything to you? I mean, do you even care about the things I said?"

Slowly, Lizzie nodded her head up and down. "Yes, Stephen. It means everything to me. I thought about you constantly these past couple of months, and now that you're here, you certainly seem older and more… more…"

"Does this mean that…?" Stephen stopped suddenly.

"What?"

"Nothing."

They sat awhile in silence, Lizzie feeling a bit self-conscious as she plucked aimlessly at the grass in the hay field. Quite unexpectedly, Lizzie jumped to her feet. "Let's go back, okay?"

Stephen sighed and then slowly stood up. They started walking back to the volleyball game, their steps becoming slower and slower. They said nothing until Lizzie laughed a low, happy sound.

"We're not exactly in a hurry to get back to the volleyball game," she said softly.

Stephen reached for her hand, holding it tightly in his own as he turned toward her and said, "Lizzie, I've thought of doing this so many times, that I'm not sure it's real. But... may I... can I pick you up Sunday afternoon?"

Lizzie smiled a small smile to herself. "You mean for a real date?"

"Yes."

"Oh, Stephen, of course. Yes, you may."

Feeling very shy, Lizzie continued walking with Stephen beside her, her hand securely held in his. It was a moment she would never forget, the feeling of having committed herself to a relationship, unsure of what the outcome would be. It was a shaky, scary, exhilarating feeling, and yet at exactly the same time she knew without a doubt, just like Mandy said, she just knew it was right. She would have to ask God over and over probably just to be positive, but so far, it seemed very, very good.

Chapter 14

THERE WAS NO USE TRYING TO HIDE ANYTHING from her family the following morning. She was the first one down the stairs, smiling widely the minute Mam turned from the stove to say, Good morning.

Lizzie thought she would suddenly burst apart if someone didn't mention her broad smile. She smiled with all her teeth showing, fairly dancing between the stove and the breakfast table. Mam was preoccupied and didn't say anything more. Lizzie cleared her throat, intending to tell Mam about her upcoming date with Stephen if she didn't notice soon.

The door burst open and Mandy hurried into the kitchen, quickly washing her hands at the small sink by the door.

"Hey, Lizzie, you and Stephen must have gone on quite a walk. What's going on? Come on, you have to tell me."

Turning, Mandy's eyes teasing, she dried her hands on the fluffy blue towel hanging on the side of the cupboard.

Lizzie took a deep breath, leaned against the counter, and adjusted her bib apron. Straightening her shoulders, she said clearly and slowly, savoring every minute of her important announcement, "I have a date with Stephen."

Mandy squealed and Mam stared, open-mouthed.

"I knew it!" Mandy shouted, throwing the towel up against the ceiling. "I just knew it! You know why? Stephen was talking to John for awhile after the game. He was probably making plans to do something with *us*!"

"Well, congratulations, Lizzie," Mam said quietly and almost reverently. "I've always felt right about you and Stephen."

Lizzie beamed at Mam, basking in her words of praise and acceptance. This all felt so very right and good, so she just continued smiling and laughing as she helped Mam with breakfast, chattering happily with Mandy about their upcoming weekend.

The door to the back porch opened as usual as Dat and Jason came in to hang their hats on the hooks against the wall.

Suddenly there was a loud banging sound, and Dat's frustrated voice saying, "Whoa! What is going on here?"

"Are you all right?" Jason asked.

Quickly, Mam moved toward the back porch. She met Dat halfway, her eyes full of concern.

"What? What happened, Melvin?"

Dat came through the door, shaking his head in disbelief.

"I stumbled across the doorstep," he said. "My legs both feel tingly, almost as if they are numb."

"Have you felt like that for very long?" Mam asked, hurrying toward him.

He sat heavily in a chair at the table, lifting one foot gingerly and flexing it.

"My feet felt that way for a few weeks, but I didn't think it was necessary to become anxious or concerned. I thought it would disappear after awhile as it had before."

Lizzie stood against the counter, her arms crossed tightly in front of her. The joy of her morning was fading away, replaced by heartbreaking pity as she saw bewilderment on Dat's face as he shook his head. She was sure now that there was something seriously wrong with him. There just had to be.

He had gone to the optometrist several weeks ago to have his eyes thoroughly examined and then the prescription of his lenses changed. But still he complained about days of foggy vision and a complete blind spot in his left eye. Mam said he would just have to learn to live with his failing eyesight because the doctor had said he seemed healthy otherwise. But now this.

Lizzie turned toward the kitchen window, staring blindly out to the horse barn. Dat had to stay healthy. He had to. Everything depended on his health and well-being to keep the farm running smoothly, the shiny, stainless steel tank filled with milk, the milk check coming in the mail to pay the mortgage payment and the accumulated bills. How in the world would they ever go on farming if he was unable to work?

She caught her lower lip and bit down hard, physically trying to keep back the panic she felt creeping up on her. We'll just be horribly poor with Dat not being able to work. There will be nothing in the house to eat. Mandy's paycheck and mine will have to go toward the mortgage payment. Mam will have to get a job. Did the church help people if their father couldn't work? What about her first date with Stephen? He probably wouldn't want to be married to someone as poor as she would be.

She could not let the wolves come any closer, tightening the panicky feeling in her chest. Turning, she shook her head as if to clear away the fear and faced Dat squarely.

"Dat, what... what do you really think is going on here?" she asked.

Mam and Mandy shared a knowing look, realizing how hard it was for Lizzie to calmly accept a situation like this.

Dat looked into Lizzie's eyes, and she read the fear in his. No, Dat, not you. You can't be afraid. You're Dat. You are the one who makes everything right for us so that we don't have to be afraid. She felt almost angry at Dat for being frightened.

"You have to do something, Dat!" she burst out.

"Lizzie," Mam said calmly.

They all looked at Mam.

"I think there really is something wrong other than a passing ailment," she said. "Chiropractic treatments have done nothing to correct the numbness in Dat's feet or help his feelings of exhaustion."

"Why didn't you tell us this before?" Lizzie asked.

"We kept a lot of his symptoms quiet because we didn't want to frighten everyone," Mam said. "We'll go see the family doctor as soon as I can make an appointment, and he'll very likely refer us to someone who can do further examinations. We really need to find out what is going on," she concluded.

Dat hung his head and sighed wearily. Mam put a hand on his shoulder as if to reassure him that everything was going to be fine. Mam seemed so solid, so courageous, so in control of this helpless, frustrating situation, that Lizzie took a deep breath, calming herself in the wake of Mam's bravery.

When Mam and Dat got home from their appointment in town, Lizzie was preparing name charts for the upcoming school year. Quickly, she got to her feet, nervously running to the window as she heard a vehicle's tires crunching on the gravel drive.

Dat was smiling as he paid the driver, and Mam carried a few bags of groceries into the kitchen, looking quite unperturbed. As Mam had predicted, the family doctor referred them to a large hospital in Maryland, but their appointment wasn't till the following month.

Dat pulled out a box of chocolate marshmallow ice cream and went to the cupboard to get out a small stack of plastic dishes.

"Who wants a dish of my favorite ice cream?" he said.

Lizzie watched Mam and Dat suspiciously, sure they were just trying to put on a cheerful front. But they both looked and acted so genuinely like her normal parents that Lizzie finally smiled, relaxing. She was so glad to see Dat didn't have a horrible, fearsome, life-threatening disease.

What Lizzie did not know about was Mam and Dat's talk late into that night after all the children were asleep. They had been told by the kind, knowledgeable family doctor that there was a possibility that Dat had MS or multiple sclerosis. They had never heard of the disease and didn't know very much about it.

They discussed the farm. Jason was old enough to work side by side with Dat on the farm. But what about a dependable income? If Dat actually had some disease that would render him helpless in years to come, they needed to discuss the possibility of giving up farming.

Lizzie did not see the tears in Dat's eyes that night

or hear Mam's fervent prayer to God to help them all, to have mercy on her poor husband and to realize the struggles in both their hearts as they wrestled with fear of the unknown.

And so, with the impending knowledge weighing heavily on her shoulders, Lizzie felt a bit subdued when Stephen came to pick her up after church services on Sunday. The day was perfect, absolutely gorgeous, one of those days when the blue of the sky was so rich, the leaves on the trees so brilliant, it almost hurt Lizzie's eyes to absorb it all. Little white clouds floated lazily in the azure sky, for all the world like little cotton balls stuck on a brilliantly hued, first-grade art project.

Stephen had curried and brushed his horse to perfection, the horse's reddish brown coat rippling in the sunlight. He had combed his black mane and tail until they flowed together perfectly and cleaned and oiled the harness. Lizzie smiled to herself when she saw the light playing on the freshly washed spokes of the black buggy wheels. Stephen disliked washing his own buggy. Probably Rebecca had done it.

Stephen stopped his horse at the sidewalk and Lizzie hurried out, waving to her parents who stood smiling on the front porch. She knew Jason was peeping out somewhere, and she hoped fervently he would be quiet. Stephen and Jason had learned to know each other during a hunting trip they had taken a few years earlier. Jason was happy to hear that Stephen had asked Lizzie on a date. Now she just hoped Jason would be discreet, at least until she was safely on the buggy.

She sighed with relief when Stephen's horse responded to his "C'mon" and tug on the reins. Soon they were well out the drive and away from the house, safely out of earshot. Just as Stephen turned to look at her, asking how her week was, an earsplitting whistle sliced through the air. Stephen pulled back on the reins, grinning as Jason charged through the milk-house door, his grin spreading widely across his face.

"Hey!"

"Hey, Jase."

"What are you doing with Lizzie in your buggy? Do you have enough room for her?" Jason asked.

Lizzie could feel her face heating up, but Stephen laughed easily, reaching out and knocking Jason's hat sideways.

"You can come along with us!" he said.

"There's no room!"

Lizzie tried to laugh, which ended in a small giggle, and she turned toward Jason, glaring at him, her eyes telling him in no uncertain terms to go away and behave himself.

As they turned onto the road, the horse picked up speed, and Stephen pushed open the door on his side of the buggy to let in a burst of warm air.

"You want your window open?" he asked.

"It is warm enough. I'll get it," Lizzie said, reaching out to pull in the window before hooking it to the clasp on the ceiling.

They rode in silence for awhile until Stephen looked over at her. He cleared his throat.

"You're so quiet today," he said.

"I guess I am, Stephen," Lizzie said. She added quickly, "It's not you or anything. It's just my Dat."

Stephen lifted his eyebrows, looking at her with so much care and concern in his eyes she thought for one wild moment she would burst into tears, sobbing and hiccupping and snorting the way she used to when she was a small child.

She didn't. Calmly, her breath catching in her throat, she told him how Dat fell through the doorway, about his doctor's visit and the upcoming appointment at the huge hospital in Maryland.

Stephen listened without comment until she had finished, then he shook his head and said, "Wow." Lizzie watched him as he shook his head again, as if he was trying to comprehend what she had said. He turned his head and watched the scenery on the other side, saying nothing. He said nothing at all for a very long time, but for some reason, Lizzie wasn't uncomfortable. The silence wasn't awkward because she knew this was just how Stephen was. Lizzie smiled to herself, thinking about all the times he disappeared and reappeared without making any sound at all.

When they came to Elam Zook's home and Stephen turned in the drive, Lizzie's heart began pounding with excitement. She tried to appear calm and composed, but deep down she knew this was quite an event, her very first date.

She felt a bit important, knowing it always caused a commotion when a couple started dating. She arranged her black apron carefully, adjusting her cape and straightening her new navy dress. Of course, she had to have a new dress. Mam always told her she looked best in dark colors like dark blue. Lizzie had chosen the rich, blue fabric because of the way the soft, thick material hung in graceful folds.

Her Uncle Marvin was unhitching his own horse as they approached, and he turned to greet them with a wide smile and raised eyebrows. Lizzie grinned back at him, casting a sidelong glance at Stephen who was trying to keep a straight face.

The whole day was special for Lizzie, and when Stephen came to ask her, a bit timidly, if she was ready to go with him to the hymn-singing, her heart swelled with pure happiness. What a feeling! It was just the greatest thing! She felt like Stephen was hers and she was his, an overwhelming feeling of belonging, of security and togetherness.

She took a deep breath, looking around at her group of friends to see who was watching, and answered a bit louder and slower than was absolutely necessary. "Yes, I am, Stephen. I'll be right out," she said, trying to bat her eyelashes and look a bit humble at the same time.

It didn't work. As soon as Stephen was out of earshot, Mandy threw back her head and laughed an unladylike guffaw of pure, unrestrained mirth.

"Oh, my! You laid that on thick enough!"

Mandy batted her eyelashes while the other girls laughed, a bit hesitantly at first, but seeing Lizzie laugh with Mandy and get up to slap her arm affectionately, they burst into laughter.

"Hey, Mandy, give her a break. It's her first date with him," Mary Ann said, coming to Lizzie's defense.

"See?" Lizzie said.

"That wasn't so bad!" Mary Ann said.

Lizzie smiled at her, a smile of knowing and acceptance. Friends were just the best thing in the world—other than Stephen, anyway.

On the way home that evening, Lizzie and Stephen talked easily about all kinds of different subjects, or rather, Lizzie did most of the talking while Stephen listened, occasionally adding his flat "Wow."

She became a bit nervous and ill at ease as they turned in the drive, wondering what would happen next. What if he didn't like the food she had prepared for a snack? She hadn't actually baked the chocolate whoopie pies herself or the cream cheese cupcakes either. Mam had taken care of all that since Lizzie hated to bake.

But there was nothing to worry about. John and Mandy had arrived home first and had already arranged an array of snacks on the kitchen table.

John and Stephen knew each other well, so they had a good time discussing numerous things until it was time for them to leave.

Lizzie walked with Stephen to the barn to help him with his horse, while John and Mandy remained on the porch swing.

She could sense Stephen's nervousness as he was hitching up his horse and buggy. He didn't say anything at all, but his movements were hurried.

Suddenly he went very still standing beside his horse, one arm crooked against the side of the harness. Lizzie stood quietly, waiting to see what he would say. Would he ask her for another date? Did he even want to continue seeing her? She lowered her head, kicking self-consciously at the graveled driveway.

"Lizzie."

Her head snapped up. "Hmmm?"

"I don't want you to continue dating if you're not sure. Okay?"

"Wh... what do you mean?"

"I mean, this is very serious for me. You know how I've always felt since the first day we met. Don't go on dating me if you don't feel the same."

Lizzie was bewildered. "But Stephen! You haven't asked me yet!"

"I'm not going to."

Her heart sank way down, miserably, horribly. This is it, then.

"Well, then..."

"Let's think about it this week. I'll probably see you Saturday evening then, all right? G'night, Lizzie."

She stepped back, bewildered, surprised, humiliated even. "G'night."

The gravel crunched under the buggy wheels as

he drove out the lane at a good clip, leaving her standing on the darkened slope before she turned to make her way slowly into the house.

"Wow," she breathed.

Chapter 15

A FEW WEEKS BEFORE SCHOOL STARTED, ON a hot August day, Charlie Zimmerman drove his battered old pickup truck in the drive, parked at the end of the sidewalk, and honked the horn loudly.

Mam and Lizzie were husking corn under the walnut tree, and when Mam saw Charlie drive in, she gasped, her hand over her heart. "Oh, I wonder!" she breathed. Quickly, she laid down the brush and the ear of corn she was holding and hurried to the pickup truck.

Lizzie watched, holding her breath in anticipation as Charlie smiled as he talked. When Mam said, "Oh, my!" with both hands held to her mouth, Lizzie dumped her corn from her lap and raced over.

"What? What?" she asked excitedly.

"Joshua and Emma have a little boy!" was all Mam could manage to say. She laughed and cried, she smoothed her apron over her stomach, pulled her covering over her ears, threw back her covering strings, and said, "Oh, my!" at least three times. Charlie beamed as she ran quickly to the barn, calling for Dat in a voice thick with tears.

Lizzie smiled at Charlie.

"Sorry, I guess she's a bit overwhelmed."

Charlie placed a hand on her shoulder, saying, "She has reason to be. She has reason to be."

Dat appeared at the barn door with Mam, a huge grin on his face. Charlie pumped Dat's hand up and down, congratulating him on his first grandson as Mam stood beside them and pulled her covering over her ears again. The three of them stood talking while Lizzie returned to the wheelbarrow load of corn, her thoughts spinning.

Emma had confided in Lizzie in a recent letter that she was "in the family way," as she put it. Amish families didn't talk very much about babies before they arrived. Lizzie hadn't even known about Mandy and Jason until after they were born.

She was very happy that Emma had a son, but this was some time to have a baby! August, right before school started, with all the canning and freezing. Someone would need to go and stay with Joshua and Emma, and although she desperately wanted to go, she knew she should stay at home and work on school projects.

That evening when Mandy came home from work, Lizzie and Mandy had a fierce argument about who would be allowed to go to stay with Emma. Lizzie wanted to go with all her heart, and so did Mandy. Mam settled it by saying she would go the first few days, and after that Lizzie could stay till the end of the week, and Mandy could go for the whole week after that. Lizzie grumbled because Mandy got to stay longer, and Mandy grumbled that Lizzie could go first.

No one wanted to see Mam stay at Joshua's for a few days, but Dat said Emma needed Mam more than the rest of the family did, and they would all be just fine without her. First, though, they would all go to Allen County to see the baby and drop off Mam.

The corn was finished in record time that evening as they chattered about the baby. When they were finished, Mandy fairly hopped up and down with her eyes shining as she ran to the phone shanty to call John with the news.

Lizzie scrubbed the kitchen floor after the last of the corn had been taken to the cold storage in town. Mandy was so lucky to have a 100 percent steady boyfriend, whom she could trust completely and tell him everything she knew.

Lizzie knew she would love to be able to share this happy event with Stephen. But, oh, no, he hadn't asked her for a date for the coming weekend. It irked her. Kind of. Why didn't he ask her out again? Probably so she would wonder all week long if he really liked her or not. He *told* her he cared about her. Then why didn't he ask her?

The next day the whole family went to see the new baby. When they arrived, Joshua's and Emma's house was quiet, the gas lamp in the living room hissing softly as the evening shadows lengthened across the house.

Mam reached the small white bassinet next to the sofa, oohing and aahing as she expertly picked up the small blue bundle inside. Emma got up from the rocking chair, beaming with happiness. Joshua's face reflected his joy as Dat exclaimed how the baby was every inch his father's son.

Lizzie took a good long look at Emma's little son, Mark, and decided he was actually really quite cute for a baby boy. He wasn't deep dark red or grotesquely swollen like some newborns. His eyes were little half moons, with a button nose, well, bigger than a cute button, but a nice nose, and his tiny little mouth puckered into a bow.

Lizzie looked at Baby Mark, then a bit dubiously at Jason. Now there was a case of one of life's greatest mysteries. She remembered very well the shock she felt when Mam came home from the hospital with Jason. He had been alarmingly homely looking, and most of his young life Lizzie had pitied him because of his wild-looking curls. But as he was growing into a young man, she thought he was the most handsome person she had ever seen, now that his curly hair was under control. He had blue-gray eyes with thick curly lashes and a kind smile that melted anyone's heart. So who knew? This cute baby might not be very good-looking at all when he got older.

Joshua and Emma both looked well and happy, so Lizzie decided it must not be too traumatic to have a baby. The biggest test was probably going to be in the coming weeks since a helpless infant could really scream. Babies yelled and cried horribly at times until you were reduced to a quivering mass of nerves and crying yourself. Like Mam had been with Jason.

Lizzie tried hard to put those thoughts to the back of her mind, focusing instead on how cute Mark was and how happy and relaxed Emma looked, her love for Joshua shining from her eyes every time she glanced at him.

❧

Lizzie returned later that week to stay with Emma and Baby Mark. She enjoyed her time with Emma immensely. Working for your sister was definitely more fun than working for someone else, Lizzie thought. It was so easy to relax at Emma's house, feeling right at home, getting something to eat when she was hungry, asking to take a nap when she was sleepy, and learning all the while to appreciate a newborn baby.

Mark very seldom cried, and when he did, Emma could always quiet him easily. She would feed him or throw a soft white diaper over one shoulder and hold him there, his soft little face snuggled against the flannel diaper. Emma rocked him in her pretty new rocker while Lizzie curled up on the sofa. They had long, serious conversations while Emma cuddled her newborn.

"But, Lizzie," Emma said, smiling, "I am *so* happy for you, starting to really, truly find your life partner."

Lizzie eyed Emma skeptically. "What do you mean, 'life partner?' You don't know for certain, Emma."

"No, I don't. That's true. But... I don't know. Mam always had this feeling..."

"Mam's feelings aren't always right."

Emma stopped rocking as she watched Lizzie closely. "Why are you so testy about this subject?"

"You mean I should be all starry-eyed and gushing about how much I'm in love? Well, surprise! Maybe I'm not."

Lizzie picked at a loose thread in the blue and white afghan on the arm of the sofa. She smoothed a finger nervously across the arch of one eyebrow as her eyes fell before Emma's.

"Don't you like Stephen, Lizzie? Nobody said you *have* to date him. I mean it's your individual choice."

"He doesn't like *me*!" Lizzie spat out, annoyed at the huge lump beginning to form in her throat.

Emma began rocking again, patting Mark's back nervously with her hand. "Now *that*, Lizzie, I do not believe."

Lizzie lifted bewildered eyes to Emma. "You don't?"

"No, I don't."

"Well, then, why didn't he ask me for a second date? He said we should both think about it for awhile. Now that was a dumb thing for him to say. It just makes it seem as if he isn't sure if he likes me, or if he wants to date me seriously. I mean, what in the world is there to think about?"

"Lizzie, it seems bold of me to say this maybe, but for someone as smart as you are in book learning—a teacher even..."

She caught her breath as she let out a low laugh. "Remember how desperately I tried to keep up with you at school?"

"No. I forgot."

"Anyway, you can be so simple and dense and blind. Lizzie, think! Why wouldn't Stephen want you to think this over? He has always adored you, no, actually, adored the ground you walked on, and you never, not once, worried about his feelings. First, there was Joe and John, then Amos, and through all that..." Emma stopped.

"Neither Joe or John wanted me," Lizzie burst out. "Amos didn't either."

"Well, you know what I mean. Mam told you over and over to pray for God's will, and did you ever? Huh? Did you?"

"Sometimes. But, Emma, I know I'm older now, but sometimes God still seems way out of reach. Honest. Sometimes when I pray my prayers bounce against the ceiling and fall right back down. I feel silly on my knees."

Emma watched Lizzie seriously. "You should

have joined the church earlier."

"Why?"

"I don't know. Maybe you would be more comfortable with God if you gave your life over to him. You never really thought about that, did you?"

"Well, not really. I didn't want to join church too early. You have to be so plain and can't do one fun thing. Besides, this joining the church thing is all about the *ordnung* and obeying the rules, and I can do that anytime."

"No, Lizzie, joining church is so much more. It's learning how to live for Jesus Christ, your Savior, after you realize that you are a sinner and want to live a better life."

"Oh."

That was all Lizzie said. How could she confess to Emma the fear in her soul? How could she tell anyone that she was scared to death to actually come right out and admit to God that she was a sinner? She was afraid of God as it was, always trying to assure herself that she wasn't all that much of a sinner.

She still couldn't quite figure this whole thing out. If you confessed that you were a real sinner who was going to go to hell, you had to depend on something to help you out of that. Lizzie still was not convinced that she wasn't at least somewhat good enough to make her way to heaven. She helped Mam with the work at home, she wasn't outright terribly disobedient, and she even helped with the milking. Now that was a chore she absolutely hated with a passion, but she did it without complaining too much.

She threw the afghan off her lap, sat up, and smiled at Emma.

"Why don't you lay him down and we'll each make ourselves a cup of peppermint tea and a toasted cheese sandwich? I'm hungry."

Emma smiled back, relieved to see the dark look on Lizzie's face turn to a lighter one.

Their cups of tea steaming between them, they sat down together. The rich, buttery smell of the sandwiches made the kitchen seem warm and homey, Lizzie thought. Even as she felt the dark cloud of doubt return.

"What?" Emma asked, as only sisters can ask, that perfect opening when one perceives that something is troubling the other.

Lizzie swirled a spoon in her tea.

"This sinner thing, Emma. I know Jesus died on the cross for us, and I understand that. The new birth they preach about is all over my head. I don't get that, really, and Mam said I don't have to, that I will in time, that we can't of ourselves become born again.

"So that doesn't bother me so much. It's just that, how do we know for sure that if we do feel like a sinner, I mean, a bad one, then how can we be certain that Jesus' blood is for us, too? I mean me, just for me?"

Emma took a bite of her sandwich and chewed slowly. She wiped the crumbs from her mouth with a napkin.

"We never are. We just have to have faith and

believe it. It's kind of like a gift that seems too good to be free, so it's hard to humble ourselves to admit that we even need it in the first place. But you'll understand more as you grow older. We don't need to understand every little thing before we try to live for God."

"I guess."

Lizzie paused before telling Emma that Mandy and she would join church the following summer, and probably by then she would be ready to start that serious journey.

"In the meantime, you'll wait until Stephen asks for another date, right?" Emma teased.

Lizzie snorted. Emma laughed as she told Lizzie about how insecure she felt when Joshua asked her out the first time.

"But he asked you again that Sunday evening for the coming weekend, right?" Lizzie asked.

"Oh, yes! I would have had a fit if he hadn't."

That was no comfort at all, but Lizzie didn't say so. She needed to get out, get some exercise, clear her head of all these troubling thoughts wrapping themselves around her.

"Emma, do you mind if I start mowing the yard? I could do it all tomorrow, but I need the exercise."

"No, of course not. Why do you want to? Didn't I help much with whatever is troubling you?"

"Oh, of course," Lizzie said, meaning every word. There was still no one like Emma to explain things to her in a clear, uncluttered fashion that made everything more hopeful. Emma was like that.

Walking steadily behind the reel mower with the grass clippings dusting her feet and the hot August sun on her back, she did feel much better. Hearing the drone of a low airplane, she stopped to watch its course across the blue sky.

Airplanes were amazing things, an engine keeping that heavy craft in the sky and moving it along at that speed. Why weren't Amish people allowed to fly in airplanes? What would be wrong with one little ride? It would be the most wonderful feeling to be flying along above the earth and looking down on the little dots that were towns or houses and barns.

She sighed, returning to her grass mowing, and thought about how much it would cost to ride in an airplane. She'd ask Joshua; he knew such things.

"Lizzie!"

Joshua was hurrying toward her, a white piece of paper fluttering from his hand. Lizzie stopped, swiping at her loose hair with the back of her hand, watching him questioningly.

"I was in the phone shanty and the phone rang. Someone wants you to call him right away!" he said, a broad grin spreading across his face.

"Who?" Lizzie asked, her mouth becoming dry as her heart started banging too fast.

"Go find out!"

Lizzie grabbed blindly at the piece of paper, trying to read the numbers while running. She stumbled down over the bank beside the road, her thoughts scattered into a jumble that made no sense. Stephen? Would he? Did he even know where she was? He would never call in the middle of the day. He was at work. It was probably Jason. Or… or the school board. Or Dat. Joshua had said *he*.

She wiped her perspiring face, and then with shaking hands she spread out the piece of paper as she sank onto the stool in the shanty. She definitely did not recognize the number. Oh, this was so terribly unnerving. She was afraid to dial and afraid not to pick up the phone.

Taking a deep breath, she dialed the number quickly, just sure she would have heart failure if it was Stephen. Or if it wasn't.

It rang twice before a voice said, "Hello!"

Lizzie's heart sank. Marvin! What did he want? Trying desperately to keep her voice from showing the disappointment she felt, she said, "Marvin! Why are you calling me?"

"Stephen wants to talk to you."

Lizzie's mouth flew open as if to protest, but there was nothing she could do as she heard him yell for Stephen.

Then, "Hello."

"Hi… hi!" Lizzie breathed.

"What are you doing?"

"I was… was mowing grass, actually."

"Oh."

Typical Stephen. Just "oh."

"Why… why are you calling me?"

There was silence for the space of a few heartbeats before Stephen told her that he was doing some concrete work with Marvin and that Marvin had told him about the new baby. Stephen paused.

"How are you feeling about our date, Lizzie?" he asked finally.

He laughed before she could respond.

"Marvin didn't think I was very smart," he said. "He thought I should have asked you out again."

Lizzie bit her lip, squeezed her eyes shut, and then opened them wide as she tilted her head back to look at the ceiling. Good old Marvin, coming to her rescue like this.

"Well, I guess that's up to you whether you want to see me again," she replied.

"You know how I feel, Lizzie," was all Stephen said.

"Does that mean you're asking me out... or... or what?" Lizzie asked.

When she hung the phone on the hook, she definitely did have a date the following weekend. Dashing into the house, Lizzie let out a most unladylike yell of excitement, causing Emma to sit up from her nap on the couch, struggling to orient herself after all of Lizzie's hollering.

Baby Mark snuffled in his bassinet as Lizzie shouted, "Stephen called. I have a date!"

Laughing wearily, Emma sank back against the cushions.

"Lizzie, you're acting as if you're the only person ever asked for a date," she said, closing her eyes.

"I don't care!" Lizzie said, flopping into a chair and gazing happily at the opposite wall. "I have another date with Stephen!"

Chapter 16

Summer days turned sticky with August's humidity, and the heat hovered like a warm, wet blanket. Even getting up in the morning was a chore, and brushing her teeth brought a small sheen of perspiration to Lizzie's upper lip. The sun was already a hot, orange orb rising mercilessly across the east pasture when she headed outside with Mandy to do yard work after breakfast. It was going to be another uncomfortable day with the thermometer hovering between 90 and 100 degrees.

English people had air-conditioned homes, that was the thing. They could escape into their shaded, cool houses where that wonderful invention purred endearingly at the window, bringing waves of refrigerated air into a miserable house. They could lounge about in perfect comfort as long as they didn't go outside, Lizzie thought.

But not Amish people. No electricity meant no air-conditioning. So summer was miserable, and you had to go about your day with a smile on your face and sweat dripping off your nose and down your back and into your eyes, especially when hoeing in the garden or mowing lawn.

The weekends weren't as much fun in the summertime, either, once the heat became this uncomfortable. For one thing, they had to wear Sunday dresses and capes and aprons, which were not designed for August heat at all. Long sleeves, a lined cape, and a black apron pinned around the waist amounted to layers and layers of heavy fabric.

Lizzie brought this fact to Mam's attention when she was getting ready one Sunday afternoon before Stephen picked her up. Her hands were moist with perspiration, and the pins would not go smoothly into the black belt of her apron. Her good humor had disappeared.

"Mam, help me pin on my apron," she said.

Mam glanced up from the *Family Life* magazine she was reading.

"It's too HOT to dress up!" Lizzie yelled as she accidentally pricked her finger with a pin.

"Now..." Mam began.

"I mean it, Mam. Think about it. We have facing on our dresses—that's two layers of dress material—and till the cape is pinned on, that's two more. Then, there are another two in the belt of our aprons. That's six layers. Six!"

Lizzie was almost screeching in exasperation, and Mam roared, helplessly caught in waves of laughter.

"Ach, now Lizzie. It's not that bad. I guess as long as the world has stood, it's been summer and winter, and we just take it as it comes."

Lizzie flounced off before Mam had a chance to help her pin her apron, deciding that if she was going to be in that kind of mood, she'd do it herself. As long as the world stood, thought Lizzie. What an ancient expression! The world didn't stand, it hurled itself around the sun at unimaginable speeds, whirling so fast it made no sense that you didn't feel one thing.

Stephen had continued to ask Lizzie for a date each weekend, and their relationship had quickly become more serious. They talked easily now, a more comfortable, effortless conversation, and it didn't really matter whether they kept small talk flowing or not. Silence between the two of them was content and easy, too.

Dat kept his appointment at the large hospital in Maryland. The doctors put him through a battery of tests to determine why his eyesight was failing and what caused the numbness in his legs and feet. He was often very tired and discouraged after his appointments, worried because his feet and eyes no longer wanted to do what his brain told them to do.

A few weeks after his examination, Mam went to the phone shanty to find out what the tests revealed. Lizzie watched her walk out the lane with a sinking feeling in her heart. Soon Mam came striding back in the driveway, her thumbs curled under her four fingers as she did when something upset her. She took up the corner of her apron and wiped her eyes before reaching the porch. Lizzie steeled herself for the absolute worst, watching anxiously as Mam approached the steps.

Lizzie glanced nervously at Dat who sat at the kitchen table, drumming his fingers on the tabletop. As Mam came through the door he looked up anxiously, his eyes seeking reassurance.

Mam shook her head, making a soft, clucking noise. "Ach, the doctor wants to see you in his office in Maryland. I guess they don't realize how much it costs for us to go that far with a driver, but he didn't give us much choice."

"How soon does he want to see me?" Dat asked.

"Tomorrow forenoon."

Lizzie dreaded her return from school that day, knowing this was the actual day they would find out why Dat wasn't well. As always, she predicted the worst, her thoughts swirling around in her mind until she was in quite a state. She wanted the day to end swiftly, and yet she did not want to go home at all.

But there was no avoiding the cold, hard truth when Mam's words hit her with all the impact of a sledge hammer.

"He has MS," Mam said, not softly or loudly, just in plain ordinary words without tears or any display of emotion at all. She just said the words, simply and matter-of-factly, like carefully laying Scrabble tiles in the proper blocks to complete a word.

Lizzie threw down her book bag, folding into a kitchen chair with a sigh.

"What does that mean, Mam?" she asked, her fingers plucking nervously at the rip in the plastic tablecloth.

Mam turned from the sink where she was peeling potatoes for the evening meal. Taking up the corner of her apron, she dried her hands on it before sitting down at the table.

Her eyes looked tired. The red veins running through the whites of her eyes were more noticeable when she took off her glasses and wiped them with the dry corner of her apron. Putting her glasses back on her face, she smiled at Lizzie, only to have one corner of her mouth drop immediately as her nostrils flared and tears came of their own accord, despite her best effort to hold them back.

"I don't know, Lizzie, really, I don't," Mam said softly. "We have plenty of literature the doctor gave us to read, so I'm sure till the evening is over we'll know more. The way I understand, it starts with a virus which somehow gets into the spinal fluid, and, in time, that messes up the brain signals, which is why Dat doesn't have the full ability to walk like he used to. Same thing with his eyes."

"But there has to be something doctors can do," Lizzie said. "Isn't there some type of medication they can give him to make it go away?"

"No. Not the way the doctor described the disease. There are many types, some much worse than others, or with some the muscles deteriorate faster, I suppose. Ach, Lizzie, I really don't know too much about it yet. I just know that we have this to live with now and we have to make the best of it."

Mam went back to peeling potatoes with a tired sigh, and Lizzie watched her, a feeling of overwhelming pity making it hard for her to speak normally. "Where is the literature the doctor gave you?" she asked.

"On Dat's desk."

So Lizzie curled up on the sofa, devouring every word she could about the disease that evidently was living in Dat's spine. Multiple sclerosis. Whoever came up with those words? she thought. Her whole being rebelled against this horrible intruder that had so rudely interrupted their lives.

She opened one pamphlet and looked at a few drawings of spinal fluid and odd-looking bacteria.

"This slowly progressive disease involves various parts of the central nervous system and presents numerous symptoms which tend to come and go, only to return again in greater severity," Lizzie read.

She found out that although a tremendous amount of research was being carried forward in the hope of discovering the basic cause, as yet there was no known cure.

Another pamphlet described in more detail exactly what was occurring in Dat's body. The lesions of multiple sclerosis which interrupt the nerve pathways are characterized by a loss of the usual insulating material called myelin, which covers the nerve fibers. In other words, Lizzie thought, little tiny scabs are messing up the nerve fibers, making everything more difficult for him to do.

She flung the glossy little folders on the arm of the sofa and marched back out to the kitchen.

"Does this mean that we have to stay home on weekends and everyone is going to be all serious and sad and I can't go camping this weekend?" she burst out, leaning against the countertop as she searched Mam's face.

Mam smiled a very small smile. "No, of course not. Dat is still alive and well and will continue to be all right for quite some time. Actually, he shouldn't be showing too many signs of the disease for up to a few years, other than his stumbling and blurry vision. So, no, Lizzie, you can go camping, of course. Our family life will just go on much the same as it always has."

"What about the farm?"

"We'll keep going as long as Dat is able. We'll see. Now go change, and you can start getting the wash off the line."

Chapter 17

THAT SATURDAY AFTERNOON STEPHEN DROVE up the lane and past the barn in a spring wagon. Two horses pulled the wagon which was covered with a tarp, forming a makeshift roof and sides so it looked almost like a modern-day covered wagon. Rebecca sat beside Stephen, smiling and waving her long, thin arms the minute she spied Lizzie.

Stephen's eyes were shining with excitement as he jumped down to hold the horses while Lizzie loaded her sleeping bag, pillow, ice chest, box of food, and folding chairs into the back.

Dat came out of the barn and shook his head at Stephen.

"Looks like a lovely pair to me!" he said, pointing to the horses.

"They'll be all right," Stephen replied, laughing.

"You better not let them see the contraption they're pulling," Dat laughed.

"That's just in case it rains."

"Hopefully it won't."

Smiling and waving, they were off, after Dat told them to be careful and behave themselves.

"That's what he always says," Lizzie said to Stephen.

"Well, at least he's friendly about us going camping," Stephen answered.

"I'll say," Rebecca added.

Lizzie's parents hadn't liked the idea of a group of youth traveling together for so many miles and camping overnight, especially in an unknown place. Stephen knew a very nice English couple, good friends of his parents, who had made arrangements for them to pitch their tents on their campground. This, however, made little difference to Lizzie's parents.

Finally, Dat spoke to Stephen's parents at church one Sunday. After a long discussion, the parents finally decided it was all right to let the youth go camping this once, but if they heard of any unruliness, they could never go again.

They were instructed in rather serious terms how to behave, Lizzie thought. They were to be very careful of traffic and take good care of the horses, especially as they pulled the wagon up the mountain. They couldn't yell or be just plain down noisy or put themselves or the horses in danger.

It was, Lizzie thought, a bit uncommon for the small group of youth in Cameron County to even have the audacity to ask their parents to go camping overnight, but those are the kind of things that made life exciting. They all sat together and talked about their upcoming adventure after the hymn-singings on Sunday evenings. Mam and Dat should realize how fortunate they were that she asked permission to just go camping. What if they all decided to go white-water rafting? Or go for an airplane ride? Camping was mild compared to that.

ᦥᣞ

The air was chilly so Lizzie wrapped a blanket around her shoulders as the horses trotted faster. They were on their way to pick up Marvin and Stephen's friend, Reuben, before heading to the campground across the West Mountain. Lizzie had never seen Stephen in such high spirits nor heard him talk as much as he did on their way to pick up Marvin.

The horses traveled together all right, although Stephen had to hold back Bob, the small chestnut brown one. Bob tossed his head up, then threw it down, worrying with the bit in his mouth until Lizzie began to be a little afraid.

"Why is that small horse so agitated?" she asked Stephen.

"He'll settle down once he gets good and tired," he answered, quite unperturbed.

So Lizzie tried not to let the little horse bother her as they picked up the two other boys and headed west. It was, after all, a perfect fall day, a bit chilly, maybe, but otherwise just a great day to be off on an adventure like this.

But Lizzie could feel Bob's agitation, and she was afraid he would wear himself out, raising and lowering his head, chomping down on the bit, prancing, stepping sideways, until the sweat turned to foam and flecks of foam coated his harness. If he would only calm down, he would use maybe only half of his energy.

She didn't blame him. It would be awful to be hitched to that long wooden tongue with a horse he had never met before, with those leather blinders on each side of his face. He wanted to run the way he was used to, run free and swift, without that weight hanging on his collar.

What if one of the horses began balking and they began drifting backward? They were going up, up, always on a slight incline, very different from the rolling up and down terrain of Cameron County.

Lizzie could no longer remain quiet, so she brought up the subject to Stephen again.

"Don't worry about it," Stephen said shortly.

Lizzie glanced at him sideways and shrugged her shoulders. All right, be like that then, she thought. She was hurt. That wasn't very nice of him to tell her off like that. She watched him again, but he was talking and laughing with Reuben without noticing that Lizzie was quiet. Actually, a bit miffed.

She wished Stephen would reassure her more verbally and help her overcome her distress about Bob. He probably wouldn't be very comforting about anything, Lizzie thought as she realized the night would be very dark so far away from any towns or houses and the campground so far away from Mam and Dat and Mandy.

Golden leaves floated to the ground, and little wrinkled brown ones scudded across the road as the breeze pushed against the covered wagon. Stephen and Marvin discussed the best places to pull off on the side of the road to let the horses rest and drink water.

Just as Stephen had predicted, the horses slowed to a walk once the road turned gradually uphill, because they needed to conserve their energy for the long haul to the top of the mountain.

The five young people settled in and relaxed, laughing and talking about all kinds of ordinary subjects. Lizzie told them about Dat's disease and how hard it was to think of him being unable to walk in the coming years, which brought quick sympathetic tears from Rebecca. She's such a dear, Lizzie thought, and not only because she's Stephen's sister, just because she's herself.

As the afternoon continued, Rebecca and Marvin got out of the wagon and were now walking behind it to make the load lighter for the horses. Up front, Reuben and Stephen were having so much fun while Lizzie sat in the back seat, her arms crossed tightly in front of her, and pouted. She tried not to pout seriously, just enough to make Stephen notice that he had hurt her feelings. But if he noticed, he gave no sign.

Bored all alone on the back seat, she cleared her throat and coughed. Nothing happened. Stephen kept having fun with Reuben, so she dug in her purse until she found her pack of chewing gum. "Anyone want a piece of gum?" she sang out.

"No, thanks!"

"Nope!"

Lizzie stuffed two big pieces into her mouth and chewed vehemently. She peered through the plastic side flap to see where Rebecca and Marvin were, but they weren't even in sight. She sighed and flopped back against the seat.

"I'm bored," she said loudly.

Stephen turned to look at her and laughed.

"You'll soon be a lot more bored than you are now, if you get bored this quickly," he said.

After he said that, Stephen laughed, bringing bright color to Lizzie's cheeks. Now she wasn't just hurt and bored. She was angry. How dare he? Her very own boyfriend.

"Let me off," she said curtly.

"Why?"

"Just let me off."

Stephen shrugged his shoulders, stopped the team, and watched as Lizzie climbed down over the back step.

"What are you going to do?" he asked, really noticing her this time.

"Walk."

"By yourself?"

"Of course."

"Do you want me to come with you?"

"No."

She soon found Rebecca and Marvin and had a good time walking with them along the leaf-strewn country road that wound its way to the top of the mountain.

They stopped almost at the very peak of the mountain and had a long, delicious lunch, while the boys watered the horses at the spring which bubbled out of the rocks. It was a beautiful spot, one Lizzie would never forget, sitting surrounded by thick foliage that provided a brilliant background to the sweating horses.

After lunch they climbed back onto the wagon and started down the opposite side of the mountain. Lizzie fought down her panic as the brakes, which were blocks of rubber, scraped and screeched against the back wheels, helping the horses hold the wagon to a safe speed.

She sat back against the seat with Rebecca, put her fist to her mouth, and whispered, "Aren't you afraid?"

"No. The horses are taking it easy. Stephen's a good driver."

But Lizzie was immensely relieved when they finally rolled into the campground. It was so good to be on level ground—on good, soft, green grass— that she chattered happily on about anything and everything. She felt so much better. She would never tell Stephen how absolutely petrified she had been.

After talking to the owner of the campground, the boys fed and watered the horses and then set up the girls' tent and one for themselves. As the sun slipped behind the mountain, Marvin and Reuben started a roaring campfire while Stephen got out folding chairs. They all started roasting hot dogs and burning marshmallows to a black crisp.

Stephen brought his chair over close to hers and sat down beside her. Lizzie smiled.

"Are you having fun?" he asked quietly and only for her ears to hear.

"Oh, yes. Except for a while back there when you were mean to me," she said, trying to pout prettily.

"Mean to you? When was I mean to you?"

"You and Reuben were laughing at me."

Stephen sat back and looked at the stars twinkling down between the leaves of the treetops. "We didn't want to make you feel bad, Lizzie, but I don't like when someone nags at me when I'm driving a horse. Especially not two horses."

"I'm sorry," Lizzie whispered.

"That's okay," Stephen said gruffly. Stephen and Lizzie sat quietly side by side until it was time for bed.

Rebecca and Lizzie had a great time in their tent, settling in for the night. They arranged and rearranged their sleeping bags and adjusted their pillows. Finally, sometime after midnight they dozed off fitfully, each trying to reach a comfortable position on the hard ground.

In the middle of the night, Lizzie awakened to a shrill scream, which sounded so much like a genuinely terrified woman that she sat straight up and grabbed Rebecca, her eyes wide open in terror. The horses were going crazy, whinnying and snorting and stamping their feet as they strained on the ropes that held them to the trees.

"Rebecca! What is it?" Lizzie hissed.

"How would I know? I didn't hear it. You woke me, grabbing my head!" Rebecca shouted.

Then at that moment another terrifying, high-pitched wail sliced through the thick darkness. The horses snorted again and whinnied restlessly.

Rebecca and Lizzie cowered in their tent, half whimpering with fright. This was awful. Was it a woman who was hurt and afraid, or worse yet, a huge mountain lion out there on the mountain somewhere, just waiting to rake its claws through the thin material of their small tent?

Just when Lizzie thought she would scream loud and long without any restraint whatsoever, she heard the boys' tent zipper, and bright spots of light moved across the campground to the horses. The boys gently steadied the horses, calming them in soothing tones.

Another ear-splitting scream rent the night air as the girls sank lower in their sleeping bags. Lizzie was close to tears as she wriggled out of her sleeping bag and quickly pushed up the tent zipper. Just as she was ready to call out to Stephen, she heard him tell Marvin that he was almost positive that sound was a bobcat.

A bobcat!

They aren't even very big, Lizzie thought. About twice the size of a house cat.

Quickly she stuck her head out and called, "Are you sure, Stephen?"

"I think so, but just to make sure, we'll walk around with flashlights after we get the horses calmed down."

Lizzie crawled back into the tent, smiling to herself about how calm and grown up and handsome Stephen looked out there, taking charge of this terrifying situation. He would protect her, making her feel so much less afraid and alone. She guessed she could forgive him for being uncaring on the way across the mountain. She definitely was not going to bring it up ever again, that was one thing sure.

Stephen was her boyfriend now, and if she wanted to continue their friendship, she would have to learn to be quiet, keeping her thoughts to herself at certain times. Emma said that was important when you got married, and she believed almost everything Emma said.

Chapter 18

MANDY THREW A PILLOW IN LIZZIE'S direction and let out a fierce yell. Lizzie reached down and picked up the pillow, firing it back at Mandy as hard as she possibly could. Tiny pellets of cold, hard snow whacked against the upstairs windows of the old farmhouse as another winter storm began to pick up speed, dropping icy snowflakes on the brown frozen landscape. Inside, Lizzie's bedroom was suffused in the soft yellow glow of the kerosene lamp, the wick turned up as far as it would go without sending black smoke billowing out of the glass chimney.

It was the week before Christmas, a busy time in the Glick household. Mam loved Christmas shopping and Dat gladly let her go ahead with it. He was no shopper, he always said, which was just fine with Mam, as she certainly was. Mam always saved money somehow, somewhere, even if it meant doing with less grocery money through November.

Lizzie just knew that on Christmas morning there would always be three or four good-sized packages piled around the drop-leaf table in the living room for each family member, while Mam hovered about, her cheeks pink with excitement. Every year Lizzie had a long list of things she wanted. This year's list included ice skates and new dresses and a warm robe, as well as things for her room, like a new picture for the wall and a nice new candle with an artificial flower ring around the base.

Oh, my! Nothing surpassed the spread of food at Christmastime. Mam was always a very good cook and a wonderful baker, but over Christmas she completely outdid herself.

Each year she would start by looking through all of her cookbooks, particularly her red hardcover Betty Crocker one. Then out would come her gray metal recipe box with the tattered yellow recipe cards that held all the wonders of Christmas. Among them was date pudding, which was so rich you couldn't eat too much, although Lizzie always managed to eat so much her stomach hurt a bit.

There was hardly an end to the rich desserts and drinks Mam would cook and bake for weeks before Christmas. She made butterscotch pie, chocolate pie, sand tarts, Grandpa cookies, Christmas layer salad, banana pudding, and Christmas cake. Mam mixed ginger ale with grape juice, or she bought soda—Mountain Dew, Pepsi, or root beer—and vanilla ice cream to make root beer floats. Which, Lizzie discovered as a child, you should never eat with olives.

Sometime Mam roasted a turkey for Christmas, and other years she baked a ham. She would always arrange pineapple rings on the ham and baste it with a bit of the juice while it baked.

The best part of Christmas dinner was the Ohio filling. It came out of the oven moist and steaming with a golden brown crust on top. The crust was the best. It tasted like toast with too much butter, Lizzie thought. Mam's version was from her native Holmes County, Ohio, and included potatoes, carrots, and celery chopped into tiny pieces, cubed bread, chicken, and chicken broth. It was so good. There was no other way to describe it except to say it was almost the best thing about Christmas food.

Mam made all kinds of cookies and candy, too. Rice Krispie treats and chocolate-coated peanut butter crackers were Lizzie's favorites.

Lizzie and Mandy always worked very hard to clean the entire house for Christmas, while Mam baked and cooked in the kitchen. They didn't decorate the house because that would be too worldly. Sometimes Mam allowed a few red candles on the windowsill or a candle set in the middle of the table.

Amish people did not believe in Christmas trees. Lizzie always wanted one though. Her favorite argument was that Laura Ingalls had one, decorated with popcorn and cranberries. Mam said Laura was English, but Lizzie said she wore longer dresses than her own. Mam said they were still English, and her nostrils flared a bit, and Lizzie knew it was time to stop pressing Mam on the Christmas tree issue. Christmas trees were fancy and not in the Amish *ordnung*.

At Christmas the festivities also extended to the youth gatherings, especially the large Christmas hymn-singing that all of the parents were also urged to attend. It was just a special time, where all the voices blended together as the group sang old German favorites.

They often sang the verses in German and the chorus in English of songs such as "Joy to the World" and "Hark the Herald Angels Sing." Lizzie's favorite was "*Stille Nacht*" or "Silent Night" in German.

Dat loved singing, and especially at Christmastime he was in his element, sitting in the middle of the room at the singing, leading many of the songs with his beautiful voice. He knew all the words to all of the songs. Lizzie was secretly proud of Dat because she knew that when he started a song, the singing would become especially rousing. Dat was probably the community's best voice.

Two days before Christmas, Lizzie and Mandy were wrapping their Christmas presents for John and Stephen. Picking out a gift for a boy was a new experience for Lizzie, and one she was decidedly not comfortable with. Mandy teased her mercilessly, which was quite funny for awhile, but now Lizzie didn't think it was so humorous anymore.

She dreaded exchanging gifts with Stephen because she was worried about how to act properly and politely. She just didn't know how and when to say the right thing.

What if she didn't like what Stephen gave her? Of course, she would fuss over it and tell him it was beautiful even if it wasn't. But Mandy laughed when Lizzie told her how she would react, being calm and polite no matter what she received.

"Your face is a dead giveaway," Mandy said. "You can't hide your true feelings."

"That's not true!"

"You'll say, 'Oh, how lovely!' and promptly burst into so many tears that you'll need a whole box of Kleenexes to keep blowing your nose," Mandy continued, clinging to the pillow that landed in her face.

Lizzie flipped back her long, brown hair, which was still wet from the shower, and scowled at Mandy.

"So. You weren't exactly thrilled with that cheap picture John gave you for your birthday," she said.

"I was! Where did you get that idea? Huh? He gave me my water set, too, not just the picture."

Mandy got up from her perch on the bed and ran a towel across her wet hair.

"You're just jealous," she said.

Lizzie shook her head vehemently. "Oh, no. Huh-uh. I wouldn't want a water set. I'm not getting married anytime soon."

"Then why are you dating Stephen?"

"'Cause I like him. He's fun to be with.

"Is that all?"

"Well, for now."

Mandy sat back down on the bed and straightened the gold bow she had tied around John's gift. The enormous box was wrapped in a dull red paper and done up with a gold bow, which looked very masculine. It was the perfect paper for a young man's present, Lizzie thought. She and Mandy had bought the same thing for their boyfriends, a small shaving cabinet with sliding glass doors and a wooden towel rack. They were very popular among the girls' friends and considered the perfect expensive Christmas gift to give to their boyfriends.

Lizzie's package for Stephen was wrapped in forest green paper. She was very happy with it, except she secretly thought the red looked more Christmasy. She would never admit this to Mandy, who was already too smug and self-assured about that package of hers.

"So, Mandy, you give John his gift Saturday evening, and I will give Stephen his Sunday evening, okay? Because you most definitely are not going to watch us exchange gifts or hear us or anything."

Mandy laughed easily. "Oh, relax. We're going to be down at the farm with his brother."

"Over the entire holiday?"

"No, of course not. John says he has something special to tell me or show me. I'm not sure what he meant."

"He's going to ask you to marry him!" Lizzie said loudly.

"Hush, Lizzie! You'll wake the twins! No, he's not. I'm not even near old enough and haven't joined the church yet."

"Oh, that's right. I forgot."

They sat and talked awhile longer as the snow pinged against the windows and the soft hiss of the kerosene lamp made everything seem homey and cozy. They talked about Dat and how they hardly ever noticed there was anything different about him since his diagnosis. It always made them sad to think of Dat's disease, but since Mam was so upbeat, encouraging Dat to keep doing all the things he was used to doing, it helped the girls to see that it really wasn't so terrible to have multiple sclerosis.

"Not yet, Lizzie," Mandy said wisely, shaking her head slowly. "But sometime it will be."

"I know," Lizzie said soberly.

They sat in comfortable silence, Mandy with her chin on her knees, her arms wrapped around her legs. Lizzie plumped the pillows and flopped back, crossing her hands behind her head.

"So, what do you say when you give your boyfriend his present? Just, 'Here,' or 'Do you want this?' or 'Open this,' or what?" Lizzie asked.

Mandy rolled over and collapsed in a fit of laughter. She laughed until she could hardly get her breath, gasping and wheezing as she slapped at Lizzie.

Lizzie laughed with her, but only because she always had to laugh when Mandy did—that's just how it was.

Wiping her eyes, Mandy said, "Yes, Lizzie, just hold out the box and say, 'Here!' "

"You're a big help!" Lizzie said, pushing Mandy

off the bed where she collapsed into another fit of giggles on the rug.

"Are you really so nervous about giving Stephen that gift?" she asked, sitting up and watching Lizzie incredulously.

"Of course I am! I never had a boyfriend before," Lizzie said.

"Don't worry about it. You know how Mam says, 'Everything will work out.' You and Stephen are so relaxed and comfortable together, I can't see why you're making such a big deal out of this."

Quite honestly, Lizzie was uncomfortable with formalities, even ordinary everyday little ways of being nice and polite and knowing exactly what to say at the exact right moment. Oh, she could talk to English people, go shopping, pay drivers, and get along all right in the world, but receiving a gift from someone or acknowledging a compliment always made her feel completely at a loss about how to act.

⁂

So when Stephen and Lizzie drove home that Sunday evening after the hymn-singing, she was in a state of panic. Stephen talked easily while she chewed desperately on one fingernail after another, nodding her head or saying, "Mmm-hmm."

Suddenly Stephen reached over and took her hand away from her mouth. "Quit that. Either you're really hungry, or you haven't clipped your fingernails in a long time."

Lizzie laughed but didn't say anything.

When they reached her home, Stephen unhitched his horse and went around to the back of the buggy. Lifting the back door, he extracted a box which was so beautifully wrapped that, even in the dim light of the forebay, it looked so expensive it took her breath away. Oh, she wondered, what was inside?

She looked at Stephen questioningly, but he didn't notice or pretended not to. Without saying a word, he started toward the house. There was nothing for Lizzie to do but follow him, and since he wasn't saying anything, she guessed she may as well remain silent as well.

Stephen said he wasn't hungry, so Lizzie asked if he wanted to exchange gifts first.

"Let's do," he said.

Sitting in the living room in the quiet house lit with the soft yellow lamplight, she took the package he handed to her as naturally as breathing, and about as uncomplicated. After putting aside the huge foil bow, she tore off the paper and found a golden glass object wrapped in white tissue paper.

She was puzzled, unable to think of anything shaped like that. The glass, a translucent golden color, had a bumpy design in it, almost like little bumps with lines between them.

Unwrapping it carefully, she held it up to the light.

"A shade! A glass shade!" she exclaimed. Quickly she dug into the tissue paper again and came up with a huge, intricately designed kerosene lamp with a clear glass chimney and a bracket to hold the big, beautiful shade.

Lizzie was so pleased she couldn't find words to express herself. John had given Mandy a blue one exactly like this, but Lizzie just figured she would never have one of her own because John came from Lamont, where everyone knew the latest style in gifts and things like that. She had tried hard to admire Mandy's beautiful lamp, even though she was thinking how perfect a gold one would be in her own room. And now she owned one!

She didn't struggle with what to say. She was too delighted about owning that perfect lamp.

"Thank you, Stephen," she said sincerely, her whole heart meaning the words. "I just love it."

"I'm glad," he said.

"Oh, I almost forgot yours!"

She handed him the large package, watching eagerly as he ripped off the bow without bothering to save it, just like boys always did when they opened gifts, Lizzie thought. He tore open the box and smiled quietly when he saw the golden oak wood of the shaving cabinet.

"Just what I need," he said.

"Really?" Lizzie asked breathlessly.

"Yes. I do need this to keep small things in my room. It's beautiful oak wood, too."

"You really like it?"

"Of course I do."

Lizzie sighed happily, and Stephen handed her a large white envelope.

"Your card."

"Oh, oh, yes, of course. I put my card for you inside the shaving cabinet."

Separately they opened the cards and read the words. Lizzie had agonized for a great length of time at the card shop in town, trying to find a Christmas card with the perfect words.

Should her card say "To the One I Love," or should it say "To a Dear Friend"? If she got the first card, it would tell him she loved him, and that would be dumb because she had never told him that. Not yet. If she gave him the one that said "To a Dear Friend," it sounded like a card she would give to Mary Ann or Rebecca or just any ordinary girlfriend.

And Stephen was definitely more than that. But to say "I Love You" on a Christmas card was a little too bold, she thought. She had finally settled on a card that said "For a Special Friend," which really was a nice safe card that didn't seem as if it was meant for the mailman or the milk-truck driver or Charlie Zimmerman.

She opened the large white envelope Stephen handed her and stifled a gasp when she saw the words, "To the One I Love at Christmas," in large beautifully written words across the entire face of the card. The inside had soft paper, almost like tissue paper, folded along both sides, and Stephen had written beautiful words about how his life had changed since they had started dating and how much she meant to him, especially at Christmastime.

Below it he had written, "I Love You, Stephen."

Lizzie remained seated, reading the card a lot longer than was absolutely necessary, simply because she didn't know what else to do. She was afraid to look at Stephen, and horribly embarrassed at having chosen that simple friendship card. Color crept into her cheeks as she watched him close the card and return it to the envelope with a soft sigh.

"Stephen, I... I..." she stammered.

He turned to look at her, and she met his gaze for only a moment before dropping her eyes in bewilderment.

"It's okay, Lizzie. It really is. I'm just glad you consider me your special friend."

She laughed softly. "Well, if you must know, I spent some agonizing moments at the card shop, trying to figure out which card was appropriate. And now your card says so much more than mine. It's just that, well, sometimes I think I must be the only person in the whole world who doesn't really understand... understand... well, what I mean, I mean... what I... what love is."

There was a long, uncomfortable silence as Lizzie sat miserably twisting the hem of her apron in both hands. Just say something, Stephen, anything, she thought.

But he didn't. He sighed again and stood up abruptly, gathering the wrapping paper that was strewn across the sofa.

"I'm hungry," he announced. "Let's go have our snack."

In the kitchen, the mood was dispelled, the atmosphere lighter, and Stephen bantered lightheartedly, as usual, while they ate the Christmas cookies and drank hot peppermint tea. After he left, Lizzie put the mugs in the sink, absentmindedly letting the flow of warm water splash on the back of her hand, her thoughts ebbing and flowing.

Why could she never find solid ground where Stephen was concerned? It was like walking through a maze or a puzzle where she could never find her way with absolute clarity. Did anyone ever love beyond a doubt, totally and absolutely committed to one other person, their only desire to spend the rest of their days growing old together?

She shook her head wearily, knowing she was tired from the long holiday so that now was not a real good time to be contemplating anything. As she made her way up the steps to her room, carrying the lamp, she felt old and weary from constantly battling her doubts and fears.

She wished Emma still lived at home so she could ask her if she ever felt unsure of herself where Joshua was concerned. Well, she was going to get some sleep and not worry about anything till morning. She ran her hand across the beautiful gold lamp, still in awe of actually owning one like Mandy's, only prettier. It had been a good Christmas, with all the presents from Mam and Dat, the love they had for each other, and, most of all, the fact that the old farm and Cameron County was their home, really and truly.

Chapter 19

LIZZIE MARCHED DOWN THE MIDDLE AISLE of her classroom, her face contorted with disgust. She reached out and grabbed Eli's arm, yanking him back into his seat. He looked up at her, his face a mixture of mockery and fear.

"If you don't stay in your seat, I'm going to have to get out my paddle," she ground out between clenched teeth. "Sit down and stay there!"

The classroom became very quiet, the only sounds coming from a few nervous pupils clearing their throats. Lizzie turned on her heel and stomped angrily back to her desk, her hands shaking as she picked up her pen.

Why were the pupils being so disruptive today? Was it the long, boring winter months that made the children restless, or were they all just trying to drive her as far as she would go? Swallowing her threatening tears, Lizzie tried to calm herself before a feeling of panic completely took control of her senses.

Normally her teaching duties were a happy time, a time of feeling fulfilled, busy, and as if she was doing a service to the children and their parents, an important part of the community. But lately, everyone and every little incident worked on her nerves, making her feel as if she was inadequate, especially with the children misbehaving, getting low grades, and ignoring their schoolwork.

She gazed out at the dark scudding clouds which hung low above the small schoolhouse. The bare branches of the trees along the creek whipped back and forth in the stiff winter wind. Shivering, she got up, grabbed the coal stoker, poked at the red-hot coals inside the black stove, and then adjusted the draft. Stifling a yawn as she called on the fourth-grade English class, she crossed her arms in front of her, keeping her back to the stove.

Hannah raised her hand impetuously, shaking it over and over trying to get Lizzie's attention.

"Hannah?" Lizzie asked, raising her eyebrows.

"I'm not finished."

Elam raised his hand, a defiant look in his black eyes.

"Elam?"

"I'm not done either."

Lizzie sighed. She longed to go home to her room, bury herself in the warmth of her comforters, and sleep. Everything was overwhelming her until there was nothing left but a great weariness. But she had to go on and make an effort to complete this long, dark, and dreary day.

Mentally shaking herself, she took a deep breath.

"Why were you unable to finish?" she asked evenly. In response, two pairs of shoulders lifted and dropped as two pairs of eyes dared her to do something about it. She knew that today was not a good time to undertake an important discipline measure because of how tired and discouraged she was, so she steadied herself and smiled.

"Well, please try harder to complete today's lesson," she said.

The afternoon finally came to a close, and when Lizzie locked the schoolhouse door and turned to climb into the waiting van, she knew this had been one of the longest days she had ever lived, especially since she had begun teaching school.

At home she told Mam she didn't want any supper and went straight to her room. Pulling pins from her cape and apron while kicking off her shoes, she dropped into bed, yanking the heavy down comforter completely over her head, and fell into a deep, blissful sleep. She didn't hear the door opening, or see Mandy stick her head through the doorway, or hear the door close carefully behind her as she went back down the stairs.

When she woke up, the light was fading in the west, leaving her room in gray twilight. Blinking, she sat up, bewildered. She knew instinctively that it wasn't morning, and yet it didn't feel like it was evening, either. She grabbed her alarm clock and saw it was only five-thirty. Then she remembered how tired she had been when she climbed into bed.

Slowly she threw back the covers, put her feet on the floor, and sat, her back rounded and her head hanging in dejection. Immediately worries and fears surrounded her, banging incessantly like a child playing with the lids of its Mam's pots and pans.

What if... what if... what if I'm dating Stephen and I don't even like him one bit? What if I mess everything up my whole life and just continue to go on this way, not knowing if I'm truly in love and if he is the right one for me?

All winter she had harbored these doubts. Christmas had heightened her uncertainty again when they exchanged cards and he had been so sure on his card, professing his true love, and she stumbled and hedged, unable to really commit herself, or at least unsure about what to say. Why was it so complicated? It wasn't that she didn't like Stephen, and she certainly did not like, or long for, any other young man. Something—she didn't know what—was not right.

She had tried opening the subject with Mandy, but her sister had been very little help. Oh, yes, she had said she went through a time of being tempted to date others, but those feelings weren't from God. It was only the devil trying to make you miserable, she said, and you had to deal with it. Mandy was wise, but she could be a bit lofty at times, making Lizzie feel as if she was seven years old.

Raising her head, Lizzie rubbed the small of her back. There was no one to talk to. Mam wouldn't give her any choice at all, because her verdict about doubts was exactly the same as Mandy's. They were all from the devil. Well, how much power did that guy have, she wondered to herself. Surely it was not only he who was swirling her thoughts like some endless electric blender whirring everything together until nothing made any sense. Besides, she couldn't think of the devil too much, knowing how badly he scared her.

Oh, God, she groaned as her head sank into her hands. Guide me. Tell me what to do.

That weekend Lizzie was in such a state of despair that she would not have minded if Stephen hadn't picked her up at all for their date.

Everything he said and did irked her, setting her teeth on edge. No, she really did not believe that this relationship could go on, and the more she dwelled on this, the more evident it became. Why, of course it couldn't. She definitely felt better, almost light-hearted and less dejected, when she thought of ending her relationship with Stephen.

So as they drove in her drive that Sunday evening, she was calm and sure. As he pulled into the forebay, she laid a hand on his arm to stop him from unhitching his horse.

He turned to look at her.

"Stephen," she said quietly, calmly.

"Hmmm?"

"There's no need for you to come in tonight, because … because … well, I would like to end our friendship this evening."

"You what?" Stephen was incredulous, disbelieving.

"I don't think we should continue seeing each other. Really, I'm not happy during the week. I'm depressed and grouchy at school, and I think it's because I'm not happy with you."

There was a long silence before Stephen sighed, his shoulders slumping in defeat. "Well, there's not much for me to say then, is there?" he said quietly.

"No."

"It won't help for me to beg, huh?"

"No."

"You feel sure this is what you want?"

"Yes."

They sat together in silence, their shoulders touching, the lights of the buggy shining on the forebay wall. The horse nodded his head, wanting Stephen to unhook the rein that held his head up.

The chains in the workhorses' stalls rattled as they lifted their heads, and a calf bawled in the distance.

"Well, Lizzie, it's hard for me to let you go, but I know it'll only make it worse if I don't give up. So..." he swallowed hard, "there's nothing I can do. You know my feelings will never change, but if yours ever do, don't hesitate to let me know."

Calmly, Lizzie threw back the buggy blanket, slid back the door, and climbed out. She could barely stand and look at him, and he averted his gaze completely.

"Good-bye," she whispered.

There was no answer, so she turned away and walked slowly across the gravel drive. She had done it. She had ended this troubling thing, and no one, not even Mam, had advised her or told her what to do. She felt independent, a bit proud of herself for having conquered her worst enemy, her doubts about Stephen.

She still felt peaceful and unperturbed as she climbed into bed, thanked God for having led her to this victory, and fell asleep a few minutes after her head touched the pillow.

❧

Her alarm clock jangled without mercy that morning, jarring her senses into wakefulness. She jabbed viciously at the shut-off button and groaned, rolled over, and then stuck her head under the comforter. Her room was freezing cold, as usual, and she just couldn't quite face the chilly air.

Then it hit her. Like the force of a sledgehammer, the thought slammed into her. Stephen was no longer her special friend. She had ended it. Dry, sour-tasting panic rose in her throat, causing her to sit up abruptly, her eyes wide open. What have I done, her mind screamed. How does he feel this morning? Will he even go to work? Does his family know? What will Rebecca say?

She had the distinct feeling that Stephen was whirling around in outer space, and she was one little black dot a million miles below on a round blue earth, and there was absolutely no way possible to ever see him again. Her whole being recoiled at the thought of Stephen disappearing forever. I won't be his girlfriend. Or his wife. Not ever.

A deep, horrible, rasping sound tore from her throat as she flung herself back on her pillow. No. No. This was all wrong. Horribly, terribly, 100 percent all wrong. If she thought she had felt despair before, she had never experienced remorse so real that it cut like the sharpest knife.

She had to do something, go tell someone. Somehow, she had to let Stephen know right this minute, no, this day. Surely she could pull herself together long enough to go to school. Grabbing her bathrobe and a handful of Kleenex, she hurried down the stairs, honking her nose noisily before entering the kitchen.

"Mam!" she burst out, wild-eyed.

Mam whirled from her usual morning place at the stove, her eyes wide with alarm.

"L...Lizzie!"

"Mam, you have to listen to me," Lizzie sobbed. "I told Stephen our friendship is over, and now..."

Mam's shoulders slumped with relief when she heard the words.

"Oh, I thought something really awful had happened. This had been awhile coming, Lizzie."

"And now..." Lizzie continued. "I can't stand it. I feel as if I'll never see him again, and it's just... just horrible!"

Mam turned off the gas burner, laid down the

spoon she was holding, and came to sit in front of Lizzie. Putting a hand on her shoulder, she rubbed it gently to comfort her, letting her sob into her Kleenex.

"There, Lizzie, now that's enough. This almost had to happen, knowing how undecided you were for so long. It's amazing how God answers prayers," she said, shaking her head.

"But Mam, I felt so calm, so peaceful when I ended it."

"Yes, I believe it. God was leading you to do that. He knew you had to know how it felt to no longer have him in order to understand the depth of your real feelings."

Lizzie looked up, her eyes swollen and her nose red as she swabbed at yet another river of tears.

"Now get yourself pulled together, Lizzie. You can make it through today."

"But...Stephen! Mam, he'll go English, or do something awful, and it will be all my fault. I have to let him know this morning that I do... Oh, Mam, I do love him."

She launched into another fit of weeping, while Mam sat quietly, rubbing her back.

"Why do you always choose the rockiest path, Lizzie? You hurt yourself so much more than Emma and Mandy. I guess each child's nature is different."

"Well, Mam, how can I let him know how I feel? I have to right now, right away, this minute."

"No, no, Lizzie. God will provide a way if you'll only calm down now. If nothing else, you can always write him a letter. Hopefully, he did say you could do that. I mean, he's willing to try again."

Lizzie's face lit up with fervent hope. "Oh, yes, Mam!"

"All right, then, get ready now, and off to school. You'll survive."

And Lizzie did survive three whole days before she and Mandy received an invitation for a surprise birthday party for Mary Ann, their friend from church. Lizzie dressed carefully, choosing Stephen's favorite color, but she was no longer in a state of panic about his well-being. She actually felt calm and quiet. Way down in the deepest center of her heart, she sensed a sure and steady bud of love unfolding, and the feeling was the most restful, abiding thing she had ever experienced. The doubts had been driven away, she guessed by God, because no other thing or person could heal and calm in such a wonderful fashion.

But her heart still thumped in agitation when she saw him standing in Mary Ann's kitchen. His usual dark tan seemed a bit lighter, and his eyes were sad as he spent the evening standing at the edge of the room, saying very little. He never said a whole lot, but tonight he barely smiled at all.

After the evening's festivities were over, she knew it was now or never, so she walked over to the group of young men.

"Stephen," she said. He turned.

"Can I talk to you?"

He didn't answer, just followed her quietly until she stopped a good distance away from the group.

"It's cold," she said, turning toward him.

"Yeah, well," was Stephen's answer.

"Stephen, I... I do want to... I mean, I'm sorry I ended our friendship. When I woke up the following morning, I knew without any trace of doubt that what I did was so horribly wrong."

She heard Stephen inhale sharply. "Are you sure, Lizzie?"

"Yes!"

Her heart seemed to stop when she felt Stephen grasp both her hands, keeping her from twisting her apron hem. He held her hands gently, and she slowly quieted under his strength.

"Lizzie, I'm not good with words. You know I don't talk about feelings easily. But... I... just hope...

Slowly Lizzie raised her eyes to his, and the steady, glowing light in his eyes showed the true love he felt in his heart.

Then, there was nothing to say. No words were sufficient. Lizzie felt a soft pressure on her hands, and then in one flowing movement she was enveloped in his strong arms. Her cheek rested on his chest, and an indescribable feeling of warmth, of being wanted and needed, of being understood, all washed over her, much like a gentle spring rain. It was sort of like she imagined Heaven to be. But Mam's words admonishing her to keep their courtship pure kept her feet firmly on the ground.

Stephen really did love her. He really, really did, and that knowledge kept her there in his arms, safe, secure, and slowly realizing that her own love for him was developing, like a rose, slowly opening to the sun's warmth. It seemed so right at this moment, close to his heart, but would she always feel this way?

Stephen said very quietly, "I can only hope you can someday return my love."

As they clung together, Lizzie began to cry as Stephen struggled to blink back his own tears. Releasing her, he stepped back, but only for a moment as they both began talking at once. He told her of the struggles of the past few days, the terrible rebellion that raged in his heart to abandon the Amish way if he had no chance with her. Lizzie could only nod her head in understanding, feeling closer to him than she had ever felt before in her life. She wanted to stay in the circle of his arms forever.

Maybe this was why the Amish people tried to teach their youth about the respectability of a clean and honorable courtship, she mused. If this is what real love feels like, oh, my! she thought happily.

Looking up at Stephen, she loved the way his straight, brown hair fell over his eyebrows and how he brushed it away every 10 minutes. His eyes shone with a new light of joy and hope redeemed, and Lizzie giggled to herself, thinking they probably were only a reflection of her own.

Suddenly her future was spread out before her as clearly as a picture. Stephen and Lizzie. No, Stephen and Elizabeth. She was all grown up now. They would probably join the church and be married in the fall and live happily ever after, just like Cinderella and her prince.

Oh, glorious thought. No more doubts. No more what-ifs. What Lizzie did not quite comprehend was the fact that they were still both human beings who lived in a real world of trials and sorrows, which would balance the joy.

Chapter 20

It seemed as if suddenly every one of Lizzie's friends started dating at once. Uncle Marvin asked Mary Ann to a singing, and they began dating soon afterwards. Just when Lizzie thought it couldn't become more exciting, Stephen's sister Rebecca began dating Reuben.

The couples often drove to the mountain on a Sunday afternoon, or had skating parties by the pond, or just spent time together as winter turned into spring. Lizzie looked forward to the weekends when she and Stephen joined the other couples in different activities throughout the community.

Lizzie soon discovered that living happily ever after, or rather, dating happily ever after, was only a fairy tale, a myth, just like lots of things in life that are far too good to be true.

She didn't feel like ending their relationship again, but this thing of dating was not always 100 percent perfect. Actually, last weekend had barely made the 75 percent mark.

That Monday morning Lizzie was in a vile mood. She didn't want to go to school, but neither did she feel like staying at home under Mam's scrutiny. Mam had a way about her that never failed to irk Lizzie if she was having problems. Mam would start by looking at her a few extra moments, then purse her lips before asking what she had done that weekend. By then, Mam already had a very good idea that she didn't have a great time, not even a very good time, so why did she ask? So Lizzie would mumble something vaguely unintelligible and wish Mam would go away and let her alone.

Lizzie held her shoulders as high and stiff as she could manage and posed her eyebrows in a perfectly worried arc as she dashed between the table and countertop, slamming her lunch box a bit harder than was absolutely necessary. No wonder, she thought angrily. It just made no sense whatsoever. Who had ever heard of walking the Appalachian Trail when you were dating? That was one of the stupidest things she had ever heard of. Imagine, leaving your girlfriend for a month while you went striding along a string of mountains just to see how far you could go. For all the world, it reminded Lizzie of that song about the bear going to the other side of the mountain to see what he could see, and only that. To see what he could see—that was the only reason.

Oh, it wasn't that she hadn't tried to persuade Stephen to give up the whole silly idea. At first she had listened patiently as he tried to explain where they would go—they, meaning Reuben, Marvin, and him. He told her in detail how many miles they would hike each day, and that it would probably be close to a month till they reached their destination.

She gasped audibly when he said that, then launched into a full-blown tirade of protests. What made him think he could do this? Why, if a young man had a girlfriend, it was his moral responsibility, no, his duty, to stay at home and spend his weekends with her. She saw Stephen's jaw set as he turned away from her to watch the scenery out the buggy window. He also let his horse run faster than was absolutely necessary, which only increased her foul mood.

When she realized she wasn't getting anywhere with him by threatening and protesting, she tried to get him to change his mind by being sweet, batting her eyelashes demurely as she told him how terribly she would miss him. Was he really sure he wanted to do this? After all, he had to think about the dangers out on those unfamiliar trails, the mountain lions, black bears, bobcats, and other dangerous creatures.

What really upset her was how he laughed at her for saying that. He laughed long and loud, with kind of a snort at the end that made her feel as if she was in first grade and didn't know anything at all. So she set her mouth in a firm line and refused to talk. If he was going to be determined to do this senseless thing, then he was going to have to suffer for it.

The rest of the way home she sat back against the corner of the seat, her arms folded in front of her, and pouted. Stephen kept asking her questions and she would answer with a small, "Okay," or "Fine," until he gave up talking to her.

Needless to say, their Sunday evening had ended on a sour note, with Stephen taking Lizzie's peevishness in stride, but never coming close to considering how she felt. He just went right ahead talking about his plans to walk the Appalachian Trail. That was the trouble with boys. They did what they wanted to do, and it was up to their girlfriends to be agreeable, and supportive even, no matter what their personal feelings were.

Look at Mam and Dat, she thought bitterly, as she slapped a piece of cheese on top of a slice of bologna. He just went and moved if he felt like it, and it was up to Mam to pack up and go along, even if she didn't want to one bit. Lizzie stifled a yawn and clicked her lunch box shut. Oh, Monday morning and the school year almost at a close, with most of the pupils being very tired of their lessons and, no doubt, their teacher as well.

She sat down hard on a kitchen chair and stared morosely out the window. Mandy had gone to work an hour earlier, so that left only Mam to finish the breakfast dishes and do all the morning chores, sweeping the house, shaking a few rugs, straightening the toy shelf, and other little duties necessary to keeping everything organized.

"Lizzie, why don't you help with the dishes until your driver comes?" Mam said kindly.

"He'll be here any minute," was her curt reply.

Nothing, not one thing, or hardly anything, went right that day. To start with, the fire in the coal stove was out completely. There wasn't even a spark, not a hope of finding a few red coals to rekindle the blaze. The schoolroom was uncomfortably chilly, so chilly in fact that you could see your breath.

Where was Elam King? Why hadn't he come to the schoolhouse as usual and stirred the coals and turned up the draught so that she was greeted with a warm rush of air when she opened the door?

Muttering to herself, she started scraping down the cold ashes, coughing as the dry coal dust irritated her throat. She bet anything there was no kindling in the coal shed, and she was not about to hike to Elam King's farm to find some.

The door opened behind her, and Elam King's breathless children hurried up to Lizzie.

"Dad forgot to fix the fire, Teacher! We have a sick cow," they announced, all in one sentence.

Lizzie told them it was all right, she'd get the fire going, when really, it was not all right. But what else could she say? It wasn't the children's fault, or Elam King's. So she would blame the cow, which was quite easy, knowing how cows tended to become sick or have a calf at the unhandiest moments.

Midmorning little Jonas cried because he wasn't finished with Friday's arithmetic lesson. Lizzie gritted her teeth, resisting the urge to grab a handful of his tangled curls and give them a good, hard yank.

He was never finished. He was just a natural-born little procrastinator who always pushed away his lessons until the very last moment of the day, and then panicked when the rest of the children put their books away to go home.

Lizzie had tried making him stay in at recess, but he was so amicable about it that it was no punishment at all. He would sit in his desk while the other pupils hurried out the door, his sunny expression never wavering as he launched into a vivid account of his weekend.

She had tried standing behind his desk, urging him almost continuously to work, but that was not the answer either. It left her feeling frustrated, and Jonas so nervous that he kept chewing on the corner of his shirt collar and repeatedly blinking his eyes, until Lizzie was afraid he'd ruin his eyesight.

Besides the problems with Jonas and the lack of a good warm fire, she felt the constant irritation of thinking about Stephen nonchalantly telling her that he planned to traipse all over creation for a whole month. She was writing on the blackboard when she heard a snicker, followed promptly by a rubber band hitting the blackboard beside her. Slowly she returned the chalk to the tray, turned calmly, and addressed the crowd of tittering boys.

"All right, who was it? Who snapped the rubber band?"

No one answered and no one lifted a hand. A complete silence fell over the classroom.

"You may as well tell me because I'll find out,"

Lizzie said, her cheeks flaming with anger. Blatant disrespect, that's what it was.

"It was me," one of the seventh-grade boys said, raising his hand, staring at her as if to challenge her to do something about it.

All the frustrations she had endured over the weekend, and especially this morning, hit her with the force of a cannon, leaving behind only blind, white anger. She marched back to his desk, grabbed his shoulder, and smacked his face as hard as she could. His head snapped back, and his expression changed to one of disbelief, then shame, as he lifted both hands to his face as if to ward off more blows.

"There! That is something I will not tolerate. You boys have been trying me to the limit these past couple weeks, and you don't even have enough respect to be ashamed of your misbehavior. I will not take it!" she said loudly, punctuating each word angrily.

The classroom instantly quieted down. In fact, it was so quiet you could almost hear the creek rippling across the rocks in the schoolyard. Little Rachel, who was in first grade, started sobbing quietly into her handkerchief as she rolled her large eyes in Lizzie's direction. The upper-graders all bent their heads, resuming their work with averted eyes.

"So everyone can just straighten up, and I mean it," she finished. She walked back to her desk, sitting in her chair with shaking knees as she absently toyed with her red pen.

An aura of alarm hung over the classroom like an impending storm, and Lizzie swallowed down her own fear, after the realization of what she had just done settled into her conscience. Suddenly, she felt like a huge, green ogre, complete with horns, who had swung her club and terrorized innocent children.

What had she done? What would the boy's parents say? She was almost positive she was in trouble now. Oh, mercy. Well, it was all Stephen's fault, really, if you thought about it. She had lost her temper because of trying to deal with him walking the Appalachian Trail. It was frustrating if your boyfriend just did what he wanted with no regard for your feelings whatsoever. It was all his fault. It was.

The remainder of the day, everyone was quiet and well-behaved. They kept their distance, knowing that this was not a good day to go to their teacher's desk to talk because she was in some vicious mood.

Before she dismissed the pupils at the end of the day, she agonized between apologizing to Alvin or standing firm. He would go home and tell his parents, no doubt about that, but, oh, well, the damage was done now. The only way was to stand firm, she knew, as he had no business snapping that rubber band.

When she got home that evening, she poured out her whole miserable day to Mam and Mandy. They listened attentively, and Mandy gasped when she told her about smacking Alvin across his face.

"Mercy!" Mam said. "Lizzie!"

"Do you think his parents will be upset with me, Mam?" Lizzie asked, fear wrapping its tentacles around her chest and squeezing.

"It's hard telling. I just don't know how they'll react to this. Why did you do it?" Mam asked.

"Because! He made me so mad!"

"You know it probably wasn't for the best," Mam said gently.

Lizzie glared at Mam rebelliously, still determined in her heart that Stephen was to blame for her outburst. So she told Mam about his plans, and to her consternation, Mam burst out laughing.

"It's not funny!" Lizzie shouted, flouncing over to the kitchen counter and lifting the lid on a stainless steel pot. Sniffing, she said, "Mmmm, chicken and dumplings!"

"Ach, Lizzie, now listen here," Mam said.

Lizzie returned the lid and watched Mam warily. If Mam said, "Now listen here," she knew there was a stern lecture coming, whether she liked it or not. Mam's serious lectures were like a dust storm in dry areas or a storm at sea. You just battened down the hatches, gritted your teeth, and hoped it wouldn't get too fierce.

"If you think for one minute that you're going to marry Stephen and never learn to give up to him, you have another guess coming."

Well, the storm was a heavy one if she said "you have another guess coming." That was her age-old tool used to drive a point home with all the force of a sledgehammer, wielded by a strong, muscular man.

"Men are like that. They are allowed to do things, and it's up to us weaker vessels to be submissive. That's why we wear a covering—to show that God comes first, and we obey him, and then our husband comes next, and we obey him as well."

Lizzie snorted and stammered, her face turning red as she tried to express herself.

"You mean … you mean, husbands can do exactly what they please, and we follow as meekly as half-dead sheep and adore the ground they walk on? No, I don't believe that, Mam, not for one minute. If that's the order of things, then I'm not getting married. Never. I'll be an old maid and teach school till I'm so fat I can't fit between the desks!"

Mandy laughed gleefully, and Mam's shoulders shook as she got up to check on the chicken and dumplings, bending to adjust the flame of the burner.

"What does your Bible say, Lizzie? Read it," she said.

"No."

"All right. If you're going to become rebellious, there's no point in discussing it. Nine chances out of 10 you'll have to learn the hard way anyhow," Mam said forcefully, the color in her cheeks heightened.

Lizzie watched Mam, knowing she had irked her. Good. If she wanted to become so high-minded about how a marriage should be, then she was not going to listen anyway. Her husband was not going to sit on his throne and touch her lowered head with his kingly scepter, while she bowed her head in total submission like some trembling servant who was grateful to breathe the same air as her beloved husband. The whole concept inflamed every fiber of her being.

"All right, Mam, I'll discuss it with you and try to listen to what you have to say, but you can't tell me that the husband is to be a lordly person who rules over his lowly wife with absolute authority."

Mam remained quiet, thinking, while Lizzie and Mandy waited. "Ach well, Lizzie, you think too much. I don't really know how to answer that. No, not really, in a sense, and yes, really, in another sense, I guess."

"You guess! You don't even know?"

Lizzie was appalled to think Mam had been married for 20 years, and she still didn't know how it was supposed to be.

"What I mean is—there is no black and white in marriage. Not really. The Bible has plenty of verses to ask us, no, *tell* us, to be submissive, a helpmeet to our husbands. Even in the Old Testament, Sarah called Abraham lord."

"That was in the Old Testament. They stoned people then. We don't do that now, do we?" Lizzie broke in.

"No. No, we don't. But the Old Testament is filled with lessons and good examples for us to follow. All right, now, I want you and Mandy to read your Bible this evening and see what you can find about marriage. Then come show me, okay?" Mam said, smiling.

She got up, asking Mandy to set the table. That officially brought the whole conversation to a close, leaving Lizzie seated high and dry in the middle of a frightening desert of constantly shifting question marks.

Well, if she was lucky, Stephen would be bitten by a rattlesnake the first few miles of the Appalachian Trail. Not fatally, of course, but just enough to make him return back to where he belonged.

She was also going to have to read her Bible tonight to prove to Mam, somehow, that total submission was absolutely not necessary, because that would be a sad way to live. Really, if that was the case, why did any girl in her right mind ever get married?

They just didn't think far enough ahead, that was all there was to it.

Chapter 21

"WIVES, SUBMIT YOURSELVES UNTO YOUR own husbands, as unto the Lord."

There it was in black and white. Lizzie's heart sank, and she swiped a finger nervously across her nose. Her hopes sank even further, like an anchor plunging to the sea floor as the rope unraveled, when she read the next verses.

"For the husband is the head of the wife, even as Christ is the head of the church: and he is the saviour of the body. Therefore, as the church is subject unto Christ, so let the wives be to their own husbands in everything."

Lizzie put her finger on the verse where she had stopped reading and gazed unseeingly out her upstairs bedroom window. There was no getting around it, hardly. Mam was right. The whole idea of marriage and submission settled around her shoulders like a suffocating wool blanket. There was no possible way that Scripture could be true.

In *everything*, it said. Not just some things, or most things. *Everything*. Every single thing. Well, what if the husband did something really dumb, like walk the Appalachian Trail, for instance, or if he turned nasty and hit his wife and yelled at her or beat the children, if there were any. Then what?

She opened her mouth to yell for Mandy, but closed it again, deciding to read further.

"Husbands, love your wives, even as Christ also loved the church, and gave himself for it."

Yes! See? Lizzie pulled up her knees, laying the Bible aside as she wrapped her arms around her legs, happily smiling at herself in the mirror.

There, that was the bottom line. If the husband loved his wife the way he was supposed to, he would give his life for her, or rather, to Lizzie's way of thinking, give up his own will sometimes. Actually, come to think of it, if he loved her very much, he would do anything she asked of him, because he was giving up his own life for his wife.

Lizzie continued reading the chapter and her spirits lifted considerably. When she reached the end of the chapter, her eyebrows were drawn down in confusion again.

"Nevertheless, let every one of you in particular so love his wife even as himself, and the wife see that she reverence her husband."

Well, that reverence word was a bit strong because it conjured up for Lizzie that kingly husband who sat on his throne, his scepter hovering over his trembling wife. But then, if he loved his wife as much as he loved himself, he would be very kind to her. He'd make her life easier if he could, like helping her with the hard work—gardening or mowing grass—and not go off hiking for three weeks. It would make it so much easier to submit to him if he acted half normal.

Ah, well, Lizzie mused. I just don't quite get it. Mam never said the husband was supposed to give his life for his wife. I bet she doesn't even know that's in the Bible. Maybe she just doesn't really want to bother with that verse, knowing her husband didn't always. If you were going to be honest about this, Dat didn't give his life for Mam when they moved to Cameron County. He knew it was not what she wanted to do. But then Mam didn't always reverence Dat either, and maybe that was because he didn't deserve it.

So this marriage thing wasn't quite as hopeless or mysterious or depressing as Mam made it sound with her submission speech. The husband had to stay in his place, too. Lizzie closed her Bible and went downstairs to find Mam working on her cross-stitch quilt patch by the light of the softly hissing gas lamp. She sat in the chair across from her and said, "Mam, you were wrong."

Mam looked up, adjusted her glasses, and smiled at Lizzie.

"About what?" she asked.

"It's not *just* the wife who has to be submissive. Didn't you ever read that part about the husband giving his life for his wife, like Christ died for the church?"

Mam put down her cross-stitch patch and sighed. She gazed absentmindedly at Lizzie as if she wasn't really seeing her at all and sighed again. "Yes, Lizzie, I know it's in there," she said softly.

"Well, then, if he stays in his place, what is there to submit to? Huh? Nothing, Mam."

Lizzie was elated, quite jubilant actually. She was immensely relieved to know that her husband couldn't just go off and do exactly as he pleased whenever he felt like it. He had a responsibility to give his life to his beloved wife, who would obey him with sweet reverence like the Bible said.

"I'm afraid it's not that easy," Mam said.

"What do you mean?"

"Well, for one thing, we're very human, and on the day we marry each other, we still have our own wills intact. Each of us has a pretty good idea of what we expect of our husband, and he has a pretty good idea of what he expects of his wife. Unfortunately, his wife is not always as he wants her to be, and vice versa. He is not all that she expects either. So we have troubles, trials, rainy days, whatever you want to call it, and it isn't all roses. That's why we have those verses in the Bible, something we can live towards, something we can hope to become, that perfect merging of two souls, two wills, two individuals who become one through marriage."

Lizzie frowned. "You sound exactly like a preacher. An English one."

Mam laughed. "Maybe I do, Lizzie, but I don't want you filling your head with sweet visions of a perfect husband who gives his life for you. Because ... " Mam leaned forward, a touch of, what was it—hardness? Bitterness? Honesty born of experience? "Very few men do give their lives for their wives," she finished.

Lizzie said nothing, and the pendulum on the living room wall clock rocked steadily back and forth, back and forth, as the gas light kept up its soft, hissing sound.

"I think I'll go to bed," she said finally.

"Good night," Mam said, a touch of wistfulness in her voice.

"Good night, Mam," Lizzie said.

≈≶

Lizzie lay awake, an open book beside her, the kerosene lamp on her nightstand flickering in the night air. Her thoughts were rapidly spoiling her peace of mind, like Jason shooting his dart gun into her brain. Those annoying little plastic, yellow darts with orange, rubber suction cups at the end, that if they landed squarely, hung there, quivering, until you pulled them loose.

So then, the truth of the matter was, men often did what they wanted, probably because they knew their wives were supposed to submit themselves and revere them. Boy, that just wasn't right. The thought made her so angry she felt like throwing her pillow against the wall. She rolled onto her side. She didn't know why that thought brought out so much rebellion and so many hateful thoughts.

She wondered vaguely where love came in. Love was supposed to be the reason for getting married in the first place. Wasn't that simply liking someone so much that you would do absolutely anything for them?

So now if Stephen were her husband, and he would tell her that he was walking the Appalachian Trail for three weeks, then, if she loved him whole-heartedly, she would say, "Oh, of course, my darling husband! You deserve to enjoy yourself on a vacation away from me, and I hope you have a lovely time."

And he would be so grateful for her sweet nature, her love and support, that he would go hiking for three weeks, have a great time, and tell all his friends what a wonderful, kind, loving wife he had at home. Somewhere along the line she had to get rid of her anger against men being the stronger vessel, the head of the house, the boss, in plain words, the king, which only brought on a fresh case of rebel-lion within her.

Oh, the whole mess was hopeless. Throwing off the covers, she stalked over to Mandy's bedroom door, yanked it open, and stuck her head inside.

"Are you still awake?"

"Mm-hmm, what do you want?"

Lizzie walked in and sat down on Mandy's bed, as she scooted over to make room.

"Oh, I can't sleep. I'm thinking too much. Did you read your Bible about marriage like Mam told us to?"

"Yes."

"Well, what did you think?"

"That's just how it is, Lizzie. It's really quite simple. We both live for each other and not for ourselves, and it'll go okay."

"It's not *that* simple!" Lizzie exclaimed, appalled at the thought of entering marriage with that tiny amount of concern. "What if your husband would want to go on vacation for three weeks, and you thought it was a dumb idea? Huh? Then what?"

Anger crossed Mandy's features, and she said impatiently, "Well, if you're in one of those moods, just go to bed. Go on. You're just mad because Stephen is going hiking, and you are acting like one huge, overgrown baby, pitying yourself, determined to justify your own selfishness with those Bible verses. Now go to bed. I'm tired."

Mandy rolled over and pulled up the covers, or tried to, but she couldn't with Lizzie sitting on them. She lifted her head and glared at her. "*Go!*" she shouted.

So Lizzie went.

Back in bed she tossed and turned, thinking and rethinking what Mandy had said. She was clearly on Stephen's side, so what was the use of talking to her? Selfish. So Mandy thought she was being selfish. Well, Mandy had better watch it. She just better watch who she called selfish. Lizzie could feel the heat rising in her cheeks as she thought about what Mandy had said about her justifying herself, and her rebellion. She was quite sure she meant that anyway.

Oh, that Mandy. She may as well be a little bearded man living high in the Himalayan mountains, a small wrinkled philosopher around whom people gathered for words of wisdom. She knew Mandy could see right through her, and she was as exposed as if she were made of air with little banners blowing that said she was selfish, childish, and rebellious.

She flipped onto her left side, reached out, and peered at the face of her alarm clock. Eleven-twenty-five. She groaned. It would soon be time to get up and she still hadn't slept a wink. She'd have to resort to counting sheep, she supposed. It was an awful thing when you thought too much, planned too much, and worried far too much about the future.

Oh, that's right, she thought. I forgot to pray. I wrestle around with all my problems and forget to hand them to God. She wished it would be as easy as two hands reaching down through the ceiling to retrieve Lizzie's bundle labeled "Troubles." The minute the bundle was in God's hands, it would be lifted up through the ceiling and gone out of sight, out of her mind, never to be seen again.

Life, however, was not that easy. Real life, real problems. Dear God, you're going to have to help me with this husband and wife thing. I will give up now and not be selfish. Help me, Lord, to be truly unselfish. Keep Stephen safe on the Appalachian Trail, and keep me safe from rebellion. Amen.

She breathed deeply, relaxing, and even giggled to herself as she dared to hope—although she stopped short of asking God to let it happen—she just hoped a mountain lion would scare them so hysterically they'd come back home two weeks earlier than they had planned. Or a bobcat. The way they screamed, it would probably work even better.

When Stephen brought her home after the hymn-singing on Sunday evening, Lizzie was a bit better prepared to hear him say that their plans were finished now, and they would be leaving Tuesday morning. She managed a small smile as he talked, listening attentively to his plans without once resorting to rebellious feelings.

"I want to be sure and thank you, Lizzie," he finished, watching her face attentively.

"For what?" she asked, in a genuinely small, quiet voice.

"For being nice about me being gone so long. I know you don't want me to go, but you're being an awfully good sport about it, and I do appreciate it."

"You wouldn't stay home for me, would you? I mean, give up the whole adventure if I didn't want you to go?"

Stephen was quiet for a very long time, before he said with a soft laugh, "Probably not."

So there. She had a notion to give him the whole lecture and bring the Bible to show him that he was supposed to lay down his own life for her. She knew that wouldn't be a good idea, mostly because they were not married yet. He had never asked her to be his wife, so really being so pointed would be a very wrong thing to do.

Lizzie wanted to assure him that it was all right for him to go, to let him know that she wanted him to have a good time. She really did, but she also wanted him to worry a bit that she wasn't happy because he was going and leaving her. So she didn't answer.

And in that silence, her own battle of right and wrong raged in her spirit. She knew the right thing to do, but she couldn't let go of her own desires to make him feel bad, at least a little. She wanted to punish him somehow for going against her will, so she remained silent while right fought wrong with a clashing of swords.

Finally, Stephen cleared his throat, watching her carefully as she sat in her self-induced little war of wills.

"Maybe I better go. It's getting late. Good-bye, Lizzie. I'll send you postcards, if I can."

Lizzie got up to go along to the barn as she always did, feeling perfectly miserable. "Wives, submit yourselves unto your own husbands," was constantly in her thoughts, but she reasoned that little bother away by telling herself she wasn't his wife. She didn't have to submit yet.

When Stephen was ready to step into the buggy, all of Lizzie's battles and miseries came crashing down around her, and she reached out to touch his arm.

"I... I'm sorry, Stephen. I *do* hope you enjoy your vacation, and I'll be patiently waiting till you come home. I'll miss you so much, but you know that, don't you?"

She was rewarded by the most loving look she had ever received from him as he told her again how he appreciated her attitude and how much he would miss her.

After he left, and the battle of her own will won, she felt as light as a feather floating on a soft white cloud. So that was the answer, she thought happily as she fairly danced up the stairs to her bedroom. If you could give up a teeny-tiny bit, God would supply all the feelings of love you needed. He filled your cup way full until it ran over the sides and made a big puddle beside it.

Chapter 22

THE GIRLS SAT SIDE BY SIDE ON THE PORCH swing, pushing their feet lightly against the concrete floor to keep it in rocking motion. It was one of those quiet twilight times, not yet dark, although the sun had slid behind the mountain for awhile already. The birds were twittering and fussing, scooping up the last mosquitoes for their babies' bedtime snacks. The barn door slammed, sending a few noisy robins into startled flight as Jason came walking across the drive and up the sidewalk to the porch.

He would turn 16 years old soon and was looking every inch the young man that he was. His shoulders and arms were heavier, the muscles showing beneath his shirtsleeves, and he had grown at least three more inches that summer, or so it seemed. Lizzie and Mandy adored him, their handsome young brother with the kind blue eyes that twinkled back at them as they teased each other or had long, serious conversations. His eyes always twinkled. He was naturally kind, Mam said.

But then, that Mam, Lizzie thought. She just loved Jason because he did anything she asked of him. If she needed manure for her flower beds, or a bit of mulch brought, or even if she came home with a load of groceries, Jason ran to help. Sometimes Lizzie felt a bit jealous about how much Mam loved Jason, but not very often, knowing he deserved her devotion, as kind as he was to her.

"Hey," he said quietly as he threw himself down on the porch steps, sighing as he ran his hands through his shock of curly brown hair.

"Hey, yourself," Lizzie answered.

"You're awfully dirty," Mandy observed.

"You would be, too. It was a long day and I'm about beat."

"You work too hard, Jase," Lizzie said.

"Shh!" Jason put his finger to his lips and rolled his eyes in Dat's direction as he came across the yard. He didn't really hobble or limp; he just had a dragging gait, almost as if he couldn't lift his feet properly.

Dat stopped at the porch, grabbing the railing before looking at Jason. "Tired?" he asked.

"A little."

"You work too hard, Jason."

Dat shook his head, a frustrated look in his eyes, his hands gripping the railing firmly. He knew he wasn't able to do some of the fieldwork anymore, and that ever so gradually more and more of the heavy jobs, as well as the responsibility of the farm, fell on Jason's young shoulders.

Mam came out to join them. The twins were in bed already. Mam was wearing her blue summer house-coat that still smelled like talcum powder, the same as it always had. It didn't matter which scent of pow-der she used, they all smelled like Mam. Even when Lizzie was a little, worried girl, Mam's housecoat had smelled the same, a soft, flowery Mam aroma that wrapped around you, comforting and instilling a sense of peace, of belonging, of love as warm and sure as the sun that rose and set each day.

"Do we have any ice cream in the freezer?" Jason asked, lifting his eyes to look at Mam.

"Oh, yes! Your favorite. I just got two half-gal-lons in town today," Mam said, as she hurried into the kitchen to fill a dish with his favorite treat.

"Anyone else?" she called out the kitchen win-dow.

Everyone had a dish of ice cream as they had a serious conversation about farming. Dat broached the subject, saying matter-of-factly that he couldn't see any sense in continuing, seeing how hard Jason had to work just to keep everything afloat. He admit-ted that the cows weren't doing as well as most of the other farmers' cows in the area, and that it was a constant struggle to keep the bills paid with enough left over to live on decently.

Mam had known for a long time what Dat was now admitting. She had often fussed to the girls, her face red as she toyed nervously with the straight pins in her dress, saying how she wished Dat would give up farming.

"He's just not cut out to be a farmer," she would say wearily, before giving in time after time, hoping that Dat would see it for himself.

Now it seemed as if Dat had finally arrived at this conclusion. Mam could not hide the excitement in her eyes as she listened to what Dat was saying, and Lizzie could tell she felt like shouting her delight at his words.

"So some changes are going to have to come," Dat said.

"Like what?" Jason asked, his spoonful of ice cream stopping halfway as he turned to face Dat.

"Well, we're going to have to make a living some-how. I have MS, which isn't that big of an issue, really, because I can still do a good day's work. But..." Dat said, his voice softening, "it won't always be this way."

Lifting his head, he looked out across the fields to the creek. "I always liked to build things, carpenter work. What do you think, Jason? Could we run a carpenter crew?"

Jason shrugged his shoulders. "You could, maybe. I don't know much about building anything, although I suppose I could learn."

"Sure you can learn. Building is just a matter of common sense and hard work. In a few months you'll probably be working circles around me," Dat smiled.

Praise from Dat was scarce, so when he did

congratulate someone on a job well done, or whatever, it meant the world to them. Jason ducked his head, flustered, not quite knowing how to handle this compliment, but Lizzie could see a small smile of embarrassment on his face. Dat had given him a real compliment, like one man to another, telling him he was a hard worker.

So the day came a few weeks later, when a tractor and trailer rolled down the country road, and were barely able to make the turn at the end of the drive. The driver had to back up and keep trying at a few different angles, barely inching his way past the wooden corner post of the fence lining the driveway. One wheel went down so far into the ditch Lizzie felt sure the whole truck would twist sideways until it snapped in two.

Dat got quite fussed up, almost running out the drive, waving his arms, trying to be helpful, which, probably wasn't of much assistance to the driver, who was used to handling his truck quite well by himself. But that's how Dat was. When he hitched up a horse, he said, "Whoa, Whoa," almost continuously. Even if the horse stood rock still, he kept saying "Whoa."

Dat was small and became agitated easily, putting in lots of effort to accomplish a task. He was also very meticulous about things, making sure everything was done to his specifications, so that was probably the reason he became so excited, knowing how he would dislike having the corner of his fence run over by a tractor and trailer.

After the truck was properly parked, the driver lowered the large steel gates, and Dat and Jason started loading cows. Lizzie felt no emotion at all as each homely-looking cow lumbered precariously up the ramp with a minimum of prodding by the shocking stick.

One good thing about cows being so dumb, Lizzie thought, was the small amount of effort it took to load them onto a truck. The only thing a cow thought about too much was chewing its cud, so they probably wanted to hurry onto the truck so they could get on with their cud-chewing.

The rest of the afternoon, different trucks and drivers rolled down the lane until every single cow, heifer, and calf had been sold. The whitewashed cow stable seemed strangely silent and eerie, with only a few ambitious barn swallows left to make it their home. The drop seemed deep and dry with no fresh cow manure or water in it, the milk house vacant and lonely.

Silence hung over the whole barn until it gave Lizzie the shivers, reminding her of a tomb. Maybe they shouldn't have sold the cows, she reasoned. What if there was no blessing in Dat's carpenter crew because he had sold the cows? What if Dat only thought he could build things like pole barns and houses, and he really couldn't? The empty cow stable gave her the creeps so she hurried out into the bright sunshine, back to the normalcy of the farm.

Dat had reminded the girls that the farm equipment and horses would also have to be sold eventually, which made Lizzie feel sad, loving the sound of those magnificent horses dragging their chains across the worn wooden boards of their feed box. There was just something about watching a workhorse eating mouthfuls of oats, with some of the grain spilling out the sides of their mouths, that was delightful to watch. The way they used their huge mouths to nibble up every little bit of grain was so amusing. They ate corn that was still on the cob so cleanly, it was almost as if they were humans eating corn off the cob. Lizzie often wondered why the horses didn't chomp down the entire cob, but Dat said they tasted bitter to the horses.

But there was hardly any use in keeping the work-horses if they had no work in the fields. If there were no cows to feed, there was no sense in making the horses plod their way around and around a field, their heads nodding, harnesses creaking, as they pulled on the thick leather tugs attached to their enormous collars, heaving with their powerful neck and shoulder muscles.

Lizzie never tired of watching a team of horses working in a field. Sometimes there were only two hitched together to pull a wagonload of hay or a cultivator. Sometimes, for heavier equipment, there were four in the harness, side by side, pull-ing together. In the spring, Dat hitched six horses to the large plow so that each horse could pull his fair share of the plow without tiring too much.

Well, she reasoned, they still had Bess, the driv-ing horse, Rocky, the better driving horse, Billy, the beloved oatmeal-colored Shetland pony, and Jason's riding horse. Dat loved riding horses, so as soon as Jason was old enough, he bought a fine Morgan stallion for him. Mam wasn't too happy about that horse, but she didn't say much, just pressed her mouth into a firm line and shook her head ever so slightly.

Jason's riding horse was named Charmer, and he certainly was that. His coat glistened in the sun, a deep reddish brown, with a rippling black mane and tail. He had three white "stockings," or white hair above his black hooves, which only made him look fancier. Dat said he was almost too nice-looking for Amish people to own him, but he said it in a twinkling, humorous way, so that Lizzie knew he was very proud of Jason's horse.

Jason was an extremely good rider, sitting back, relaxed in his saddle, moving with his horse as if they were one. Lizzie and Mandy were thrilled to watch Jason and Charmer, exclaiming to each other that surely no other girls in Cameron County were lucky enough to have a kind, handsome brother like theirs, especially now, with his riding skills developing every week.

Shortly after selling all of the cattle, Dat hired a driver with a heavy pickup truck and bought ladders, scaffolding, saws, and all kinds of tools and equipment to begin building things for customers. He placed an ad in the local paper, made phone calls, and had business cards made. It wasn't long before he had a few months' work waiting for his crew.

Dat was the kind of person who thrived on changes, any kind of new and different changes that occurred in his life. So this carpentry business was just as challenging and exciting for him as farming had been when the family first moved to Cameron County. He didn't seem to be sentimental about the cows once they were gone, never saying too much about missing them and instead taking this new endeavor in stride.

Lizzie teased him about the cows, saying he didn't like them as well as he wanted the rest of the family to think he did.

"I miss milking cows, Lizzie," he said.

"I bet you don't."

"I do!"

"Not too much!"

Then Dat had to laugh, and, as he always did, he blinked his eyes in that certain way, which meant, Behave yourself. But what he said was, "Now, Lizzie!"

So she felt better about the empty cow stable, glad that Dat and Jason enjoyed their work building things. Dat loved going away every day, traveling away from home and seeing the sights along the way, talking to different people, just getting out and about. He often brought home a watermelon or cantaloupes from a farm stand along the way, or candy for KatieAnn and Susan. The supper table was always filled with lively conversation about the progress of a building, an eccentric customer, or a wreck on the highway.

These were happy days on the farm. Dat built a small room off the dining room that was mostly windows, with a skylight in the ceiling, which made it a greenhouse of sorts. Mam was overjoyed with her new room. She spent many happy hours in it, growing all her own plants for her ever-expanding flower beds around the yard.

Her favorite were her "cheraniums," as she called geraniums. Because of Mam's origins in Ohio, she always pronounced her "g's" and "j's" with the "ch" sound. Jacob was "Chakob," and jelly was "chelly," and so on. She never changed the sound or pronunciation of her words, tossing her head impatiently when the girls teased her about it, and she never fully accepted the eastern Pennsylvania Dutch. She always rolled her "r's," and said, "Fact!" to exclaim about something and "Ei, nay" when she wanted to be emphatic, driving a point home.

Mam was a bit different from proper eastern Lamton Amish, but that was who she was, and she never changed. She still clung to some of the old traditions from Ohio, in spite of the ever-changing world around her. Joshua genuinely liked Mam, as did Stephen and John, although they remained shy, staying away from Mam and Dat, as is the Amish tradition when youth are dating. But the times they were there for Sunday supper, Lizzie would often catch Stephen chuckling to himself as Mam fussed away in her Ohio accent.

Lizzie was glad that Mam and Dat were resilient and brave. They took life and made the best out of what God handed them. Mam had a deep-rooted faith and believed that whatever happened in their lives held a special purpose, a deeper meaning, a lesson from God that they didn't always comprehend.

So when the cows were sold and Dat quit farming, Mam felt it was a reward for being submissive to something she had fiercely resisted. She was blessed now with a happy husband who worked well with his son and with a farm she had grown to like. Not love. Mam never loved the old farm, but she accepted it resignedly, appreciating every new thing Dat built for her.

After the cows left, life on the farm changed drastically for Mam. She had no men to cook for, no milk house to keep clean, and her days turned quiet and peaceful as she went about her work while Lizzie and Mandy were off at their jobs.

And, of course, not getting up in the morning to help milk was one of the best things that had ever happened to Lizzie in her entire life. Never again would she have to stumble out to a smelly cow stable, in frigid temperatures, as well as on sweltering summer evenings when she detested every cow permanently.

Mam said it was a blessing to be given a life without cows, which was probably true, but anything in life is like that, Lizzie thought. If some source of irritation is no longer around, of course it's a blessing, but to Lizzie it was more than that. If was a gift. An undeserved gift.

Chapter 23

ONE WARM SPRING DAY, SHORTLY BEFORE Stephen left to hike the Appalachian Trail, he drove in the lane to pick up Lizzie for their weekly date. He had slid both buggy doors back and fastened both windows to the ceiling, held there with leather straps. Bob was already wet with sweat from traveling the three miles to Lizzie's house. The buggy shone a brilliant black, the gray canvas washed spotlessly clean. The blue interior made Stephen's eyes bluer than ever, and Lizzie's heart skipped a few beats when he smiled at her.

"Hello, Stephen," she said, smiling back at him.

"How are you, Lizzie?"

"Too warm," she said emphatically, plopping down beside him on the seat, lifting her apron to cool herself. She still wasn't happy that he was leaving her for a month to go hiking, but she was excited about their date today and decided not to let his upcoming trip spoil her mood.

"It's not too warm. I love this weather."

"Do you really?"

"Sure. Makes you feel good to sweat. I tie a red handkerchief around my head at work. Soaks up the perspiration."

Lizzie imagined this and laughed.

"So, what are we doing this afternoon?" Lizzie asked.

"I thought we'd ask Reuben and Rebecca to go to the dam for a boat ride. It would feel nice and cool on the water."

"It would be cooler IN the water," Lizzie laughed.

"I could push you off the boat if you want."

Lizzie punched his arm while Stephen clucked to his horse, and they started slowly out the drive. That was the nicest part about having a boyfriend, Lizzie thought. This slow, easy pace and never having to hurry became the best part of Sunday afternoons. She looked forward to this time each week—riding around in the breezy buggy, just the two of them, enjoying each other's company, talking easily, laughing, getting to know each other better.

"Whose boat?" Lizzie asked.

"We're building an addition for Mr. Wright who lives on the other side of the dam. He has a big aluminum boat he takes out on the water quite often, and he said I'm welcome to use it anytime I want."

"Really? Are we going to use it today?"

"Mm-hmm."

"Wow!"

Lizzie loved the whole idea. Water didn't scare
Lizzie. She was a good swimmer, having learned in
the river in Jefferson County, so the boat ride didn't
worry her at all. Actually, on a day like this, it would
feel wonderful to fall into the lake. Of course, boys
and girls weren't allowed to go swimming together,
and falling into the lake would be considered exactly
that, even with her dress on. And her cape and apron
and covering.

"Reuben and Rebecca will meet us at Maybury,"
Stephen said.

"Do they have their own team? What will we do
with the horses? Isn't too hot to make them pull us up
the mountain? What about the flies that are so pesky
to horses in hot weather? Do you have fly spray?"

"Whoa!" Stephen laughed.

"What?"

"Yes, Reuben and Rebecca have their own team.
The horses can be put in Mr. Wright's barn. And,
yes, it is too hot to go the whole way up the mountain, but we'll only go a short way till we turn down
the road that goes to the dam." He paused.

"Oh, and, no, I don't have fly spray, but this guy
has a barn so they'll be fine."

Lizzie relaxed then, enjoying the ride to the little
town of Maybury, a small grouping of houses, two
churches, a post office, a tractor business, a general
store, and gas station, all tucked cozily near the bottom of the mountain.

Reuben's team was already parked by the general
store, and the purple skirt of Rebecca's dress hung

out the buggy door. Stephen stomped on the brakes, and they lurched to a stop beside them.

Reuben and Rebecca leaned forward in unison, equally big smiles on their faces.

"Hi!"

"Hello youself!"

"It's too hot for the horses!"

"We're not going up the mountain very far."

"Ready?"

"Do you have any food?"

"I packed a whole pile."

"Let's go!"

They wasted no time pulling out of the parking lot, and the horses trotted steadily through the town of Maybury and out toward the dam. The dam sat on a huge reservoir with the concrete embankment holding the water in a large valley between a high ridge and the mountain. It was a beautiful clear lake, continually fed by springs and creeks from the mountain to the north.

The horses sensed the adventure, their ears pricked forward, their necks arched, as they trotted close to the mountain. On the left, they passed a happy little creek that gurgled and tumbled along over smooth, slippery sandstone, quieting to a soft sigh in deep, dark pools beneath overhanging hemlock branches. Cattails swayed in the hot breeze, and bumblebees and butterflies hovered along the banks. Wild strawberries grew in profusion, the sun gently coaxing them up and out of the wet fertile soil.

Stephen made a sort of groaning sound, which

startled Lizzie.

"What?" she asked.

"Those deep pools are probably loaded with big heavy trout. Wish it wasn't Sunday and I had my fishing pole."

"That's all you think about," Lizzie said, in what she hoped was a pretty, pouting little voice.

"Oh, no, it's not."

"What else do you think about?"

She hoped with all her heart he would say something like "sitting by that deep pool with you" or that "you are as pretty as the wildflowers" or that "you are much more important than the fish." Which she definitely was, she thought.

Stephen adjusted the reins, thought a bit, then said dryly, "Where I would get good bait."

He roared and laughed when Lizzie made an exasperated sound, then slid his arm across the back of the seat and pulled her close.

"No, Lizzie, I think of you much more often than I think of fishing. Especially on Sundays, because I can't fish then."

Lizzie sat up straight and grabbed a handful of his long, sun-streaked, brown hair and pulled with all her might. Stephen easily pulled her hands away, yelling how much it hurt, but they were both laughing until the buggy wheel dipped down into a culvert. Stephen tugged at the reins to straighten out the buggy.

"Hey!" Reuben called from behind them. "You better watch where you're driving!"

And then the road wound steadily uphill and the horses slowed to a walk. They kept a steady pace, their heads moving up and down, up and down, the harnesses creaking against the shafts as the horses drew the buggies steadily up the mountain.

They came to a dirt road that turned down the side of a ridge, and before long, Lizzie could see the sparkling blue waters of the lake shimmering between the trees. Water was like that. It wasn't really blue, it just reflected the blue of the sky. It wasn't gray or black either. Sort of silver, but really no color. And yet it was so beautiful.

They arrived at a small brown house set in a little wooded cove by the lake. It was the cutest thing Lizzie had ever seen. Sort of ramshackle, not really kept up very well, but still very homey and cozy and friendly. Even the two large cats straddling the arm of the wooden porch rockers were smiling.

Blue morning glories wound their way up the side of the porch, and a bed of yellow snapdragons were nestled between large, pink hollyhocks. Dandelions and orchard grass grew among them, but it was all very colorful and gave the whole place an air of serenity and relaxation.

The door opened gently and a bent, grizzled old gentleman came to the porch.

"Hello there! Get down. Get down! Come on in."

Mr. Wright helped them put the horses in his little barn filled with banty roosters and pigeons. Then he showed them his boat which was rather large, much to Lizzie's relief. Not that she was afraid of the water. It just seemed safer, especially if they were going to have their lunch in the middle of the lake.

Reuben and Stephen carried the boat down the bank to the lake, and they all climbed aboard a bit gingerly. Rebecca held one side of the cooler containing the food and Lizzie the other.

There were three seats in the boat, but the four of them could easily fit two to a seat, each couple facing the other. After a few tries, they got the oars in the oarlocks, and with a swift, smooth push of the oars, Stephen steered the boat toward the middle of that deep, cool water.

Rebecca told Stephen he had better not go too close to the lip of the dam. Just suppose if they went down over that great steep expanse of concrete, they'd all be killed.

Stephen pooh-poohed that idea, but Lizzie felt the same apprehension, although she bit down hard on her lower lip to keep from nagging him along with Rebecca.

Reuben trailed his hand in the cool water, flicking it at the girls, which was just fine with Lizzie. It was so hot Lizzie guaranteed you could fry an egg on the seat of the boat. Her cape felt like it was made of wool, her dress was itchy and she could have screamed, she was so uncomfortable.

Why in the world would they sit in the middle of the lake with no breeze on this startlingly hot spring day? She was hungry, the sun was hot, and she was thirsty. She wished she was a fish. Stephen would care more about her then.

"Hey, it's too hot!" Rebecca yelled in a very unlady-like voice. Lizzie burst out laughing.

The boys agreed and rowed to the north side of the lake where the merciful shade welcomed them with open arms, the boughs of the huge oak and maple trees forming a sort of canopy for their picnic.

Rebecca poured ice-cold meadow tea into plastic cups, which Lizzie drank gratefully. As soon as her cup was empty, she asked for more. In all the world, there is nothing more refreshing than meadow tea on a hot day, Lizzie thought.

They ate thick roast beef sandwiches with slabs of Swiss cheese and lettuce from Rebecca's garden. Rebecca had thought to pack small Tupperware containers of mayonnaise and mustard which made the sandwiches taste so good.

Lizzie had packed a bag with potato chips, home-made dill pickles, peanut butter chocolate chip cookies, and large red apples, polished until they looked like a picture in a storybook.

The whole picnic lunch was so delicious, the cookies melting in Lizzie's mouth and then washed down with that wonderful ice-cold meadow tea.

Stephen's eyes held hers as they ate, and she felt such a closeness to him. For the very first time in her life, she thought she might know what it felt like to be in love. Not just kind of, or sort of, but for real.

When everyone was finished eating, they packed the remains of the lunch carefully into the cooler, and Stephen announced that they would row around the lake again to see if they could find any fish. Oh, great, Lizzie thought resignedly, remembering the sun's rays beating down on her six layer of fabric. Oh, great.

"You guys better row as fast as you can," Rebecca said loudly. "It's hotter than ever out on the lake."

"We will," Reuben assured her.

And they did. They cruised around the lake, the boat creating an actual wake like a speedboat, only a lot smaller and gentler. A nice, wet breeze cooled the girls. Stephen yelled at regular intervals whenever he spied the flash of a trout or the yellow speckles of a sunfish, bemoaning the fact that he had no fishing rod.

Rebecca and Lizzie sat back and let their hands trail in the deep, cool water as they chatted and watched the boys handle the oars, propelling them along. It was a wonderful day. It was so good, in fact, that it made Lizzie's heart hurt with the fullness of it. Rebecca was her best friend, Stephen might just be the love of her life, and Reuben was such a dear, very good match for Rebecca.

For the very first time in her life, she wondered when or if Stephen would ask her to marry him someday. They could live in the little brown house by the lake, if Mr. Wright would just sell it to them. She would weed the flower beds and paint the porch rockers. She laughed. But then, living here by the lake would have one big disadvantage. She would have to compete with the fish for Stephen's love and attention.

The Recipes

Lizzie's Favorite Recipes

Sand Tarts

Makes 12 dozen cookies

DOUGH:
2 cups granulated sugar
2 sticks (½ lb.) butter, softened
1 tsp. baking soda
3 eggs, beaten
2 tsp. milk
3½ cups flour

DECORATIVE GLAZE:
1 egg beaten
½ cup milk
colored sugar

1. Mix all dough ingredients together in a large bowl until smooth.

2. Chill dough overnight.

3. Roll thin on floured surface.

4. Cut into shapes with cookie cutters.

5. Mix egg and milk together to make Glaze. Brush tops of cookies with glaze mixture.

6. Sprinkle with colored sugar.

7. Bake at 375° for 8 to 10 minutes.

Banana Pudding

Makes 15-20 servings

3 3½-oz. pkgs. instant vanilla pudding
5 cups milk
8 oz. sour cream
1 large container frozen whipped topping,
    thawed
2 8-oz. boxes vanilla wafers
12 to 15 ripe bananas, sliced

1. Make pudding according to box instructions

2. Assemble in large serving dish in layers, starting with vanilla wafers, sliced bananas, and pudding. Continue to alternate layers, making as many layers as you wish.

3. Cover. Refrigerate until ready to serve.

Christmas Salad

Makes 15-20 servings

⅔ cup dry lime gelatin
3½ cups cold water
20-oz. can crushed pineapple, drained, with
    juice reserved
2 Tbsp. dry clear gelatin
⅔ cup cold water
8-oz. pkg. cream cheese, softened
1 cup heavy cream, whipped until stiff and
    sweetened to taste
3½ cups cold water
⅔ cup dry strawberry gelatin

1. Mix lime gelatin, 3½ cups water, and crushed pineapple, drained (juice reserved), in bowl.

2. Pour into 9 x 13 baking pan.

3. Chill until firm.

4. Heat pineapple juice to boiling point.

5. Dissolve clear gelatin in ⅔ cup cold water. Stir in pineapple juice. Cool.

6. Stir softened cream cheese into clear gelatin until smooth.

7. Fold in whipped cream.

8. Spoon on top of lime-pineapple layer.

9. Mix strawberry gelatin and 3½ cups cold water together. Chill until firm.

10. Spoon over top of creamy layer.

11. Refrigerate until completely firm.

12. Cut into squares and serve.

Christmas Nut Cake

Makes 12-15 servings

CAKE:

2 cups granulated sugar
1½ sticks (12 Tbsp.) butter, softened
4 eggs, separated
1 cup milk
3 cups flour
4 tsp. baking powder
¾ cup walnuts, chopped
vegetable oil

CARAMEL FROSTING:

1½ cups brown sugar, packed
1½ sticks (12 Tbsp.) butter
⅓ cup milk
1 tsp. vanilla
confectioners sugar
¼ cup walnuts, crushed

1. To make Cake, thoroughly cream sugar and butter.

2. Separate egg yolks and whites.

3. Add 4 egg yolks to sugar and butter and beat well.

4. Add milk, flour, and baking powder. Beat well.

5. Beat egg whites in a bowl.

6. Fold egg whites into batter.

7. Mix in chopped nuts.

8. Divide batter by pouring into 3 round cake pans that are oiled and dusted with flour.

9. Bake at 350° until toothpick inserted in center of each pan comes out clean, about 30 to 35 minutes.

10. Meanwhile, prepare Frosting by cooking brown sugar and butter over medium heat.

11. Boil for one minute.

12. Add milk.

13. Continue cooking until it boils again, then remove from heat.

14. Let cool completely.

15. Add vanilla.

16. Add confectioners sugar to thicken frosting to desired consistency, about 3-4 cups.

17. Frost cooled Cake.

18. Dust with crushed walnuts.

Chicken Filling, or Lancaster County "Roasht"

Makes 15 servings

1 stick (¼ lb.) butter
2 cups celery, chopped
2 loaves bread, cut in cubes
3 cups chicken, cooked and shredded
1 tsp. salt
1 tsp. pepper, or less, to taste
6 eggs, beaten

1. Melt butter in large skillet.

2. Sauté celery in melted butter.

3. Combine all ingredients in a large greased baking dish.

4. Bake, uncovered, at 350° for 1 to 2 hours.

5. Stir occasionally until nice and brown.

Grandpa Cookies

Makes 10 dozen cookies

2 sticks (½ lb.) butter, softened
3 cups brown sugar
1 cup sour cream
5 eggs, beaten
4¾ cups flour
1 Tbsp. baking soda

1. Cream butter and brown sugar together well.

2. Add remaining ingredients, finishing with baking soda. Mix well.

3. Drop by big teaspoonfuls onto cookie sheets. Big round cookies are best.

4. Bake at 375° for about 12 minutes.

5. Frost with caramel frosting or plain vanilla icing.

Date Pudding

Makes 20 servings

PUDDING:
1 cup chopped dates
1 tsp. baking soda
1 Tbsp. butter
1 cup boiling water
2 eggs, beaten
1 cup flour
1 cup sugar
1 tsp. vanilla
¾ cup chopped nuts

SAUCE:
2 cups water
1 stick (¼ lb.) butter
1 cup brown sugar
½ cup flour
2-3 Tbsp. water

whipped topping

1. In a large mixing bowl, pour boiling water over dates, soda, and butter. Mix together well.

2. Let cool.

3. Add eggs, flour, sugar, vanilla, and chopped nuts.

4. Place in greased baking pan.

5. Bake at 325° for 30 to 35 minutes. When a toothpick inserted in center of Pudding comes out clean, the Pudding is done. Allow to cool.

6. Cut Pudding into 1" squares.

SAUCE:

1. Combine water, butter, and brown sugar in saucepan. Bring to boil.

2. In a small bowl, blend ½ cup flour with 2-3 Tbsp. water until smooth.

3. Stir into hot syrup mixture and bring to a boil again. Stir frequently to keep it smooth and to prevent sticking.

4. Cool completely.

5. Layer ⅓ of the squares of cut-up Pudding into a trifle bowl. Top with ⅓ of the Sauce. Top that with big spoonfuls of whipped topping.

6. Repeat those layers twice, ending with whipped topping. Chill and serve.

Chocolate-Covered Ritz Crackers

Makes 20 servings

1 box Ritz crackers
1 medium jar creamy peanut butter
1 lb. milk chocolate wafers

1. Make cracker sandwiches with peanut butter spread between two crackers.

2. Melt chocolate.

3. Dip cracker sandwiches into melted chocolate to coat completely.

4. Lay dipped crackers on waxed paper. Allow to cool completely.

TIP

Successfully melting chocolate means never allowing it to get too hot. Melt in a double boiler over boiling water, stirring repeatedly. If the temperature is too high, the chocolate will turn into hard clumps.

Chocolate Pie

Makes 16-18 servings

8 oz. pkg. cream cheese, softened
1¼ cups sugar
2 tsp. vanilla
½ cup cocoa powder
¾ cup milk
16 oz. container frozen whipped topping,
   thawed
2 large, or 3 small, pre-made graham cracker
   pie shells

1. Beat together cream cheese, sugar, and vanilla.

2. Add cocoa powder alternately with milk.

3. Fold in whipped topping.

4. Spoon into two large or three small pie shells.

5. Cover. Refrigerate for at least 3 hours before serving.

Dressing
(Mam's Ohio Filling)

Makes 15 servings

2 loaves bread, cut in cubes
1 stick (¼ lb.) butter, melted
6 eggs, beaten
5-6 cups milk
1 cup chicken broth
2 cups chicken, cut up
1 cup celery, cut up fine and cooked until
    tender
½ to 1 cup carrots, cut up fine or grated,
    and cooked until tender
1 Tbsp. chicken bouillon
½ tsp. pepper
1 tsp. seasoned salt
2 Tbsp. parsley

1. In a very large bowl, toss bread cubes with melted butter.

2. Spread bread cubes on 2 baking sheets.

3. Turn oven to 350°. Toast bread for about 20 minutes, or just until nicely browned.

4. Combine eggs, milk and broth in large bowl.

5. Gently stir in rest of ingredients.

6. Bake in a large roaster or baking pans at 350°, uncovered, for 1½ to 2 hours, stirring occasionally, until hot and crusty on top.

The Glossary

Cape—An extra piece of cloth which Amish women wear over the bodices of their dresses in order to be more modest.

Covering—A fine mesh headpiece worn by Amish females in an effort to follow the Amish interpretation of a New Testament teaching in I Corinthians 11.

Dat—A Pennsylvania Dutch dialect word used to address or refer to one's father.

Der Saya—To wish someone God's blessing.

Dichly—A Pennsylvania Dutch dialect word meaning head scarf or bandanna.

Doddy—A Pennsylvania Dutch dialect word used to address or to refer to one's grandfather.

Driver—When the Amish need to go somewhere, and it's too distant to travel by horse and buggy, they may hire someone to drive them in a car or van.

English—The Amish term for anyone who is not Amish.

In-between Sundays—Old Order Amish have church every other Sunday. This is an old custom that allows ministers to visit other church districts. An in-between Sunday is the day that a district does not hold church services.

Mam—A Pennsylvania Dutch dialect word used to address or to refer to one's mother.

Maud—A Pennsylvania Dutch dialect word meaning a live-in female helper, usually hired by a family for a week or two at a time. *Mauds* often help to do house-, lawn-, and garden-work after the birth of a baby.

Mutsa—an Amish man's suit coat.

Nehva-sitsa—a wedding attendant.

Ordnung—The Amish community's agreed-upon rules for living, based upon their understanding of the Bible, particularly the New Testament. The *Ordnung* varies some from community to community, often reflecting the leaders' preferences and the local traditions and historical practices.

Risht dag—The day of preparation for an Amish wedding. Since Amish weddings typically take place at home, this is the day when the family prepares much of the food for the wedding and sets up the benches and tables used during the ceremony and the meal that follows.

Risht leid—the four Amish couples who prepare the *Roasht* for an Amish wedding.

Roasht—Chicken filling. Mam prepares both a Lancaster County and an Ohio roasht.

Running around—The time in an Amish young person's life between the age of 16 and marriage. Includes structured social activities for groups, as well as dating. Usually takes place on the weekend.

Snitz Pie—Made from dried apple slices, Snitz Pie is often served at the lunch which follows the Amish Sunday church service.

Vocational school—Attended by 14-year-old Amish children who have completed eight grades of school. These students go to school three hours a week and keep a journal—which their teacher reviews—about their time at home learning farming and homemaking skills from their parents.

The Author

Linda Byler grew up Amish and is an active member of the Amish church today. Growing up, Linda loved to read and write. In fact, she still does. She is the author of *Running Around (and Such)*, the first novel in the "Lizzie Searches for Love" series. She is well-known within the Amish community as a columnist for a weekly Amish newspaper. Linda and her husband, their children, and grandchildren live in central Pennsylvania.

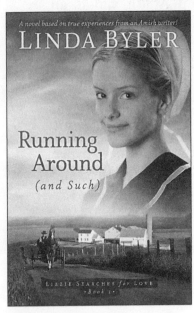
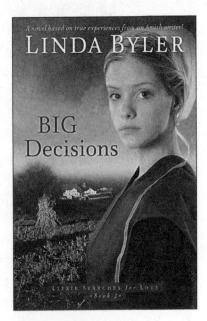